THE CASCADE WINNERS

*Sharon,
My fellow writer
and good friend
All the best
with your creative
work.
—Hanna*

THE CASCADE WINNERS

HEMLATA VASAVADA

The Cascade Winners
Hemlata Vasavada
Copyright © 2014 Hemlata Vasavada
www.hemlatavasavada.wordpress.com
email; vasavadahn@gmail.com

Published by Armchair ePublishing.
www.armchair-epublishing.weebly.com
Anacortes, WA 98221

The opinions expressed in this manuscript are solely the opinions of the author and do not represent the opinions or thoughts of the publisher. The author has represented and warranted full ownership and/or legal right to publish all the materials in this book.

All rights reserved. This book may not be reproduced, transmitted, or stored in whole or in part by any means, including graphic, electronic, or mechanical without the express written consent of the publisher except in the case of brief quotations embodied in articles and reviews. Thank you for respecting the hard work of this author.

Book excerpts or customized printings can also be created for specific needs.
email; vasavadahn@gmail.com

Book layout, eBook, .epub and .mobi conversions by Armchair ePublishing; www.armchair-epublishing.weebly.com
Cover illustration: Tony D. Locke, Armchair ePublishing

ISBN-13: 978-1497300712
ISBN-10: 1497300711

DISCLAIMER
Names, characters, places, and incidents in this novel are fictional. Any resemblance to actual individuals is coincidental.

DEDICATION

This novel is dedicated to our friends in Skagit Valley who made us feel at home when we moved to the area in 1972, and to the former employees of Skagit Steel, known at different times as Skagit/Bendix, Skagit/Continental Emsco, Skagit Products, and Skagit/Smatco.

ACKNOWLEDGEMENTS

The credit for my "singlehanded" accomplishment goes to many hands. This book would not have been possible without the support of my husband, Nitin Vasavada, and stories of his experiences in the engineering office and on offshore drilling rigs. He deserves thanks for reading and correcting my several drafts.

Much gratitude goes to Nitin's friend and former boss, Edward Mangold, friends Peter and Sherry Kelly who shared stories of their work and office politics, and Ed's wife, Sylvia, who joined them in reading my manuscript and encouraging me. I'm thankful to Nitin's friend, Thomas Doan, for providing photographs of the equipment.

Our friends, retired Boeing engineers Arun Desai, Jagdish Hajari, and Jay Surati, deserve thanks for referring the book: Legend & Legacy: *The Story of Boeing and its People*, and for answering my questions about the company's Super Sonic Transport program.

For forty years, members of Skagit Valley Writers League have inspired me to achieve my publishing goals. The members of my Tuesday and Wednesday critique groups have been my writing lifeline. They have praised and criticized my work, coaxed me during dry spells, given me suggestions to improve my manuscript, and have accompanied me on the journey through rough drafts to the final version. A million thanks to Ann Brittain,

Flo House, Frances Evlin, Heidi Thomas, Jean Molinari, Jennifer Ecker, Kay Haaland, Loretta Saarinen, Patricia Bloom and Robbie Shinn. My friend, Linda Adams deserves my gratitude for being my one-person fan club.

Credit goes to Teleia Geddess for editing my first draft and Judie Landy for editing my final manuscript.

My niece, Ami Dalal deserves special thanks for creating my Website. My deepest appreciation goes to our daughter Anita and her family, and our relatives and close friends for their support and encouragement for this project.

YOUR PURCHASE HELPS FUND
SCHOLARSHIPS RIGHT HERE
IN WASHINGTON!

Lotto

Overall Odds 1 in 27.1 ($1 play)

TERMINAL NUMBER 00190645
190645   738-031173383-115701

A. 03 04 08 11 27 29
B. 02 05 06 09 21 30

          Mon Dec09 13
014862   PRICE $1.00

SIGN ON BACK OF TICKET BEFORE
PRESENTING TO RETAILER

PROLOGUE
1987

A knot formed in Norma Gunnersen's throat as the movers carried out the last of the boxes to the truck. The door closed with a bang. The moving van rumbled, then lurched forward spewing swirls of black smoke.

Blinking back her tears, through the haze, Norma glanced at the Cascade/Eagle Energy office. "Thirty years of my working life packed in those boxes. All gone."

Harold moved to her side. "I know, honey." He squeezed her hand. "Let's go home."

Norma turned to the three secretaries standing beside her. "Take care now." She hugged them one by one, then plodded to the car and sagged into the passenger seat.

When Harold drove out of the parking lot, Norma looked at Mount Baker rising out of the Cascade Range for which the company was named. The snow-covered mountain still looked magnificent, but the office was lifeless, and the seventy-five-year old machine shop was silent without the humming of the machines. Cascade was Norma's family. This was where her grandfather and father had worked in the machine shop, this is where she had made friends and met her husband.

After her close friends left Cedarville for new jobs, a void had filled Norma's heart. Today, the hole of their absence grew deeper. Without her friends, and without her job, Norma felt unanchored in her own surroundings.

Norma spotted the Eagle Energy "expert," who had supervised the transfer of the project books and drawings from the Cascade office to Eagle Energy in Houston, locking the empty building. She bent down and picked up the *Cedarville Gazette* that she had thrown on the passenger side of the car, and read:

THE END OF CASCADE PRODUCTS

The family owned business started in 1902 and made equipment for the logging industry and later bomb shell casings during World War II. In 1962, Springfield Steel of Illinois bought it. Under their management, it expanded, giving this small town international recognition for designing and manufacturing deck machinery for offshore drilling rigs. At one point it captured forty-percent of the world market and employed 850 people. The company was sold to Eagle Energy of Houston in 1980. Now Eagle Energy is transferring the project books and drawing from the engineering department to Houston. They are selling the machines, buildings and land in Cedarville. Some employees have already moved to Houston or elsewhere for new jobs. Many more have lost their jobs."

Norma sighed, and set the newspaper aside.

Harold asked, "How about buying a lottery ticket, then eating at the Gateway Diner?"

"Okay." Norma didn't have the energy to go home and cook.

Her mind went back to the last day of bridge game and dinner with Steve and Vera, Keith and Alicia and Bryan and Jane. No one was in a mood to play. She brought out the goodbye cake she had made for them. Vera had said, she wished they had won the group lottery so they could have stayed here without any worries of job.

Jane and Alicia had wondered aloud if perhaps their group could have won someday. They had asked Norma if she would continue to play the same lotto numbers once a week. They promised to send the money with their Christmas cards. How could Norma refuse this request from her dear friends?

Buying the lottery ticket once a week would keep Norma connected to her friends.

She wished she had a video player she could rewind, and relive the Cascade years.

THE CEDARVILLE GIRL
(1956-1963)

CHAPTER ONE

NORMA

A banner announcing the Fourth-of July picnic hung at the entrance to the Cascade Products compound in Cedarville. Norma set the cashbox and raffle tickets on the table and prepared to greet the employees and their families as they arrived. This company had done so much for her family. First her grandfather had worked here, then her father, and now she too worked here. She sat down, smoothed the wrinkles from her blue skirt and watched a group of nine-year old girls, giggling and nudging each other as if someone told them a hilarious joke.

Recognizing a neighbor's daughter, Norma called, "Hello, Stacy, what's so funny?"

"We saw pictures of steam and gas donkeys. But they didn't look like donkeys. They're dirty old machines."

As a little girl, Norma too, used to chuckle at the captions of those photographs of the logging machines. "Girls, I want to tell you something. When I was your age, my dad told me that a forest engineer in India said these gas and steam donkeys could do the work of ten elephants."

A curly-haired girl grinned. "It's a good thing that we have the machines because we don't have no elephants."

"Hey, we need to go practice for the three-legged race," another girl said.

They trotted away. The running children, the red, white and blue balloons, and the smell of hot dogs and buttered popcorn brought back memories of the time when Norma used to come to the company picnics with her parents. How she loved looking at the pictures, especially the photograph of her late grandfather with the owner and the first ten employees.

A tap on the table brought Norma back to the present. She looked up and saw a tall, red-haired man in jeans and a plaid shirt staring at her. "Hello! Do I need a ticket for the picnic?"

His eyes, intense and green, pierced her heart. "Oh, yeah. I mean no," Norma stammered. "The entrance is free. But if you'd like to buy a raffle ticket, it's only a dime."

"What's the prize?" the handsome stranger asked.

"Mr. Clemens, the owner, has donated the use of his houseboat on Lake Chelan, in Eastern Washington." Norma hoped he wouldn't hear her thumping heart. "The money will go toward the hospital fund."

"I'll buy a ticket, but only if I get the winning one." He winked and handed her a dime.

Her hand brushed his when she gave him a raffle ticket, and warm blood rushed to her cheeks. He smiled, then turned and strode across the open field.

Later, Norma took the cashbox to the office and joined her parents, who were helping at the lemonade booth. She scanned for the tall, red-haired man.

After lunch, Mr. Clemens announced that it was time to pick the winner of the raffle. He called a little girl, "Grace, come here and pick a ticket."

The child came, picked a ticket and gave it to Mr. Clemens, who looked at it. "308."

Chapter One

"That's me!" The red-haired man loped to the front, waving his ticket high in his hand.

Mr. Clemens looked at the stub the man handed him and glanced at its other half in his hand. "Well folks, Harold Gunnersen from St. Paul, Minnesota, is the winner. He just started work in our accounting department. Harold, this shows how good we are to newcomers." He presented the gift certificate to him. "Congratulations."

Certificate in hand, Harold came to Norma. "Thanks for selling me the winning ticket."

"Congratulations." Norma managed to say, then introduced her parents. "My mother, Olga, and my father, Per Pedersen."

Her father extended his hand. "Congratulations! You from Minnesota? We have relatives there."

Harold shook Dad's hand. "Yes, I grew up there. My parents and brother are still there."

Norma's mother came forward. "How do you like it here?"

"It's only been a month, and I have no family. You know, the job is good." Harold looked at Norma, then brushed his red hair back with his fingers.

Mom said, "Mr. Gunnersen—"

"Harold, please," he interrupted.

"Well," Mom continued, "Whenever you feel like a home-cooked meal, please come over to our place."

"Thank you." He smiled and turned to Norma. "I'd enjoy that."

* * *

While arranging the files on her desk at the office, Norma thought about Harold. She would see him talking to the engineering manager at times. It had been four months since she had met him. The few times he had come to dinner, he seemed content to watch "I Love Lucy" and "Gunsmoke" on television. Sometimes he played a few hands of bridge with her and her parents. Norma wondered if he would ever ask her out. But for now, she needed to concentrate on her job.

She carried a blueprint that an engineer had asked her to deliver to the machine shop. As a child, she used to draw pictures of the machines and had dreamed of becoming a draftsman. But her adviser at Cedarville Junior College had steered her toward typing and shorthand, saying that drafting was not for women. She had thought of going to another college where teachers would let her study drafting. Norma said out loud, "I want to be a draftsman—a woman draftsman." It sounded silly even to her ears, so she shoved the idea out of her mind and went for secretarial training.

After she graduated, she was employed by Cascade Products as a secretary for the engineering department. When she filed blueprints for hoists, cranes and deck machineries, she often wondered if she could have drawn them. But she was happy filing calculations and customer correspondence in the project books, and learning about new designs and technology.

As she walked across the parking lot to the machine shop, Norma looked up for a glimpse of Mount Baker, but a blanket of October fog obstructed her view. The tops of the cedars and alders had taken on a gray tone, contrasting with their deep green below. She came to an abrupt stop as she bumped into someone and dropped the blueprint. "Oh, sorry."

"Me too. Sorry." Harold bent, picked it up and held her hand briefly before handing them to her. "You know, I was just on my way to your office to ask you something."

His touch electrified her. She looked up at him. He had to be at least six inches taller than her 5' 7". What did he want to ask?

Harold smiled down at her. "Have you heard of the movie,

Chapter One

The Seven Year Itch? It's playing at the Lido. Would you like to go with me this Saturday?"

"I read about it in the paper." Norma blushed. "Is anyone else going?"

Harold cocked his head. "You know, I'm just asking you. But if you're uncomfortable going with me alone, I can ask another couple to join us."

Norma wished she could take her words back. "Oh, no, I'd like to go with just you."

No way did she want a chaperone. A date, finally!

* * *

On Saturday, Norma donned a navy blue jacket over her red silk blouse and scrutinized her appearance in the mirror. In spite of the lipstick and rouge she had applied, she wondered if Harold would be put off by her pale skin.

Her mother patted her back. "You look beautiful."

"Oh, Mom, you're just saying that."

She heard a car pull up. Her father called, "Harold's here."

Norma slipped on her high-heeled pumps and hurried to the living room. Harold's eyebrows rose and he smiled. He stood. "Mr. Pedersen, I'll bring her back right after the movie and dinner."

Her parents waved to them as they left.

Harold held open the door of his blue Chevy, waited until she settled in, then got into driver's seat and started the car. The smell of cigarettes mingled with Harold's cologne felt wonderful. He parked the car near the theater and came to open her door. He put his arm around her shoulder as they walked inside the theater. Her heart jumped like the kernels in the popcorn-maker they passed in the lobby. When they sat, he placed his hand at the base of her neck. Mesmerized by his proximity, Norma hardly noticed the predicaments of Marilyn Monroe and Tom Ewell on the screen.

* * *

Norma couldn't concentrate on her work as she sat at her desk, thinking about Harold. She loved his warmth and humor and loved being with him, but he had never said how he felt. She took a deep breath and returned to typing the operation manual for the hoist the company was shipping to Alaska.

She felt a hand on her shoulder. By the gentle touch, she knew it was Harold. "I'd like to take you out to dinner this evening." His rich baritone sent a thrill through her.

"I'd love to." It was Valentine's Day. She had thought of giving him a card, but didn't want him to think she was being too forward.

"How about that place in Anacortes, you know, the Seaside Hotel? I'll pick you up at six." He lightly squeezed her arm before he turned to leave.

Later, at the restaurant, Harold and Norma were seated in a secluded area. The red table cover, white napkins and heart-shaped candle created a festive mood. The aroma of basil and oregano spread to the dining area. Harold took her hand in his for a while then let it go. "I'll be back in a minute."

When he returned, the jukebox was playing a recently released Elvis song, "Love Me Tender." When the song was over, Harold took her hands. "Will you marry me?"

Norma's heart melted. She had played the scene a million times in her head. Now that he had actually asked, she knew her answer was "Yes" but she couldn't make the word come out. A lump formed in her throat, as she blinked back her tears and conveyed her answer only with a smile and a nod.

Harold squeezed her hand. "I love you."

Chapter One

"I love you, too," Norma managed to say before her throat tightened again.

He reached in his pocket, took out a blue velvet box and flipped open the lid. Slipping the diamond solitaire ring on her finger, he kissed her hand.

"Oh, Harold, I'm overwhelmed." Unable to contain her joyful tears, she dabbed her eyes with her handkerchief.

"I want you to know that I've followed proper protocol. I got permission from your father. And your mother helped me pick out your ring."

Norma's voice trembled. "My folks really like you, but how about your parents? Are they okay with you marrying someone from so far away? I mean, they haven't even met me."

Harold caressed her hand across the table. "You know, when I went home for Christmas, I took your picture with me. I told them about you. They'll meet you at the wedding."

"Wedding! And when's that?" Norma tried to tease him.

Harold lit his cigarette. "Well, you've asked me several times when I plan to use the week I won on the houseboat on Lake Chelan. I think I should use it before this Fourth of July, when someone else wins that raffle. Do you think we could get married in June and spend our honeymoon on the houseboat?"

"Looks like you've planned the wedding and honeymoon all by yourself."

"Come on, honey, I'm just talking about the possibilities. The planning is up to you."

Honey! The word sounded so sweet. Norma squeezed his hand. "I was only joking."

Her daydreaming mind had already started to plan her wedding dress and the honeymoon.

CHAPTER TWO

NORMA

The irritating "drip-drip" of the leaky faucet echoed as Norma scrubbed the kitchen floor. What could she expect from an old rental house? Five years of marriage with Harold had many joyous moments and many unpleasant ones. They had a son and another child on the way, but recently, all Harold did was to grumble about his new boss, the gloomy and rainy town of Cedarville, the Democrats and President Kennedy.

Three-year-old Eric left his father on the couch and toddled toward Norma. She picked him up and gave him a banana. Her son took a big bite, then shifted the banana piece in his mouth from one side to the other. Norma felt her unborn child move inside her. Fortunately, Mom took care of Eric, so Norma could continue to work. Her mother had assured her that now that her father had retired, they would help with both the children. Norma sighed. If only Harold would snap out of this slump.

Eric wriggled from her arms and ran to Harold. The child's face was covered with mashed banana, residue from the huge bite that he couldn't quite keep in his small mouth. "Eric, come here," Norma called. "Let's wipe your face." If she didn't run after him,

Chapter Two

he would rub the gooey mess all over the sofa.

Harold laughed, picked Eric up and took him to the kitchen sink. He turned on the leaking faucet. "I should have fixed this."

Norma rubbed her neck to ease the tension flaring inside her head. She tried to understand Harold's excuses for not buying a house. He wasn't happy with his job after this Calder person became his boss. His father had just been diagnosed with lung cancer. But he could at least fix the faucet.

Suddenly, Norma felt as if rubber bands were twisting her stomach and back. She groaned and sank on a chair.

"Honey, are you having labor pains?" Harold asked.

Norma nodded. Harold sat next to her. Soon another cramp tightened Norma's stomach. She looked at the clock. It had been only fifteen minutes since the last contraction. "Oh, oh, we better go to the hospital."

They dropped Eric at Norma's parents and rushed to the hospital. While they waited for the doctor, Harold massaged Norma's back and wiped her sweaty forehead with his handkerchief. She looked into his green eyes. So what if he couldn't make up his mind about buying a house? At the moment, Norma treasured his gentle touch and soothing voice.

Two days later, they came home with their daughter, Anne. Norma's parents and Eric were waiting in the living room. Eric ran to Norma. She hugged him and showed him his little sister, then sat down on the sofa with her children. Norma smiled at her parents sitting across from her. Harold slid beside her. A telephone ring interrupted their togetherness when Harold went to answer it.

Norma heard him say, "Hi, Mom." His mother was probably calling to see if they were home from the hospital. But from Harold's side, all she could hear were question, "When?" and "the University Hospital?"

Harold put the receiver in its cradle and trudged to the sofa. "Dad's in the hospital. They have to remove his bad lung."

Norma struggled to find the right words to comfort her husband. "You should go there. I wish I could come and help your dad, but I can't." Norma caressed the baby.

"Don't worry about Norma and the children," Norma's Dad said.

Her mother added, "Harold, your parents need you right now. We'll take care of things here."

* * *

In anticipation of his return from St. Paul, Norma cooked Harold's favorite dish, fried chicken. She dressed Eric and Anne in fresh clothes. Hearing the familiar car horn, she rushed to the porch, Eric running behind her. Harold got out of the car, scooped up Eric, then put his arm around Norma and kissed her.

"We missed you. It's great that your dad's surgery went well."

Harold set Eric down. "I'll explain later."

After dinner, when the children were in bed, she asked him, "So, is Dad okay or not?"

"The surgery went well, but the doctor said the statistics on lung cancer aren't good." Harold lit a cigarette. "Mom wanted me to stay there longer. My brother and his wife said Minnesota Ironworks, where they work, has an opening for an accountant." He took a drag. "I applied and gave my parents' phone number. This morning, just three hours before my flight, they called me for an interview."

"What?" Blood rushed to Norma's cheeks and her eyes burned. "You didn't even talk to me about it first?"

"Honey, I applied because Olaf suggested. It's not like they're going to hire me."

Chapter Two

"What if they do offer you a job? Were you going to tell me after you packed your bags?" Norma's fingers scratched at the sofa.

"For God's sake, all I did was interview with the company. If they hire me and you don't want to go, we won't go. You know, they called me for an interview this morning before my flight. How could I have talked to you about it? You want me to get your permission before I apply for any job from now on?" He frowned.

The smoke from Harold's cigarette stung Norma's eyes. She stormed into the kitchen and furiously scrubbed the counter. "Do what you want. Who am I to interfere?"

Harold put his cigarette stub in the ashtray and came to her. "Remember what you told me before I left for St. Paul? That you wanted to help Dad during his recovery. While I was there, I started thinking that my parents would want us closer to them at this point."

Norma stopped cleaning and looked at her husband. "I guess they would like that."

"But I'm not moving without a job. So relax." Harold reached for her hand.

Norma let him hold it. Maybe she had been too hard on him. She wouldn't want her husband to have any guilt or regret if he couldn't be near his father during his illness. She too would like to spend time with her father-in-law, whom she respected, and she was sure seeing his grandchildren would cheer him up. But a permanent move so far away? Well, until a job offer came, there was no sense in fretting over it.

A week later, Harold handed Norma a registered letter from Minnesota Ironworks. Norma read the terms of employment. The salary was more than he made at Cascade. Norma's stomach rumbled as if it were filled with rocks. "I know you want to go there."

Harold wrapped his arms around her. "Are you willing to go?"

"I want to go for a short time to help your dad. But, I won't be able to find a job with two small children. Isn't housing more expensive in St. Paul?"

Harold's eyes narrowed. "We'll be able to manage. I think if I take this job at this salary, it'll be easier to get higher salary anywhere else later. What do you want me to do?"

Norma sagged onto the sofa. If he didn't know what to do after stirring up this whole job thing and disrupting her life, how did he expect her to know the answer? "I suppose it will help your career."

"You know, for a while we can stay with my parents. That way we can save up enough for a house. We should keep our furniture in storage here."

Norma swallowed hard. While she was thinking of going to St. Paul for a short time, he was already talking about buying a house there. How in the world would she handle living with her mother-in-law? Well, if she truly wanted to help her ill father-in-law, she had to stay there. They would do their duty and save money in the process. "I guess that's the best option for now." Norma combed her hair with her fingers. Had she just agreed to go to St. Paul? Not only will she be leaving her parents and friends, but her coworkers—her other family at Cascade.

Harold's eyes, narrow while discussing the offer, widened immediately. "You're the best, honey. It's not just the job, but the timing is right."

* * *

After three days of driving in the August heat, Norma arrived in St Paul with her husband and children. With the baby in his arms, Harold rang the doorbell of his parents' white, colonial home.

Chapter Two

Holding Eric's hand, Norma stared at the dry, yellow lawn, such a contrast to the lush yard back home.

Harold's mother, Astrid, greeted them at the door. "Dad has been waiting for you." Astrid hugged each of them, then took the baby in her arms. "So glad you all came to stay."

Lars Gunnersen put his hand on the armchair. "Good to see you, Norma. I'm glad you brought them all, son." His breath caught and he lapsed into a fit of coughing. He extended his withered arm toward Eric. "Hey, pumpkin, come to your grandpa."

Eric clung to Norma. He was perhaps as shocked to see the change in the old man as Norma was. At Christmas, when they had visited, Lars Gunnersen was a healthy man. He seemed to have aged ten years in the last eight months.

Astrid placed Anne in her husband's lap. Norma clenched her handkerchief. Before leaving Cedarville, Norma had asked her doctor if her children could catch cancer from Lars Gunnersen. Dr. Hobbs had assured her that cancer wasn't infectious. Still, hearing her father-in-law's hoarse voice and coughing made her wonder about her children's health in this house.

Tears ran down the old man's cheeks. "My precious grandchildren! I was afraid I wouldn't get to see Anne, or play with Eric. Thank you both." He looked at Norma and Harold.

* * *

As the months passed, Norma dismissed the notion about her kids catching cancer. She was happy Eric could entertain his grandpa, and in turn, he kept the toddler busy. But every day Norma noticed her father-in-law getting weaker. He needed help with walking, and his arms were losing strength too.

During Norma's past visits her mother-in-law would watch her with critical eyes. Now, she seemed to be too glad to have her help. She no longer made snide remarks and often left for church activities, trusting Norma to take care of Lars.

Once when Norma took the soup to her father-in-law, she noticed his hands shook and he had trouble navigating the spoon to his mouth. She asked him if she could help, and seeing him nod, started feeding him. She loved him and tried to make him comfortable in his last days.

As winter settled in and the snow hardened into ice, the gloomy house started to close in on Norma. She stared at the Christmas decorations she was supposed to put back in the basement. Astrid had insisted on having a tree, decorations and the festive dinner, even though her husband was in his last stage of life. Finally, Christmas was over.

Norma longed to have a day alone with Harold, but in the five months they had been here, her mother-in-law had never once offered to take care of the children so Norma and Harold could go out. Harold's brother and sister-in-law didn't help either. Instead, each Saturday or Sunday, Olaf and Barb would visit, supposedly to see Lars Gunnersen, then sit in the living room all afternoon, smoking cigarettes, drinking beer, and talking shop with Harold.

On Saturday, when Olaf and Barb came for a visit, they peeked into Lars Gunnersen's room, then settled in the living room with their cigarettes. Norma wanted to bring the newspaper article she had read and shove it in their faces. It said that smoking caused lung diseases, including cancer. She wondered if that had caused her father-in-law's illness. Norma's throat felt scratchy and her eyes burned. At least the kids were taking their naps, away from the smoke.

Harold brought in three bottles of beer and set his on the coffee table. As if an afterthought, he turned to Norma. "Honey, would you like some iced tea or cola?"

"No, thanks." Norma shook her head.

Chapter Two

Norma had hoped Harold would come sit with her, instead, Astrid Gunnersen came into the room and sat next to her. She asked, "Did Harold tell you that he had a crush on Barb when they were in school?"

Barb was sitting between Harold and Olaf, Harold's shoulder touching hers. Olaf pulled her toward him. "But I won her."

Norma looked away from the brothers and their trophy, and massaged her temples. Harold asked, "Honey, do you have a headache?"

"I'm going to go lie down." She turned on her heel and left.

Harold and Barb worked in the same office. Barb was a career woman and probably didn't think much of Norma's lowly secretarial job. Now even that was gone. While she was stuck in the house with Harold's ill father and two small children, he was having the time of his life with his old flame.

Before going upstairs, Norma peeked into her father-in-law's room. He was lying in his bed, his eyes open. She went in and checked his pulse but couldn't feel it. Her hands trembled. She rushed to the living room. "Call the ambulance! Dad's unconscious."

Olaf ran toward the phone while others bolted to the room and gathered around the bed. When the medics arrived, they gave the verdict Norma had feared. Lars was gone. During the five months in St. Paul, she had helped feed him and had given him his medication. She had learned to appreciate his gentle kindness and infinite patience. His sad gratitude for every little thing she did for him tugged at her heart.

* * *

Every New Year, Norma made resolutions to improve her family's well-being, and her own, but this year she couldn't think of any resolution that might help her situation. The year of 1963 brought an aching loneliness as the bitter cold outside crept into her.

When her parents had visited for Lars Gunnersen's memorial service, Norma wanted to tell them about Harold working late, Barb, and the times she had contemplated leaving him. But she just couldn't bring herself to complain about him soon after his father had passed away.

Loneliness gnawed at Norma after her parents returned to Cedarville. With Lars Gunnersen's death, the reason for her presence in St. Paul had vanished.

In early February, Astrid went to Eau Claire, Wisconsin, to visit her sister. Norma had her mother-in-law's car if she needed to go out. But who would want to bundle up two kids, get dressed, struggle with heavy snow boots, and brave the stinging winds just for a few groceries? It might have been different if she had a friend to visit. Harold could pick up the staples and the produce. Besides, the Gunnersen freezer was full of beef and chicken. While the kids played, Norma plopped on the sofa and closed her eyes.

Four-year-old Eric shook her. "Mommy, Daddy wants to talk to you."

She opened her eyes. "Oh, did I fall asleep?" She took the receiver from Eric. "Hello."

"Are you okay, honey?" Harold asked.

"Why do you ask?"

"Eric said you were sleeping. I called to see if you need anything from the store. I'm leaving work early. We'd better stock up on food. You know, there's a major storm warning."

"We need milk and eggs. If you think of anything else, you can get it," Norma replied.

She set down the receiver, got a glass of milk for Eric and a bottle for Anne. She wanted to prepare a decent meal for them, but she just plopped on the sofa, staring at the snowflakes.

Chapter Two

Harold came home and patted Eric who seemed to be struggling with a puzzle, then picked up Anne from the playpen. "Honey, what's wrong?"

"What do you mean?"

"You've been so tired. You don't know what's in the house and what we need to buy. You don't talk to me…"

Norma bolted up. "Are you making a list of everything I haven't done for you so you can leave me?"

"What?" Harold's face flushed. He sat Anne down in the playpen and handed her a rattle. "I can't discuss anything with you anymore. For the last three days I reminded you to call the real estate agent, so we could look again at that apartment we liked. What happened?"

Norma clasped her hands. Though Harold's mother had said they could stay with her as long as they needed to, he had suggested they rent their own place where Norma would be more comfortable. But if they moved into their own place, it would mean settling permanently in this dismal terrain. Norma sighed. "I don't want to look for a place. I want to go back."

Harold put his hands on her shoulders. "Would you and the kids like to go visit your parents for a couple of months? You know, the weather will be better in April when you return. We'll move into our own apartment then."

His "you knows" aggravated her anger. "I know you want to get rid of me and the kids so you can mess around with Barb."

"What?"

"Don't you 'what' me. You and your old flame are always together. You're all over her and even when I'm right there in the room you ignore me."

Harold shook his head. "If I had something going with her, would I even touch her in your presence? I swear, I've been faithful to you."

Norma clenched her jaw. "Maybe you're not sleeping with your sister-in-law, but it sure looks like you want to."

He took a pack of cigarettes from his pocket. "What's wrong with you?"

"Wrong with me or you? I gave up my job, my family and friends to come here, and look how you've treated me." She stalked to the bedroom.

Harold came and took her hand. "I know you're homesick. You and the kids are cooped up in the house. You need a break. It will be different in the spring."

Norma swallowed her tears and nodded. "I want to go for now. What happens later, I don't know."

* * *

Back in Cedarville, even with her parents and friends nearby, the emptiness in Norma's heart consumed her. The gray clouds and constant drizzle of Western Washington made the future look as bleak as the white blizzards and freezing snow of Minnesota. She missed her husband and his warm touch. Unlike her friend Wendy's husband, Harold always brought his paycheck home, and had opened a joint account with Norma. Last month in St. Paul, when she didn't have the motivation to do anything, he had prepared meals for them, and played with the children. But when she thought of his behavior around Barb, her heart burned with rage.

Norma spent most days sitting around, wondering what the future held for her. All she wanted was to sleep or sit and let the time pass by so she wouldn't have to make a decision about whether to reclaim her old life here or return to St. Paul. Her parents thought she was visiting to escape the cold. If they suspected something, they hadn't asked. Happily, they entertained Eric and Anne.

Chapter Two

Her mother nagged her about seeing her friends and former coworkers, but Norma made one lame excuse after another. Once she figured out whether she should go back to Harold or not, she would talk to her parents, but not now when her mind was so foggy.

One Saturday afternoon, her mother and a friend took Eric and another child to see Lady and the Tramp. Her father was out in the yard. After putting Anne down for a nap, Norma aimlessly turned on the television and watched a clip of Marilyn Monroe in the Seven-Year Itch. A knot formed in her stomach remembering the movie that she had seen on her first date with Harold. It soon would be seven years since they got married. Through teary eyes, she looked out, saw her father talking to someone on the porch, and escaped to her room.

Soon she heard her father. "Yes, it would be nice if you talk to her. Although she's here for just two months, getting out and meeting her coworkers might be good for her." He called, "Norma, Mr. O'Reilly is here to say hello."

She wiped her eyes, combed her hair, and went back to the living room.

The plump, middle-aged, personnel manager from Cascade Products smiled. "Hi, Norma, heard you were visiting, so thought I'd come and say hello."

"Hello, Mr. O'Reilly." Norma shook his hand. "Would you like some coffee?"

"That would be nice, thanks."

Norma went to the kitchen and brought back three steaming cups.

Mr. O'Reilly took the cup from her. "I don't blame you for getting out of the Minnesota winter." He took a sip. "The engineers really miss you. After you left, their department has gone through two secretaries. Now they've hired a third one. When your father said you were here, I wondered if you'd agree to come temporarily and train this new one."

Norma sat up straight, self-confidence coursing up her spine. Her boss recognized her work. Then she remembered hearing her father as he was entering the house with Mr. O'Reilly. Daddy must have begged him to hire her. How embarrassing.

Mr. O'Reilly continued. "We need to complete the list of all the project books and drawings before the bigwigs from Illinois come."

"Who's coming?" Norma asked.

"Springfield Steel is buying Cascade." Mr. O'Reilly set down the coffee cup. "Mr. Clemens thinks it's good. Larger companies have better benefits for their employees."

Per Pedersen asked, "Will they change its name? Will Mr. Clemens still manage it?"

"The name will become Cascade, Division of Springfield Steel," Mr. O'Reilly replied, "Mr. Clemens is retiring but will remain on the board of directors. His son will become vice president and a new president from Springfield will join us. We've been assured that we'll retain control of day to day activities. But there is so much to be done. And new orders are piling up too. So, I thought I'd ask if you'd come and help."

Norma folded and unfolded her napkin. Even if her father had initiated the meeting, Mr. O'Reilly seemed sincere in his job offer. "Mr. O'Reilly, I would like to work while I'm here."

"Well then, come Monday and fill out the paperwork."

During Harold's weekly phone call, while Eric described a scene from The Lady and the Tramp, of dogs slurping spaghetti, Norma kept wondering how her husband would react to her job offer. Would he be angry?

But when she told him, he said, "Honey, that's great. Training other secretaries! You know, that'll look good on your resume."

Chapter Two

Norma chewed her lower lip. Did he want her to stay here and let him live in peace in St. Paul? Was he expecting her back in April? She couldn't talk about it when the kids and her parents were nearby. "I'll give you the details in my letter."

* * *

As Norma settled into her old job, her bleak moments grew fewer and fewer. At home she started playing with her children again and reading books to them. She still vacillated between staying in Cedarville and going back to St. Paul. She had written to Harold about how much she was enjoying her job. Harold wrote back that he hoped she would find another interesting job in St. Paul when she returned, and he missed her and the children. Norma caressed the letter. She loved him and didn't want to break up her family.

Two weeks later, Harold called. "Guess what? I wrote to Mr. O'Reilly at Cascade. He replied that Calder, the comptroller who caused all the problems for me has left. You know, he said they are looking for an accounting manager, and asked me to apply."

Norma's pulse quickened. He wanted to come back. She pulled in a breath. She almost asked about Barb, but bit her tongue. "But, how will your mom feel? How about your brother?"

"Olaf is busy with his family and I want mine. You know, Mom has made plans to travel with her women friends. If I get this job and we settle back in Cedarville, she'll visit us."

Us! Norma swallowed her tears.

* * *

Three weeks after their telephone conversation, Norma went to the Sea-Tac airport to pick up Harold. He had received a job offer from Cascade, and was coming back. When he got off the plane, he wrapped her in his arms and kissed her. "It's good to be back with you. How are the kids?"

"Fine. Eric wanted to come to the airport, but it would have been way past his bed time. I promised he could see you first thing in the morning." The silent, angry part in her wanted to say that the baby didn't remember him or miss him, but she said, "Annie is growing so fast, you won't recognize her."

After he picked up his bag, they walked to the parking lot. Harold threw the suitcase in the trunk and pulled her to him. "Honey, I love you."

"You haven't bothered to say that in a long time." Norma fought back her tears, but they trickled down her cheeks.

"I'm sorry you feel that way." He wiped her face with his handkerchief and buried his face in her hair. "You feel so good. Let's remember our good times and start fresh."

For a moment, she wondered if she had overreacted about Barb and everything else in St. Paul. Perhaps she should give their marriage another chance. She rested her head on his chest, savoring the warmth of his flannel shirt and the steady beat of his heart.

COLLEGE FRIENDS
(1963-1971)

CHAPTER THREE

KEITH

Perspiration trickled down Keith Wilson's temples as he waited for the commencement ceremony at the High School auditorium on an unseasonably warm June day. Soon the strains of "Pomp and Circumstance" filled the hall. Keith steadied the mortarboard, and marched down the aisle with the class of 1963. He glanced at his parents perched on the edge of their seats, Grandma clutching her handkerchief, and Grandpa peering through his camera viewfinder. Keith reached his chair and sat carefully. He hoped his voice would cooperate when the time came to deliver his valedictory address. The thought of standing in front of 600 people and speaking made his legs tremble.

He had written and rewritten his speech, and practiced it over and over. He remembered his grandfather's advice, "Take a deep breath, then just say what you have to say. You are top of your class. You have no reason to be nervous."

But Keith had reasons. White students accused him of getting better grades because according to them, the teachers expected less from him. Like the time the jock got him in a corner and said he got the top grades because the teachers took pity on him. A few of the black kids in the class didn't like him and called him a "brownnoser." He wished he could fit in either his father's Negro race, or his mother's Oriental race.

When the principal called his name, he walked to the podium and retrieved his speech from his coat pocket. The paper rustled in his trembling hand. He held on to the lectern to support his wobbly legs, and began to read from his notes. Did his voice sound as shaky to others as it did to him? Finally, toward the end, when he thanked his parents, grandparents and teachers, his voice became normal.

* * *

A few days after graduation, when Keith returned home from his part-time bagging job at the Food King store, he inhaled the aroma of fried fish and vegetables. Quickly washing his hands, he went to the kitchen. "Mmm, Grandma, your tempuras make my mouth water."

His mother's parents, Grandma and Grandpa Kunigama, had come from California for his graduation and had stayed on. He enjoyed his afternoons with them while his father was at his job at the lumber mill and his mother at the florist doing her artistic flower-arrangements.

Grandma hugged him. "Come, let's eat."

"Son, your grandma loves to cook." Grandpa slurped his miso soup. "Your uncle and aunt don't appreciate her cooking."

Keith nodded. His uncle and aunt ignored and insulted his parents. His mother had told him that her dentist brother and his wife, who did the accounts for the Kunigama farm, looked down on her and her husband, because they didn't go to college or own a business. Keith suspected it was also because his father was a Negro.

Chapter Three

After lunch, Grandfather patted his stomach, then rose from his chair. "I told your father I'd weed the garden."

"Grandpa, I'll help you."

"No. You stay and rest after your hard work." His grandfather massaged Keith's shoulders, then left.

Keith carried the dishes to the sink while Grandma put the kettle on to boil water. She measured the tea and added hot water to the teapot. When she handed a cup to Keith, he again noticed her pale skin in contrast to his dark hand. Had he inherited his mother's Japanese complexion and his father's features, he could have passed as a white guy. Instead, he got his mother's delicate lips and nose, and his father's dark color and round eyes.

His grandmother took a sip of her tea. "You're just like your father, helpful and polite. I liked George from the day he and his parents came to work on our farm. Your grandparents were good, hardworking people." She shook her head. "They died too soon. Just like us, they would have been proud of you."

Keith had heard about the tribulations of his father's parents who had worked on a farm in Mississippi. When the good farm owner sold his property in 1939, he gave the Wilsons money to leave the area. They traveled to Sacramento, California, where Grandpa Kunigama offered them a job. His father and grandpa Wilson worked in the fields, and Grandma Wilson became a maid in the Kunigama house.

Sitting at the cozy dining table with his mother's mother, Keith finally asked the question that had been gnawing at his mind, "Grandma, did you want Mom and Dad to get married?"

A furrow formed on his grandmother's forehead. "Your grandpa wanted to take Miyoki to San Francisco to meet Japanese boys. Then we heard that we'd be taken to a camp because the Japanese attacked Pearl Harbor." She sighed. "I'd noticed the way your father and my Miyoki looked at each other. I knew Miyoki liked George, so I suggested the marriage. 'How dare you think of mixing races? What will happen to our standing in society?' Your grandpa shouted at me."

"So why did he agree?"

"We wanted to keep our Miyoki away from detention in case they treated us like the Jews in Germany. We trusted George's parents." Grandma paused, then continued, "And we agreed that if she had to stay with a family with a young man, it was better to have her married."

Keith chewed on his lip. He wanted more answers. "Grandma, would you have agreed to the marriage if you didn't have internment hanging over your head?"

"We wanted Miyoki to marry a nice Japanese man. But times were bad. Now we know that your parents are happier together than many Japanese couples I know. They respect each other and they've raised a perfect child." His grandmother came to his side and patted his shoulder. "But don't let it go to your head."

"What go to his head?" grandfather who had shuffled into the kitchen, asked.

"That he's a perfect child." Grandma tousled Keith's hair.

"Well, that he is." Grandpa slapped Keith's back. "Now don't call him a child. He's going to the University of Washington soon and will become a famous doctor or lawyer."

Still flanked by his grandparents, Keith hoped they would understand if he didn't choose to be a doctor or a lawyer. They were paying for his college and expected him to get a professional degree, but he wasn't sure about his goals. He was good at physics and math, but he also wanted to study astronomy and literature.

Keith gulped his tea. He hoped he could live up to their expectations.

CHAPTER FOUR

BRYAN

Bryan Stafford loaded his old navy-blue Thunderbird with clothes, books, and photos of his family and friends.

His father embraced him. "Keep the flashlight next to you in front. Where's your road map? And the map of Seattle?"

Somehow, his father's question didn't bother him. "Dad, I'll reach there well before dark." Bryan pointed to the passenger seat. "And I have the flashlight and the maps right there."

His mother came forward and hugged him. "Call us collect when you reach your dorm."

Doug, his brother, pushed him playfully on the shoulder. "I'll visit you soon."

Bryan slid in the front seat and started his car. All during the summer, he had looked forward to living independently. Now that he was getting his much-desired freedom, he wondered if he'd made the right decision. But he was accepted at the University of Washington! Smiling, he tapped the steering wheel and stepped on the accelerator.

Mowed wheat fields dried by the harsh Eastern Washington summer sun, reminded Bryan of last year when he and his buddies had set up sleeping bags by the golden fields. The radio played Rick Nelson's "Everybody's Running in a Mad Mad World." The songs from the radio and flickers of high school memories danced in Bryan's mind. After several hours, he stopped at a rest area, got out, stretched his legs, and ate his sandwich and banana. Mom's lunch felt like a feast.

After more than five hours of driving, Bryan finally reached the University of Washington campus or U-Dub as they called it. He found a parking space on a street bustling with students loaded down with books and bags. Feeling tightness in his back and legs, he decided to walk a bit before unloading his luggage. He roamed along the Campus Parkway where a bronze statue of George Washington gazed down at him. When he saw the cafeteria sign outside the Husky Union Building, he went in.

Feeling refreshed after a cup of coffee, Bryan went to a pay phone and made a collect-call to his parents, then walked to Lander Hall. The resident adviser checked his name and gave him the key for his room. Bryan climbed the three floors carrying his luggage, and saw two names: BRYAN STAFFORD and KEITH WILSON tacked on the door. He opened it and stared at the barren room—two beds without sheets and pillows, and two bare desks. Bryan went down to bring up the last of his belongings, wondering what his roommate would be like.

He climbed the flight of stairs with a box of books and photos, and opened his door, panting. He stopped short as he saw a lanky, colored kid bending over a box, a black man by the window, and an Oriental woman dusting the desk. Bryan took a step back to recheck the room number. Yes, this was his room. Could this black guy be his roommate? The colored students he had seen on television were football players, but this kid didn't look like an athlete. How did he get into the University?

Bryan set his box down on the floor. The three turned to him.

Chapter Four

The young man came forward and extended his hand. "Hi, I'm Keith Wilson."

Bryan blinked to clear his thoughts, then shook the extended hand. "I'm Bryan Stafford." He quickly wiped his hand on his jeans.

The man and woman introduced themselves as Keith's parents, George and Miyoki Wilson. Looking at the two men standing next to each other, Bryan noticed that Keith's complexion was a shade lighter than that of his father.

The woman took bed sheets out of a box. "Bryan, which side do you prefer?"

Bryan was surprised there was no Oriental accent in her voice. He tapped the metal post of the bed next to him. "This is fine." He took out his sheets.

The older man stepped forward. "Let me help you."

Dad would never do that. It certainly was easier to make the bed with the man's help.

Bryan tried to unpack his boxes and organize his closet while watching Keith and his parents. He checked his watch. It was almost six.

The Oriental woman spread a comforter and plopped a pillow on Keith's bed. "Let's go have dinner now. Bryan, would you like to come with us?"

Bryan hesitated. Before he could answer, the black man said, "If you have no other plans, we would love for you to join us."

Bryan didn't want them to feel that he wouldn't go with them because of their race. "Sure. Thanks."

At The Dragon Palace, Bryan tried to listen to George Wilson but his mind wandered to Martin Luther King's "I Have a Dream" speech he had heard on television last month. If Bryan ignored the skin color, just as Dr. King had advised, Keith's father was not much different from his own. His father worked in aluminum plant, Keith's father worked in a lumber mill. His mother worked part-time in a bakery, Keith's mother worked part-time in a flower shop.

Yet, he wondered if he could live in the same room with this stranger. What would his friends think? Or his mom and dad?

* * *

In his orientation, Bryan met several students from a fraternity. A sophomore said, "Hey, Bryan, I feel sorry for you, being stuck with a colored roommate. Forget about him and your dorm. Come have fun with us."

Bryan looked forward to belonging to this group. For two weeks during rush, he was wined and dined by the seniors, and was told about the advantages of fraternity fellowship.

He went to the initiation party. A senior filled glasses with beer. "Okay, chugging contest. Ready, set, go."

Bryan had partied with his high school buddies. He could handle beer. He looked around and saw other freshmen downing their drinks in just a couple of swallows. He drank, then burped. One freshman gulped his drink and turned his glass upside down to the cheers and applause of the older students.

"The winner! Now round two." Mugs were refilled from the keg in a corner. A frat brother glared at Bryan and another freshman. "Hey, these kids need a stronger dose."

Another senior stepped forward with a bottle of whiskey and added a slosh to his glass. Bryan took a gulp. The burning liquid threatened to come out his nose, but he held his breath, closed his mouth, and forced it down. Determined to show that he could compete glass for glass, he took another swig. And another.

The stereo blared, "It's Now or Never."

Bryan's head began to pound with the beat of the music. His

Chapter Four

stomach churned faster than the record on the turn table. Sour taste filled Bryan's mouth. The room started to spin. He felt like throwing up. Spotting the door, he bolted through the dancing throng and hammering music.

He staggered through the Seattle mist, wondering which way his dorm was. He slumped on the grass and suddenly heard voices. Were the frat brothers coming after him? He had heard how freshmen were tossed into the Frosh Pond. "Man, I gotta get out of here," he muttered.

Bryan scrambled to his feet and saw the dorm building emerge from the fog. His steps quickened. The whiskey came up with a sour taste in his mouth. He squatted by a bush and threw up. He struggled to put one foot in front of the other, tripped and fell. Everything turned black.

When Bryan opened his eyes, sunlight flooded the room. He groaned with pain.

"Good morning. How are you feeling?" Keith's voice came from a corner.

Bryan tried to sit up, but pain ricocheted between his ears. "Darn. My head!"

"You have a bump. It must be painful. Last night, you had fallen near our dorm. When I got back from the observatory, I saw you. Greg helped me get you to our room."

"Ugh. Couldn't have. I left the party early." Bryan rubbed his eyes. "What time is it?"

"It's past noon. Your parents called."

Oh, no. "What did you tell them?"

"That you couldn't come to the phone right now. They said they'd call after church."

Bryan massaged his forehead and crawled out of bed. He went to brush his teeth and shower, hoping to wash away the remnants of last night. What would bother his parents more, that he had a colored roommate or that he got drunk?

***

During his visit home at Thanksgiving, Bryan sat with his family to watch the news broadcast of President Kennedy's assassination. As the television showed Martin Luther King and his followers mourning the president's death, Bryan's father walked up to the television and fiddled with its rabbit ears. "These Negroes are good people. Not like the Black Panthers."

Bryan thought of Keith who adored President Kennedy. In the past two months, they had become good friends. They had the same classes and shared their interests in literature, tennis and physics. Was this a good time to tell his parents about his roommate's race? Words tumbled out of his mouth. "Yes, some of them are very nice. Like Keith."

"Your roommate?" His mother gasped. "They made you share a room with a colored?"

His father jolted out of his chair. "It's one thing to treat them well. But to put you in a room with a Black Panther radical is just not right."

"Keith is not a radical." Bryan clutched the armrest of his chair. "At first, I was shocked that I had to share a room with this guy. But he's good, and a straight A student. He has helped me many times. He answered the phone for you. What did you think of him?"

"He sounded good enough." His mother shook her head. "But how can you judge a person over the phone?"

His father's face flushed red. "I'll call the dean to find another roommate for you."

"You don't need to, Dad. The first quarter is almost over. It's a matter of few months now. Next year I can rent an off-campus apartment with my friends."

"Well, if it's only temporary, I guess it's okay." His father raised his brows. "But you tell me if you want to get out of that room early."

Bryan nodded and relaxed his clenched hands.

CHAPTER FIVE

KEITH

Keith stared at his class schedule. His sophomore year was almost over. Now he had to declare a major. He wanted to study planetary physics, but his grandparents were paying for college and they expected him to become a doctor. Out of respect for them, he had taken biology. But the smell in the lab and dissecting the fetal pig was nauseating.

During Christmas vacation, with great trepidation, he had told his parents and grandparents, "I can't take biology. It makes me sick. I want to major in planetary physics."

His grandfather frowned. "How will you make a living?"

Keith had thought of a quick answer. "NASA needs people with that kind of degree."

His father suggested, "Maybe you can become an engineer. NASA hires engineers."

Sitting at his desk in the dorm, Keith tapped his pencil against his forehead. Getting an engineering degree wasn't such a bad idea, especially if it made his parents and grandparents happy. He could still study the planets and get a career at the same time. He had already taken calculus and physics for his astronomy courses, which also fulfilled the requirements for engineering college. He nodded. That's what he would do.

Besides, he and Bryan could continue to study together. Bryan told him that even before he came to Seattle he had decided he wanted to be an engineer. Keith smiled. How things had changed. He had not thought he would ever study with Bryan. When they first started college, Bryan was busy partying and being a Frat guy. Even Greg, who had helped "walk" a drunken Bryan to the dorm room, had asked Keith how he put up with this party creature. Somehow, Bryan changed after the initiation incident. Now he and Keith had already rented an off campus apartment with their friends Ron and Greg.

All Keith needed now was a nice girlfriend, like Anjali, his lab partner who shared his views and understood him. But then Anjali went to India to get married. His housemates and their girlfriends sometimes tried to set him up. But most girls Keith dated, seemed interested in him only because of his skin color. As if they were looking for a shock reaction. He wanted a girl who could share his views on religion, politics, culture, and would love him neither because nor in spite of his race.

* * *

Keith looked out the window of his living room at the blooming rhododendrons. It was already the spring of 1967, and after four years of studying machine design, strength of materials, applied mathematics and such subjects, he would have his degree in mechanical engineering in June. Although he was aiming for the aerospace field, his adviser had suggested that a basic mechanical engineering degree was better for getting a good job.

The Boeing recruiters were at the campus and Bryan told him he was going for an interview. "Hey, Keith they're hiring a bunch of people. Why don't you try too?"

"I want to work at NASA."

"Buddy, Boeing has an aerospace division that designs parts for NASA."

Keith combed his hair with his fingers. He had been thinking that with luck, after gaining some experience, he might even work his way up (or down) to Houston. But most NASA people had PhD's. For now, he needed a break from his studies. "I think I should try at Boeing."

The next day, Keith collected his credentials, donned his suit and tie, and checked himself in the mirror. "You're looking sharp," Bryan said.

Keith was one of the last students to make it to the interview. The recruiters asked him about his studies and other interests.

"I have majored in mechanical engineering, and also studied astronomy. I'm interested in the lunar vehicle that Boeing is designing."

A man with round rim glasses and crew cut hair answered, "At present, we're looking for engineers for the development of the Supersonic Transport. The government has agreed to provide funding for the SST for us to compete with the TU-144 that the Soviets are working on, and the Concorde that the British and French are designing."

"SST sounds like a great project." Keith said.

After answering the questions they asked, Keith decided if they gave him an offer, he would take the job. Employment was hard to come by, and Super Sonic Transport was a cool idea. Maybe a job at Boeing could lead to his dream job at NASA.

CHAPTER SIX

BRYAN

Standing at his desk, Bryan marveled at his luck. Although Boeing had been recruiting engineers with master's and PhD's from all over the world, they had selected him right out of college. Three days before he received his bachelor's degree with the class of '67, he got a job offer. He had bounded to the living room and waved the letter at Keith. "Boeing wants me!"

Keith had grinned and raised his envelope. "Me, too."

As he left for his orientation, he looked around at other engineers in the hall, their heads bent on their desks. Although nervous at first, when he saw other new hires, Bryan relaxed.

Mr. Davis, the lead engineer, a heavy, oval-faced man, nodded for them to take their seats and smiled. "I want to formally welcome you. Supersonic aviation is not new. The military has been using SST, but commercial planes involve more research and resources." The man stretched his suspenders as if extending his chest in pride. "Now, Boeing may not have been the first, but we've always been the best—whether it's jet transport or 737 models—we've sustained and outsold our competitors."

Bryan recalled the televised unveiling of the SST mock-up, which had looked like an image from "Star Trek." A smile crossed his face. Now he was one of the engineers who would work on this plane of the future.

The lead engineer distributed the handout sheets. "We're going to be the third to manufacture the SST. But ours will be faster, better, and efficient. An aluminum aircraft can only handle the heat generated at the speed of Mach 2.2. Our goal is Mach 2.7. We plan to build it with titanium."

Bryan's mind whirled as he calculated silently. Mach 2.2 was 1,450 miles per hour. Boeing was aiming for a speed of Mach 2.7, almost 1,900 miles per hour!

* * *

Although work was going well, Bryan felt a vacuum when his girlfriend, Wendy, left him. Why was this happening to him? At the office, he set aside the frustrations of his love life and rechecked his calculations before his meeting with Mr. Davis. Bryan was glad he had a good boss. He had heard complaints about how some supervisors took credit for the ideas of their subordinates, or never explained the projects to them. John Davis was different. He explained design concepts, listened to Bryan's ideas and gave credit to him during meetings.

Bryan looked at his watch and hurried down the hall to make a copy of his calculations. As he approached the Xerox Machine, he noticed a woman standing by the copier, her back to him. His eyes traveled from her shoulder-length, auburn curls, down the black dress enhancing her curves. This must be the new secretary the engineers were raving about. He stood spellbound. What a babe!

A muscular man stepped up and tapped her on the shoulder. "We need to leave early today. I'll meet you in the parking lot at four."

Chapter Six

"You don't need to remind me again." The woman didn't even look up.

The man nodded to Bryan as he left.

Turning from the copy machine, the woman nearly collided with Bryan. "I'm sorry, I didn't see you. Do you need to use the copier?"

"I can wait." Bryan couldn't look away from her expressive blue eyes. He summoned his courage and introduced himself. "I'm Bryan Stafford. I work in the stress analysis group."

"I'm Jane Peters." A smile lit up her face. "The machine is all yours."

All day at work and later in his apartment, Jane's beautiful face invaded Bryan's mind. He tried to remember if she was wearing a ring. Was the man her boyfriend or husband? He hit his pillow. "Damn! This perfect woman is already taken."

* * *

As weeks passed, trips to the copy machine in hopes of running into Jane became Bryan's favorite pastime at work. Jane told him she had a teaching degree, and was certified to teach typing and clerical skills. She was working as a secretary until she could find a job in her field. Questions about her companion whirled in Bryan's mind. Were they married? Living together? He shook his head to clear his thoughts. Just a month ago, he had been brooding over his broken relationship, and now he was pining after a girl who probably belonged to someone else.

Bryan rose from his chair to make his usual mid-morning trip to the copy machine. Before he could leave, Claire, the matronly engineering secretary, stopped at his desk. "Jane and Dan were in a car crash this morning. They're in the hospital."

"Oh, no." Bryan pushed away his chair. "Are they seriously

hurt?"

"Jane has a few bruises, but her cousin has broken ribs."

Bryan relaxed. At least she wasn't badly hurt. He asked, "Cousin? Was another person riding with them?"

"No. Just Dan. The guy in accounting." Claire explained, "Jane lives with him and his wife since this is only a temporary job for her."

"Oh." Bryan let out his breath. Cousin—the word never sounded so wonderful. "I hope Dan recovers soon."

Claire pushed her bifocals up her nose. "I'm going to visit them this evening. I thought I'd take flowers. From our group. Would you like to contribute a dollar?"

"Of course." Bryan reached in his pocket for his billfold. "Do you mind if I tag along?"

* * *

Even months later, Bryan remembered the welcoming gleam in Jane's eyes when she had seen him at the hospital. When she returned to work the following week, he asked her out. They had been dating for eight months now, longer than he had dated any other woman. This Friday, he couldn't wait to leave work as he fantasized his evening with Jane—dinner and seeing *Midnight Cowboy*.

While waiting for her, Bryan stopped by to chat with his friend, Ted Graber. The old draftsman was nicknamed "Boeing Encyclopedia."

"So, what's the history lesson for today, Ted?" Bryan teased him. Seeing Jane coming toward him, he smiled and nodded to her.

Ted, who was rummaging through photographs and newspaper clippings in his desk drawer, looked up. "Hi, Jane, look

Chapter Six

what I found." He handed her a picture. "I thought you might like to see Rosie the Riveter during the war years. But not all Rosies were riveters. They were inspectors, expeditors, even security guards." The lines around his eyes crinkled. "Some Rosies came from Alaska after the army closed down their brothels. To make money on the side, they conducted their old business in the tunnels at Plant Two."

Jane slipped her hand into Bryan's. He squeezed it. "Ted, tell her about that tube couple."

Ted gave a hearty belly laugh. "It was during the production of B-29s. Since the plane's bomb bay was not pressurized, the crew had to crawl through a long tube to reach it. These tubes were stacked in a pyramid shape between wooden wedges, and were taken one at a time for installation. A Rosie and her man crawled inside a tube. Meanwhile a worker pulled out the wedge. The tubes rolled everywhere and the one with the couple rolled more than 70 feet. Can you imagine how much explaining they had to do?"

Jane smiled. "That's quite a story, Ted."

Ted put his newspapers and photographs inside the drawer and stood. "Time to go home or else I'll have a lot of explaining to do to my wife."

Bryan laughed. "See you Monday." He picked up his briefcase. When they were in the parking lot, Bryan put his arm around Jane and whispered, "How about a tube-tryst?"

Jane blushed and rolled her eyes.

* * *

People in the office seemed preoccupied with the Apollo Eleven moon landing scheduled for the evening. An engineer across from Bryan's desk joked, "What happens if Armstrong and Aldrin reach the moon and the Russians have already taken their parking space?"

Bryan chuckled at the comparison of moon landing to the parking woes at work. He spotted Jane approaching his desk. "Did you hear the joke?"

"Yeah. Really funny." She whispered, "I've something to share. Can we go out to lunch?"

"Sure." Bryan picked up his car keys. As they walked to the parking lot, He asked, "So, what's the news?"

"Remember the interview I had at Cedarville High School some time back?" She handed him a letter. "I got this yesterday. It's the kind of job I was looking for."

Reading the letter of her job offer, Bryan's jaw clenched. "Isn't it too far? How are we going to see each other? Are you taking it?"

"Of course. My job here is temporary and this new one is in my field."

"Well, you made your decision. What can I say? Good luck." He didn't want to act like what the women these days termed, a "male chauvinist pig" but, if like those feminists, Jane expected him to move with her to the boondocks, she had another "think" coming.

You knew I didn't want to be a secretary all my life. I was going to ask you to help me find an apartment between Seattle and Cedarville. But you're being such a jerk."

Bryan sighed. Was he cursed in love? On the return drive to the office, Bryan waited for Jane to break the silence, but she didn't. When they reached the parking lot, Jane got out, slammed the car door and left.

While driving to his apartment with Keith, Bryan told him about Jane's new job.

Keith shook his head. "Buddy, you really are upset. Let's watch the moon landing together. It will get your mind off your

Chapter Six

problem. I have some beer, and I'll order a pizza."

"Okay. I've nothing else to do."

Later in Keith's apartment, Bryan picked up the *Seattle Times* from the table. Big day for July 20, 1969. Along with the Apollo Eleven coverage, there were stories of Vietnam War deaths. So many people were dying and America was celebrating the moon landing.

Keith set two beer bottles, paper plates and pizza on the coffee table. They had just started eating when the announcement came, "The Eagle has landed."

Keith whistled. "Hooray."

"I don't care about your damn moon." Bryan bit into the hard pizza crust. "Neil Armstrong might have taken a giant leap for mankind, but here men are leaping to wars and coming home in body bags."

Keith sat up straight. "Did something happen? I mean to one of our classmates?"

"I don't know." Bryan shoved the paper toward Keith. "But look here."

Keith sighed. "They keep talking about ending the war and nothing so far."

Bryan massaged his temples. While he went to college and got a nice job, other young men were sent to Vietnam to face death. On the other hand, Vietnam looked like a good choice now, with Jane moving far away.

* * *

Time was flying at supersonic speed at work, but it crawled like a slug for Bryan after Jane moved to Cedarville. Several months had passed before he overheard another secretary talking to Claire about a note she had received from Jane. Later, Bryan went to

Claire and asked for Jane's phone number. He decided to swallow his pride and give her a call. No harm in asking how she liked her new job. He wasn't actually going to apologize to her.

Bryan drove home from work and picked up his mail. On top of the pile of letters, he saw an envelope from Selective Services. Inside his apartment, he ripped open the envelope and read. His hands trembled. The letter said that his name had been drawn under the lottery system. He had to report for basic training in three weeks.

He threw his draft notice on the table and stormed out into the rain. A block away, he saw a red and white road sign where someone had added "WAR" underneath the "STOP." Bryan had never joined anti-war movements or burned his draft card, but he certainly hadn't expected to go to war either. He probably could get a deferment because of his job. But he didn't want to think about that now. He wanted to get away from everything.

He plodded to the Octopus Tavern.

The thumping rock music and smiling barmaids took his mind off his fear of impending war-days in Vietnam. He ordered a Scotch, took a sip, then a second.

His name had been selected in a "lottery system." He snorted, "Some lottery." Shirley Jackson's short story, "The Lottery," in which each year a lottery winner was stoned to death, flashed into his mind. Instead of stones, nowadays the lottery "winners" were sent to a hostile land to face bullets.

CHAPTER SEVEN

KEITH

From his living room window, Keith saw Bryan stagger into his apartment. Was he sick? Or did he just return from a bar? Bryan hadn't gone on a drinking binge since his first year in college. Keith wanted to get the Sports Illustrated that Bryan had borrowed. Might as well go over, get the magazine, and check on him. The door to his apartment was ajar. Strange! Bryan never left the door open.

Keith went inside and heard the shower running. As he reached for the magazine on the coffee table, a sheet of paper fell on the floor. He picked it up. Draft notice? Dear Lord, not him! He tossed it back on the table. Seeing Jane's phone number on a piece of paper, he memorized it and dashed back to his apartment.

"Damn! What a rotten thing to happen." Keith plopped on his sofa with his head in his hands. The same heaviness he had felt at the assassinations of Martin Luther King Jr. and Robert Kennedy overcame him now. A shiver snaked up his spine.

With pounding heart, he dialed Jane's phone. When Jane answered, he swallowed the lump in his throat. "Hi, this is Keith. I … I… I wanted to tell you Bryan has been drafted."

"Oh, my God." Jane's voice broke. "I haven't spoken to him for months. Has he told his family?"

"I don't know. It looks like the letter arrived today. I'll call Doug right away."

Keith called Bryan's brother who was a sophomore at the University of Washington.

"I'm coming over to talk to Bryan," Doug said.

"But you can't. Bryan doesn't know that we know."

"What the hell do you mean? Was he going to war without telling us? How do you know?"

Keith cleared his throat, searching for words. He had not only snooped into his friend's mail, but had broadcast it. "Doug, listen to me. I went to his apartment to get my magazine and saw the draft notice on his coffee table. He was acting weird this evening."

"Keith, we have to do something."

"Why don't we meet tomorrow? Jane is coming. Let's get him talking first."

When Keith went to bed and tried to sleep, his stomach burned, as if he had eaten a cup full of crushed red pepper that came with the pizza.

* * *

The past two weeks had evaporated so soon. Keith, Doug and Jane had gathered at Bryan's apartment and talked about his options—getting deferment because of his job, fleeing to Canada.

"Nothing is going to work. I'll just go and get it over with." Bryan had remained stoic. "Think of it this way. More people die in car crashes than in Vietnam."

Now, Bryan was leaving for Spokane to his parents before going to Biloxi for his basic training. Keith glared at the looming gray clouds that hung above Sea-Tac Airport and the wet morose

Chapter Seven

runway below. He took a deep breath and hugged his friend. "I'll probably see you in Vietnam soon." Before he choked up, he moved aside for Doug and Jane to say their goodbyes.

Bryan gave his car keys to his brother and hugged him. "You take good care of my car."

When Bryan and Jane embraced and kissed, Keith and Doug walked away to give them privacy. Doug said, "I'm glad they made up. They're so right for each other."

Keith nodded then waved to Bryan as he left for the plane. He began a rational, hopefully comforting speech for Doug and Jane, "They won't position him with the soldiers. He'll be given a safe desk job." But Keith wasn't sure whether his rambling had convinced them of Bryan's safety. It certainly hadn't convinced him.

* * *

Keith's work at Boeing dragged on with more objections about the presumed effects of the SST on environment. He understood the public's concerns about noise and air pollution. Any activity could disturb the ecological balance, but would inactivity solve the problem? The recent environment-related improvements had increased the engineering costs. Now Congress objected to their new estimate of four billion, much larger than the original. Keith chewed on his pencil. Wasn't it better to spend the money on transportation rather than a war that was killing young men and taking them away from their families and friends? The government called it "defense spending," but who were they defending? He set aside his calculations and reread Bryan's letter that his friend had asked him to share with Ted.

Just as Keith stood to take Bryan's letter to Ted, his supervisor called him to his office. When Keith entered, Mr. Baudry gestured for him to sit. Hunching forward, the boss began, "As you know, we've been asked to cut our group by ten percent." He handed Keith a piece of paper.

Keith stared at his layoff notice. He had expected it for some time, still, he was shocked.

"As you know," the boss continued, "qualified laid-off engineers are being absorbed by other departments. You should contact Charles Jackson in Minuteman Missile System group. I'll put in a good word for you."

"Thank you for the reference." Keith stood, forced a smile and left the room.

He went to Ted's desk and gave him Bryan's letter. Keith showed him his layoff notice.

"I'm sorry, my friend." Ted scratched his chin. "SST is doomed. It's neither a commercial project, like the 747, nor a defense project like missiles and bombers. At least those who get laid-off earlier will have a better pick of jobs than those who go later."

"Actually, Mr. As-You-Know said I could get a job at the Minuteman Missile division."

Ted slapped the file on his desk. "Frankly, I'm so upset with the management, when I get my pink slip, I won't even try for another division."

"Well, Ted, you're retirement age anyway. How long have you been working here?"

"Close to thirty-five years. My father worked here before that." Ted showed Keith a photograph of the old shipyard where William Boeing and Conrad Westervelt launched their first seaplane, the B & W. "My father told me, in the early days, the Navy had ordered fifty planes, but only half of them were sold when World War I ended and their orders got cancelled. Mr. Boeing paid out of his pocket to help the workers. My father took a voluntary pay cut."

"Can you imagine any employee taking a pay cut now?" Keith asked.

"Nowadays people are not loyal to their companies." Ted shook his head. "But the executives don't care about their employees or give up their shares either. It's a damn shame."

Later, at home, Keith turned on the television. Listening to the news of more war stories, and the young dead, he shook his head. He hoped President Nixon meant when he said "Peace is at hand," and Bryan would come home safely. Keith turned off the television and picked up the class schedule of the University of Washington from his coffee table. The fall quarter was about to start. He had been a part-time student for more than a year. If he took a full load, he would finish his master's in three quarters. Instead of going through the hassle of changing departments at Boeing and facing yet another uncertain future, perhaps he should complete his degree. And, it was good that he had been saving for a rainy day. It had just arrived.

* * *

Keith had plunged into the fall quarter, taking some humanities courses along with his requirements for a master's in mechanical engineering. One quarter was already behind him. In the winter quarter, he decided to take a Buddhism course that a friend, Yokimo Sato, had suggested. While growing up, he had learned about neither his mother's Buddhist nor his father's Baptist religion. When his grandfather Kunigama passed away, Keith's heart had burned with guilt for not paying more attention to his wise grandfather. Perhaps he could make up for it now.

On a February morning, when Keith walked toward his Buddhism class, the frosted lawn still showed traces of winter, but the crocuses by the sidewalk heralded spring. He sat in the back row and listened to the professor, who talked about meeting the Dalai Lama in India, where the Buddhist leader had taken refuge after China had invaded Tibet. The professor wore a casual shirt and jeans, but he exuded the serenity that Keith associated with monks in saffron robes.

"Buddha," the professor explained, "didn't dwell on the unsolvable metaphysical questions of God and the hereafter. He saw the root of human suffering in ignorance, which according to him, could end with knowledge."

Keith took notes as the professor explained the fourfold scheme—of recognizing the suffering, identifying its cause, establishing a goal to end it, and cessation of suffering by following the right path. How logical it all sounded.

He kept on jotting down notes even after the professor left, so he wouldn't forget the key points. Yokimo came over and teased him, "Are you writing a treatise?"

"Yokimo!" A voice interrupted before Keith could reply. He looked up to see an attractive woman wave and walk toward them. "Hi, stranger, haven't seen you in months."

The two women hugged. Yokimo said, "Alicia, Have you been in hiding or what?"

"Why don't we catch up over lunch?" Alicia glanced at Keith and turned back to Yokimo. "But, if you've plans, we can get together another time."

"Let's do lunch. Oh, this is my classmate, Keith Wilson." She turned. "And this is Alicia Devries." Yokimo asked, "Keith, would you like to join us?"

"If you two don't mind, I can grab a quick bite with you." Keith collected his pen and notebook wondering if he'd be intruding. Well, Yokimo had invited him and he needed to eat.

At the Husky Union Building, they picked up their

Chapter Seven

sandwiches and tea cups and took a table. Yokimo stirred sugar into her tea. "Alicia's parents are also first-generation immigrants like my parents and your grandparents."

"Let me guess." Keith swallowed a bite of sandwich. "They came from Holland."

Alicia smiled. "Good deduction."

Yokimo continued her chatter. "So, Alicia, how's your photography coming?"

Alicia took out an envelope of prints from her backpack. "I took these pictures last year for our catalog. We place the catalogs at the entrance of the field during the Tulip Festival. Actually, we've already mailed them to a few places."

"Beautiful." Yokimo passed the pictures to Keith. "These are from her parents' farm."

As he admired the pictures of yellow, purple, red and white tulips, he decided he would take his parents to see the flowers. His mother would enjoy them. "When is the season?"

"The usual season is April, but the weather has been mild, so the flowers might bloom by the end of March." Alicia pushed her eyeglasses back on her nose and narrowed her brown eyes.

Keith listened to the gentle voice, and gazed at her smooth skin and brown neck-length hair tucked behind her ears.

* * *

It had been more than a month since Keith met Alicia. Seeing her in Buddhism class and later having lunch with her and Yokimo made him want to spend more time with her. But she was so busy during the tulip season and he didn't want to bother her.

On a sunny Sunday in early-April, Keith drove his parents to the tulip fields.

"It's like a rainbow on earth," his mother gushed as they drove past field after field.

His father said something about the acres of incredible blooms, but Keith couldn't concentrate on the flowers that carpeted the landscape or what his parents were saying. He drove, thinking about seeing Alicia again.

Later, as they walked toward the displays in the Devries Garden, Keith heard Alicia's voice. He spotted her in a group standing in front of a colorful array of tulips. "You can enjoy the daffodils, tulips and then irises from March until May. The height of each variety and the time they bloom is noted in the catalog. Some are early blooms, some are late blooms. Please take that into consideration when you order your bulbs. Plant the shorter ones in front, mid-size next, and then the taller ones."

She looked around. A huge smile spread across her face as she saw Keith. She waved. He savored her eloquent glance and waited for her to finish her presentation before approaching her.

A hand clasped his shoulder and he turned to see Bryan's girlfriend. "Hi, Jane!" He hugged her. "What are you doing here?"

"I'm here with some teachers. I live just five miles away." Jane gracefully walked over and introduced herself to his parents.

Jane looked elegant in her burgundy pantsuit and shoulder-length hair. Keith's eyes wandered back to Alicia. Dressed in her jeans, T-shirt and tennis shoes, she looked beautiful. The crowd had moved on, so Keith and his companions went to her. He introduced them, "This is Jane Peters, and my parents, George and Miyoki Wilson. You explained the planting and arranging of the bulbs very well, with your directions, I think even I could attempt it."

Alicia looked at Keith's parents and smiled. "Hello, nice to meet you. Hope you're enjoying the tulips. Excuse me, I need to go." Alicia turned and walked away.

Keith stared at the windmill wondering why Alicia seemed so

Chapter Seven

cool. She was radiant just a while ago when she had spotted him. Had he offended her? She already knew about his Japanese mother and black father, so that couldn't have caused her indifference.

* * *

It had been weeks since the visit to the Devries Gardens, and Keith didn't get a chance to see Alicia. He called her once but her roommate said she wasn't there. He might have to ask Yokimo to find out why Alicia was avoiding him.

After the Earth Day gathering, as Keith walked across the street with Yokimo and a group of engineering students, a car sped through a nearby puddle. Yokimo stepped back to avoid the splash, slipped on the wet pavement, and landed on her arm.

Keith reached down to help her. "Are you okay?"

"Ouch!" Yokimo struggled to her feet. "I just stumbled." She lifted her arm.

"This could be a fracture," John, a student from the group said. "We better take her to Harborview. My car is parked down the street. I'll bring it around."

Yokimo groaned, "I suppose it won't hurt to get it checked."

John dropped them at the emergency entrance of Harborview Medical Center. "Call me when you need a ride back. Keith, you know my number?"

Keith nodded and helped Yokimo to the lobby, where they waited with a variety of people. A bearded man next to them reeked of beer and tobacco. Yokimo cradled her injured arm and asked Keith, "Instead of calling John again, can you call Alicia? She'll give us a ride back."

"Sure." Keith stood. This would give him a chance to see her, and maybe find out why she was avoiding him. He called her from a pay phone outside the hospital.

Alicia answered and promised to be there in a few minutes.

Twenty minutes later, Alicia dashed into the emergency room. Just as she reached for Yokimo's hand, a nurse called her name and took her to the examination room.

While waiting in the lobby, Keith's attention was split between an insipid sitcom on television and complaints from other patients. His mind whirled with questions for Alicia, who sat next to him flipping through a magazine. He cleared his throat. "Still busy with tulips?"

"No, they're gone." She looked up. "By the way, I ran into your girlfriend the other day."

"Girlfriend?"

"Yes. The one who came to see the tulips with you."

"Jane Peters? She's not my girlfriend." His heart thudded. Is that what Alicia had had been thinking? "She's my buddy Bryan's girlfriend. He's in Vietnam."

Her face turned red. She chuckled. "First, I saw you with Yokimo, but she told me you were like cousins. Then I saw you with Jane. I thought you had a whole flock of girlfriends."

He laughed. "I was coming from the Earth Day celebration with Yokimo when she fell."

"Oh, I was there too. It was a huge crowd. And for a group that talked about saving the earth, they sure made a mess with their beer bottles, pop cans, and fliers."

"I think their motto is, 'Do as I say, not as I do.'" Keith laughed.

Alicia smiled, showing her dimples. Keith relaxed. As they chatted, his admiration grew for her simple tastes, her interests in literature and other cultures, and her loyalty to her friends.

He hardly noticed that two hours had passed before the emergency room doctor came out and told them, "Her X-rays show no fracture. I've given her a prescription for pain. Make sure she rests and doesn't drink alcohol. She'll be ready to go home in a few minutes."

"I'll stay with her tonight and make sure she follows your orders," Alicia told the doctor.

* * *

Yokimo's accident had brought Keith closer to the girl of his dreams. In late spring, after watching a matinee, Guess Who's Coming to Dinner at the campus, he and Alicia walked hand-in-hand to the HUB and sat at a table. Keith brought two cups of tea, then asked, "Do you think your parents will act like Spencer Tracy and Katherine Hepburn?"

He loved her, and his parents liked her, but he hadn't met Alicia's parents and wasn't sure what they would think of his biracial heritage.

"Seeing you won't be a surprise for them." Alicia put her hand on his. "I've shown them your picture. They would like you to come for dinner. My Dad was so happy when I told him you're getting a master's in engineering. He values education."

"Hey, lovebirds!" Yokimo called. "Don't forget, I took a fall to get you two together."

Keith grinned. "We'll be grateful to you forever."

"Keith," Bryan's brother, Doug strode to their table. "I was looking for you. Bryan is back in Spokane."

"What happened? Is he okay?" It must be serious because he wasn't supposed to come home yet. Keith chewed on his lip.

Doug sat down beside him. "His jeep in Da Nang overturned. He fractured a rib and tore some ligaments in his shoulder. They sent him to a hospital in Thailand, then to Spokane."

Keith worried about his friend. "Can I call him?"

"Heck, yeah. When I talked to him, he asked about you." Doug turned to Alicia. "And I told him about the new love in your life. I was thinking, after exams we could go to Spokane. Jane said when her summer vacation starts, she'd go too. Maybe we can all go together."

Keith let out a breath of relief. From what Doug said, Bryan's injury was not life threatening. "Let's do it." He couldn't wait to take Alicia to meet Bryan.

* * *

Keith woke up in the middle of the night with stomach cramps. What a time to get the flu. He cursed the stars as he made several trips to the toilet. His plans to take Alicia to see Bryan disintegrated. He couldn't leave the room, let alone drive to Spokane.

For three days, he barely managed to get up to drink some tea and lie down again. Eventually, he was able to sleep through a full night. He awoke to a persistent ringing. It couldn't be the alarm, since he was through with his classes. The clock radio was quiet and showed eleven a.m. He rubbed his head. It must be the doorbell. He staggered to the door.

Alicia stood there, all smiles. "I brought some chicken soup for the patient."

He resisted his desire to embrace and kiss her. "You shouldn't be here. The place is a mess and full of germs. Thanks for the soup though."

She pushed open the door wider and stepped in past him. "After three days, I'm sure your germs are safe. Last night when I called, you said you were feeling better."

"Better, yes. But not recovered." Keith brushed his fingers through Alicia's hair. "My mother wanted to come over, I said no. But I guess there is no stopping you."

"Why don't you take a shower? I'll clean up in here and warm

Chapter Seven

the soup for us." Alicia strode into the kitchen.

After a hot shower and a change of clothes, Keith felt better. He sprayed Lysol disinfectant around the house to combat any lurking germs. He embraced Alicia. "Now I feel alive. And hungry."

Aromas of oregano and lemon in the chicken broth whetted his appetite, but he still worried about being able to keep food down. It was so nice to see Alicia and he appreciated her efforts to cook for him. Alicia served him soup and toast, then brought her plate and sat across from him. Keith hesitantly swallowed one spoonful, then another. It didn't threaten to come up.

"You should rest now." Alicia cleared the table.

"My energy returned as soon as I saw you." He reached for her hand. "I wanted to take you to Spokane to meet Bryan. I'll call him and see if we can go next week."

"First you get well. Why don't we watch the tennis match?"

"Good idea." With his arm around Alicia, Keith turned on the television, fiddled with the channel knob, and adjusted the rabbit ears. They returned to the sofa.

They stayed in that blissful state until the doorbell rang. "Who could be here now?" Keith groaned. He barely had a few hours alone with Alicia.

"You stay seated. I'll be back." Alicia opened the door.

"Aren't you going to ask us in?" A male voice asked.

"Bryan?" Keith pushed himself up from the couch.

His friend stood in the doorway, his arm in a sling. He looked thin in his loose T-shirt and baggy pants. Keith strode forward. Bryan put his good arm around Keith's shoulder.

"Hey, buddy, good to have you back." He turned to Jane and Doug. "Come on in."

Doug cuffed Keith's shoulder. "Thank me for suggesting that he ride over with us."

"Thanks. For once, Doug, you had a good idea. Jane, thank

you, too. I'm sure you had something to do with this." He drew Alicia close. "Bryan, I still have to formally introduce her."

"We met at the door. But since you want the formality …" Bryan shook Alicia's hand.

After everyone settled in the living room, Alicia asked, "Would you like some coffee?"

"That sounds great." Bryan nodded.

While the women busied themselves in the kitchen, Bryan and Doug talked about the television shows and new cars. Keith finally asked, "So, tell me, buddy, how did this happen?"

"Let's talk about where I go from here. I'm hoping Boeing will reinstate me."

Keith leaned back in his chair. His friend didn't want to talk about his injuries or his experiences in Vietnam. To make matters worse, he was oblivious to the situation at Boeing. "They're laying off a lot of people. Even Ted lost his job after thirty-six years."

"I still want to go talk to John Davis at Boeing. I'll go to Cedarville and check out Jane's pad. Next week, I'll come stay with you and go see Davis. I hope I can pick up where I left off."

"Sounds like a plan. I'll start working on my resume. I need to find a job too," Keith said.

* * *

Keith drove Bryan to the Boeing office to see his former boss. Since Bryan had made an appointment with Davis, they were able to get inside the parking lot. Keith waited in the car, reading newspaper articles about Boeing layoffs and Vietnam War protests.

Soon Bryan walked out of the building. "It doesn't sound promising. The SST is as good as gone. I asked him about the 747. That would've been ideal for me in Everett, closer to Jane.

Chapter Seven

But he didn't sound hopeful there either."

"Sorry, buddy." Keith folded the newspaper. On his return from the war, instead of a welcome, Bryan faced war protests and loss of the job he loved.

Keith started the car. "After my layoff, I decided to finish my master's. Maybe you could do that, too."

"Davis gave me this card of the director of Engineering Corporation of America. The company hires temporary help, job-shoppers." Bryan slumped in his passenger seat. "But it looks like those openings won't be at Boeing."

"How about sending our resumes to this ECA office?"

"I don't know. I'm not that keen on getting temporary assignments all over the state." A knot formed on Bryan's forehead. "My parents have been telling me that I should get my MBA. Since jobs are hard to find, maybe I should do that."

"Makes sense. Especially when you can share Doug's apartment. Next year, the job market is sure to improve."

* * *

A week after Keith had mailed a resume to the Engineering Corporation of America he got a call for an interview at their office in Seattle. In the lobby, Keith checked his tie, then rearranged his resume and credentials in his hand. A man came to the door and asked him to come in. Inside the interview room, he glanced at the four men sitting around the table who nodded for him to sit in the vacant chair. The atmosphere was much more intimidating than the campus interview with the Boeing recruiters five years ago. He handed his application, diploma, and reference list to the man on his right. The man appeared to check each paper before passing it on to the next person. As they all took turns with the papers, Keith wiped his sweaty hands with his handkerchief.

What was going on in their minds? When the application and other credentials finally made it around the table, the balding man to his left kept Keith's resume and application and returned the diploma to him.

The man in the middle chair rested his elbows on the table. "Your grades are impressive. It seems your first and only job was at Boeing. But with your mechanical engineering background, you would surely adjust to the demands of other industries."

Keith nodded. "The same engineering principles can be applied to different product lines. My skills are transferable."

"Have you heard of Cascade Products?" one man asked.

Keith shook his head. "No, sir."

"It used to be a small company that manufactured logging equipment, then diversified and started designing and manufacturing deck machinery for offshore oil-drilling platforms. About eight years ago, Springfield Steel acquired the company. It has grown quite large under them. We're getting the most requests from Cascade for job-shoppers—temporary hires."

Keith hesitated. "I'm sorry, where did you say Cascade Products is located?"

"About seventy miles north of here, in a small town called Cedarville."

Cedarville, Alicia's hometown!

One man handed him a sheet. "These are our terms. You'll be employed by us and paid through us. If you sign the agreement, I'll call Cascade right now to confirm."

Keith studied the contract. "I'd like to give it a try."

Alicia was studying photojournalism at the University of Washington. After she graduated, she wanted to help her parents in their bulb farm. If he got this job, she would be ecstatic.

The man who had gone to make the phone call returned to the table. "Can you start next Monday?"

Chapter Seven

"Yes, sir."

"Here are the instructions for getting there. Take your transcripts and this copy of our contract. They'll try you out for a week. If it doesn't work out, we'll find another location for you."

Keith stood, shook everyone's hand one by one, and thanked them. His feet barely touched the ground when he returned to the car.

THE CASCADE YEARS (1971-1987)

CHAPTER EIGHT

KEITH

The Seattle drizzle continued as Keith Wilson drove north on I-5. He hummed along with "Dawning of the Age of Aquarius" and grinned. With a new job and Alicia in his life, it was a new age for him too. The sun peeked through the clouds and he caught a glimpse of a rainbow.

After an hour-and-a-half on I-5, he took the exit for Cedarville and continued for a few miles. He slowed down when he saw huge steel winches—larger than any he had ever seen on the ferries or tow trucks —and drove around the chain link fence into the parking lot. Before he got out, he checked his tie and picked up his briefcase with the appointment letter from ECA. He walked to the personnel office and introduced himself to the secretary.

The woman quizzed him, "Engineering Corporation of America sent you?"

"Yes, Ma'am." Keith fingered the knot on his tie. Not that he was shabbily dressed. Obviously, she didn't expect a colored engineer.

She rose from her chair. "I'll take you to the Director of Engineering."

As he followed the secretary, Keith glanced around at the other employees. Their homogenous whiteness was such a contrast to the varied races at the Boeing plant and the University of Washington. Would they accept him here?

At the director's office, the secretary introduced him to a round-faced, blue-eyed man. "Mr. Meyer, this is…"

Couldn't the woman remember his name? "I'm Keith Wilson."

"Thank you, Janice," When the secretary left, Mr. Meyer turned to Keith and extended his hand. "Hello, I'm Carl Meyer." After shaking his hand, he gestured for Keith to sit, then took his own seat. Propping his elbows on the desk, he glanced at the resume. "So, you used to work at Boeing for their Supersonic Transport. Do you have any experience with winches?"

"No, sir. My first job after graduation was at Boeing. When the SST was canceled, and I was laid off, I went for my master's. My engineering skills are transferable. I have experience in stress analysis."

"We can certainly use that. We have a backlog of anchor-handling equipment, mainly winches and fairleads for offshore platforms. You must have an idea about the product."

Keith knew that winches were used to hold offshore vessels in place during exploration and drilling operations, and fairlead guided a rope or winch cable. "I have a general idea."

"We have orders from two companies for mooring winches. We have designed several of these." He shuffled through catalogs of deck machinery and anchoring equipment and showed Keith a photograph of a steel drum. "Cascade built this during World War ll. An oil company had bought this from the Navy surplus, and used it for mooring. We have to redesign it for larger winches that can spool a mile long, two-inch wire rope." He rose from his chair. "Today you acquaint yourself with the job. Tomorrow you start the grind. Follow me. I'll introduce you to the engineering

Chapter Eight

secretary. She'll help you get started." He smiled.

Relaxed by the man's friendly attitude, Keith slipped his finger under his collar to loosen the grip of his tie. He took the catalogs and walked with Meyer, hoping this engineering secretary was not as brusque as the first one he met. Meyer stopped at a desk in the hall. "This is Norma Gunnersen. She's been here for more than fifteen years. So if you need any old manuals or blueprints, she is your source." He turned back to her. "And, Norma, this is Keith Wilson. He needs a desk."

Norma shook Keith's hand. "Welcome to Cascade." She pointed to open space behind a black board. "We can set up a desk over there for you. Is that okay?"

"That's fine." Keith nodded. As if he had a choice.

Meyer winked at Keith. "I'm sure you'd like to be in the midst of the action. Besides, if the draftsmen have any questions they'll come to you first."

Keith smiled.

Norma took him around and introduced him to draftsmen and other engineers. They appeared to be amicable. If they were put off by his dark skin they didn't show it. Finally, Keith settled at his desk and pored over the catalogs Meyer had given him. His career had certainly taken a different turn. Instead of calculating air resistance for planes, he would now be calculating the diameters for drum shaft and the power required to pull anchors on the ocean floor. Instead of Mach speed, he would have to slow his pace to feet-per-minute. In college, he had wanted to explore the skies, now he would work on the machinery that explored the depths of the sea.

"Keith!" He looked up and saw Meyer, who said, "Let's go to lunch."

The director of engineering was asking him to lunch. Quite a change from Boeing, where he'd been just one of the many recruits, and no one cared whether he ate or not.

During lunch, when Meyer found out that Keith drove more than seventy miles from Seattle, he suggested, "It would be better if you moved closer to work. Hold on a minute." He put his BLT sandwich on his plate, went to the front of the restaurant and returned with the *Cedarville Gazette.* "Seven years ago, when my wife and I moved here from Chicago, there were no rentals in this farming and fishing community. Now, I've seen some ads. Check them out."

Keith had planned to commute until he was sure the company was going to make him a permanent employee. Trying not to be rude, he opened the page to the classified section. "Thanks for the newspaper, sir."

"Hey, no 'sir' business here." Meyer cuffed Keith's shoulder.

* * *

Within two weeks, Keith got tired of driving an hour-and-a half each way and made appointments to see two homes with rooms for rent. After work, he drove to the first address and rang the doorbell. An older woman opened the door and stared at him. Keith said, "Hello, I called earlier about the room."

"Sorry, the room is already rented." She closed the door in his face.

Keith shook his head and returned to the car. He had to expect that in this small, all-white town. This wasn't the segregationist South, and "Negros" or "Colored" were now called "Blacks," but the attitudes remained the same.

After several visits to possible rentals and getting similar reactions, Keith thought of requesting the ECA office to find him another assignment in Seattle or Tacoma where the sight of a Black-Oriental man wouldn't shock people. His boss at Cascade

Chapter Eight

was helpful and his coworkers were friendly, but if he couldn't find a place to stay, how could he work in Cedarville? Alicia had said he could stay with her parents. But he didn't want to stay there while she was still studying in Seattle. Besides, their house was at least twenty miles from the office.

At work the next day, Keith settled in his chair and concentrated on his job. He flipped through the project notes of a smaller winch and checked the numbers to use as a guide for designing a larger winch. He filled out a table with the new data and took the form to the computer analyst for calculating the size of the gears and shafts.

On the way back to his desk, he talked to Norma. "Thanks for finding the old project books, Norma. Reading the correspondence and specifications from the engineers to their customers and seeing the calculations will help me with this new project. Now if only I could find a place to rent . . ."

"What kind of place are you looking for?"

"One or two bedroom apartment, or basement or whatever. There are several basement apartment listed, but I guess they don't want to rent to me."

"Sorry, you are having such a hard time." Norma put her elbow on the desk and rested her face on her hands. "Actually, my mom is thinking about renting her house. After Dad died, when Mom had a heart attack, we asked her to move in with us. I'll talk to her. You probably don't want to rent a house, though."

Norma seemed sincere in her offer to show the house. "Depends. How much is the rent?"

"I'll talk to my husband and my mom. You know how old people are. She said she wouldn't mind renting, but I don't know what she'll do. I'll let you know tomorrow."

"Thanks." Keith figured Norma was gently preparing him in case her mother refused.

* * *

The next evening, Keith met Norma and her husband, Harold, at Norma's mother's home. The old renovated house, especially the yard in the back, appealed to him. Though not a gardener himself, he could imagine his mother's joy at seeing the vegetable patch and rhododendron bushes. And Alicia? He could almost see her hazel eyes grow wide at the sight of the trellis covered with pink roses. Still, the house might be too expensive. "The rent for something so spacious must be high."

Harold ran his hand on his chin. "I've been checking the rental ads in the paper. You know a house this size rents for about two-fifty a month."

Just 250 dollars for this big house? Keith remembered his father's advice that the house payment—rental or mortgage—shouldn't exceed one-fourth of his monthly salary. This was only $25 more than what he was paying for his apartment in Seattle. "It's a great place."

Norma adjusted her slipping purse on her shoulder. "Would you like to come to our house and meet my mother? You can ask her any questions you have about the place."

"That sounds good. I'll follow you." Keith wanted to make sure Norma's mother wouldn't change her mind after seeing him.

Upon entering the Gunnersens' home, Keith inhaled the aroma of baked bread and put his hand over his stomach, hoping it wouldn't growl. Norma's mother, Olga Pedersen, welcomed him. "Hello, Keith, Norma told me about you."

"Hello." The wrinkled hand Keith held reminded him of his grandmother Kunigama. "Mrs. Pedersen, you have a lovely home. If it's all right with you, I'd like to rent it."

"When I came to live with Norma, I thought it was temporary."

Chapter Eight

Keith expected her to say she wanted to move back to her own home, but Olga said, "Now I'm resigned to the fact that I can't stay alone any more. Instead of leaving the house vacant, it's better if someone lives in it." She took her glasses off and wiped them with her handkerchief.

Right then two children came running to the living room. Norma hugged them. "Hi, sweethearts, this is our guest, Mr. Wilson. Keith, here are Eric and Anne."

The boy murmured, "Hello."

Norma ruffled Eric's hair. "He had a birthday last week and he's eleven now."

Eric went and sat by his father. "And my sister is not even eight."

The girl clung to her mother. "I'm hungry."

Olga took her granddaughter's hand. "Come I'll get your dinner." She turned to Keith, "Would you like to join us?"

Although touched by the old woman's invitation, Keith wasn't sure what to do.

Norma reassured him, "Mom cooks plenty. You are welcome to stay."

"You must try her meat loaf," Harold added. "She says she doesn't want to depend on us. Does she look like she is our dependent? She's here when the kids get home and has dinner ready when we come home." He chuckled, "Mom, you should rent your house so we keep getting this fine service."

Olga patted her son-in-law's hand. Keith thought of Alicia's mother. He hoped he could have such a close relationship with her. Harold stood and slapped Keith's back. "Let's eat."

During dinner, Norma asked, "So, Keith, what kind of things do you like to do?"

"Oh, I like hiking and reading. I play cards sometimes."

"What card games?" Olga Pedersen asked.

Norma set down her fork. "Keith, Mom, isn't trying to quiz you. It's just that she loves bridge and hasn't found a foursome to play in a while."

"In college, my three housemates and I used to play bridge. But I haven't played for a few years."

"Then you have to move nearby so we can have a foursome." Norma turned to her mother. "Wouldn't you like that?"

"That would be great." Olga smiled.

"So, you have cinched the deal." Harold chuckled. "Is it for the house or cards?"

Keith couldn't help but join in the laughter.

After dinner, Keith thanked everyone and stood to leave. Harold followed him to the door. "If you like the house, I'll draw up the rental contract and bring it to work."

"Yes, I love the house. Thanks."

Keith had not only found a rental, he had made some friends.

* * *

Keith watered the plants and mowed the lawn in his new rental home. Alicia had promised to come to him before going to her parents for the Labor Day weekend. Her parents had also invited Keith and his parents for dinner this evening.

Hearing a car door, Keith ran inside the house, slipped a tiny velvet box into his jeans pocket and rushed out the door. He pulled Alicia into his arms, then stepped back. Her eyes glistened as he bent to kiss her.

Inside the house, before Alicia could settle on the sofa, Keith grabbed his camera. "Let's go to outside. I want to take your picture."

They went to the yard, their fingers entwined. Alicia stood against the backdrop of the trellis. Through the camera lens,

Chapter Eight

Keith gazed into her eyes that matched her shiny brown hair. Then he glanced at her tie-dye blouse and denim shorts. They complemented the few pink roses that were still there. He pressed the shutter.

"Okay, let me take your picture." Alicia started to walk toward him.

"Don't move. I'm not done yet." He set his camera on a nearby plastic stool and stepped closer to her, took the box from his pocket and opened it. His eyes locked with hers, but he couldn't utter a word.

Alicia's hand flew to her mouth as she stared at the ring. What was she thinking? Would she accept his proposal? Keith's heart fluttered.

After what seemed like hours, she said, "Oh, sweetheart."

"We did talk about getting married after I got a job. So, will you marry me?"

Alicia wiped a tear with the back of her hand. Her mouth curled up at the corners and her eyes twinkled. "Yes, I'll marry you, Keith Wilson." She held out her hand.

Keith slipped the ring on Alicia's finger and wrapped his arms around her. As they walked inside, he bent down and nuzzled her neck, trying to savor her proximity before they had to leave for dinner at the Devries. "Do we have to go tonight?"

"Yes, we do," she whispered. "Remember your parents are coming there."

Keith made a face. "Then they'll come home with me and you'll stay with your parents. I want you with me."

"We have time." Alicia turned and kissed him. "And I'll be back on Monday before I leave for campus."

In late afternoon, Keith lay in bed savoring Alicia's scent while she took a shower. The thought of dinner with both sets of parents made Keith jittery and happy at the same time. Now that he and Alicia were officially engaged, her mother would nag them to set a wedding date. There would also be the issue of deciding on a church. The Devries belonged to the Dutch Reform Church. But Alicia couldn't stand the rigidity and had stopped attending services. What would his parents want? His father hadn't attended his Baptist church and his mother hadn't followed her Buddhist religion.

Alicia came out of the shower, wearing Keith's white bathrobe and sat beside him on the bed. He combed her wet hair with his fingers. "Sweetheart, how do you want to handle questions about the church?"

"We won't worry about it now. Today, we'll announce our engagement and tell them we'd like to get married after Christmas."

Later, in the Devries' living room, Keith took Alicia's hand. "We have an announcement."

"We're engaged." Alicia waved her hand displaying her ring.

"That's great news. Cheers!" Dad raised his wineglass. "We're happy to see you both take this step. Alicia, I already feel like you're our daughter."

Mom hugged Alicia.

Hennie Devries embraced Keith. "Welcome to our family." Then she smiled to Keith's mother. "Miyoki, it's wonderful to see our children so happy together. Keith is like a son to us."

"But, Mom, you already have a son," Peter called.

"Peter, you can surely use a big brother." Zosef Devries patted his son's back. He turned to Keith. "Now that you're officially his brother, guide him into choosing proper college courses so he can get a good job."

Keith winked at Peter sitting on the sofa. In the few months that they had known each other, Peter treated Keith like a friend.

"Now, children," Hennie said, "you know it takes time to plan a wedding. Have you decided on a date?"

Chapter Eight

"We're thinking of December, after my exams," Alicia replied. "Maybe, right after Christmas."

"Where do you want to get married?" Hennie asked, "What church?"

Seeing Alicia's knotted forehead, Keith reached for her hand.

"Hey, sis, remember how once we attended this Unitarian service?" Without waiting for an answer, Peter continued, "Even Mom goes there sometimes and likes the minister, Adele."

"Really?" Alicia raised her brows. "Mom, you never told me that."

"What do you think of Adele?" Hennie asked.

Alicia's eyes sparkled as she explained to the Wilsons, "She's a nondenominational minister. She has studied Eastern religion also." She squeezed Keith's hand. "We can write our own vows."

Keith nodded, flooded with relief that a conflict between Alicia and her mother about the church was averted. And it was good his parents were accommodating.

"Let's know how we can help you," Mom offered to Hennie.

Hennie smiled. "Believe me, Miyoki, I'll need your help. Keith said you do artistic flower arrangement. The Japanese arrangements are so pretty. What are they called?"

"Ikebana," Alicia answered for her future mother-in-law and smiled.

"We have our garden, but daffodils, tulips and irises don't bloom in December," Hennie said.

Mom patted Hennie's hand. "Don't worry I'll do the flower arrangements."

Watching the mothers, the smiling fathers, and feeling the warmth of Alicia's hand in his, made Keith's heart soar with joy.

CHAPTER NINE

BRYAN

Three days after Christmas, Bryan stood next to Keith as his best man. His eyes wandered from the poinsettias and carnations to the lavender candles and crepe paper decorations until he spotted Jane in the front row. Their friends' wedding would really put pressure on him. He had been going with Jane before Keith and Alicia met, and yet their friends were making a lifetime commitment.

Jane's not-so-subtle hint echoed in his ears. "I wonder how long Alicia would have waited if Keith hadn't proposed?"

Bryan pulled in a breath. Jane didn't seem to understand his problems. After he came from Nam, he was shocked that he couldn't get his job back at Boeing, so reluctantly enrolled in the MBA program at the University of Washington. Now, he had his degree but how could he make a commitment without a job in sight? Jane herself had pointed to a billboard in Seattle referring to Boeing's massive layoffs: THE LAST PERSON LEAVING TOWN, PLEASE TURN OFF THE LIGHTS.

He shook his head. Better concentrate on his wedding duties. He smiled at his friend. The hall filled with music as the flower

Chapter Nine

girls entered and moved down the aisle sprinkling rose petals. Seeing Alicia's long white lacy dress, Bryan imagined Jane wearing it. His gaze met Jane's lively blue eyes and he smiled. One day he would get married to her.

* * *

Before Bryan received his MBA, Keith had suggested that Bryan apply to Cascade Products. "Buddy, I know you have your heart set to work in aeronautics. Some people think of Cascade as 'dumb iron engineering.' But my job is quite challenging. With an MBA, does it matter if you're in marketing for planes or deck machinery? At least give it a shot."

Although Bryan had ignored the suggestion at first, finding a job had been harder than he had imagined. After the New Year, he sent his resume to Cascade.

Four days later, he received a call from the Cascade office. Now here he was for an interview. The secretary took him to the office of the director of personnel.

A tall man with square jaw greeted him. "Hello, I'm Adam Jones." He shook Bryan's hand indicating the man next to him. "This is Carl Meyer, Director of Engineering."

Bryan shook hand with a chubby man wearing a white shirt and maroon tie. Meyer smiled and pointed to a seat. On the desk, Bryan saw the resume he had mailed. Its white paper with black print looked bland on the rich mahogany desk covered with colorful catalogs of marine deck machinery, mechanical engineering books, and a yellow telephone. He opened his briefcase, took out his diplomas and transcripts and handed the papers to Jones, who glanced at them and passed them on to Meyer.

Meyer seemed to study his credentials. "Hmm. I see that you

are interested in a job in marketing. Did you see our want ad in *The Seattle Times* for design engineers?"

"I saw it this weekend after I had sent my resume."

"How do you feel about design work?" Jones asked. "Isn't that what you did at Boeing?"

Bryan leaned forward. "Yes, sir. But in my MBA, I majored in marketing and sales."

"There's no job available in marketing at present. Our marketing office is in Houston, corporate office is in Springfield, Illinois, and the offshore design and manufacturing facilities are here." Meyer leaned forward on the table. "In the near future we plan to open a marketing position at Cascade. It'll smooth the process for our engineering and manufacturing departments. At present, we're looking for design engineers for fairleads and related equipment. You must have an idea of what the work involves."

"I have a general idea." He knew fairleads were used to guide ropes or winch cables to the ocean floor. The engineering job wasn't his first choice, but if he took this job for now, it could become a stepping stone for a marketing position when it opened up. "I'm sure the design work is equally interesting. My friend Keith Wilson says it is quite challenging."

Jones handed him some papers. "If you are interested, here is the application form. You can fill it and mail to us."

Bryan took the papers from Jones. Meyer picked up Bryan's resume. "I see that you've used Keith Wilson as a reference."

"Yes sir." When Bryan had included Keith's name along with that of his faculty adviser and former-boss at Boeing, Keith had laughed, saying he had no influence with hiring.

"How long have you known Keith?" the personnel director asked.

"We've been friends since our first year in college." Bryan did

Chapter Nine

a quick calculation. "Nine years."

"He's a great engineer." Meyer gave a paper to Bryan. "This is a copy of the job description for the engineering position."

"Thank you." Bryan put the copy and his credentials into his briefcase and stood. "I was wondering if I could say hello to Keith."

"Go ahead. He recently became a permanent employee and a senior engineer." Meyer stood. "I'll show you his cubicle."

Bryan went in the direction that Meyer had pointed and stuck his head into Keith's cubicle. "Hi. I like your new office."

"It's small but better than the sitting in the hall." Keith gave a big smile. "How did it go?"

"If you have time, why don't we go to lunch and I'll tell you about it."

"Good idea." Keith picked up his wallet. "My treat."

At the restaurant, after they ordered lunch, Bryan told him the job was for design engineering not marketing. He gave Keith the job-description sheet.

Keith read it and whistled. "Wow! Project Engineer for fairleads."

"What?" Bryan turned the page around and read it. When Meyer gave him the paper, he had stuffed it in his briefcase. "I didn't even read it."

Guilt weighed heavy on his chest. Keith had only recently been made a senior engineer who had to report to a project engineer. "How did that happen? You have been working here for more than a year."

Keith took a sip of water. "Maybe if you get this position, you'll forget about ever trying for that Boeing job."

"Meyer said you are good at what you do. Why wouldn't they give the position to you?"

"Listen, buddy, I'm working with winches and we already have a project manager for that. I came through ECA as a temporary engineer, and only recently became a Cascade employee. I'm happy they made me a senior engineer. You applied directly to them just when this position opened up. Makes a difference."

The waitress brought their lunches. Bryan took a bite of his pastrami sandwich. "Well, if I get this job, it would be good to work with you. And I'll be closer to Jane."

CHAPTER TEN

NORMA

As Norma typed the parts list, she felt someone was watching her. She looked up and saw a young man with collar-length hair and long sideburns standing by her desk. "Hello"

"Hi, I'm Steve McGill from manufacturing. I need to see Keith Wilson to clear up a problem on a blueprint."

"I'll take you to his cubicle." She glanced at the boyish man. "I'm Norma Gunnersen. I don't remember seeing you before."

"I was transferred from Springfield last month." Steve combed his hair with his fingers. I don't know anyone at work that well."

He sounded lonely. In spite of his hippie appearance, he was soft-spoken and polite. Norma thought of her son. In five or six years, Eric might go to college in a different town. Who would help him? Turning to look at Steve again, Norma felt an urge to hug him and help him adjust to the area. She had invited Keith and Alicia, and the new engineer, Bryan, and his girlfriend, Jane, for dinner Saturday. She decided to invite this young transplant too.

* * *

On Saturday evening, Norma set the table for the guests, then spread garlic butter on the French bread. Her mother had prepared baked red snapper with spinach stuffing and Keith and Bryan had each offered to bring a bottle of wine. From the family room, Harold, who was with the kids as they ate their macaroni and cheese, announced, "Here they all come. You know, they must have synchronized their watches."

When the guests entered the house, Norma introduced Steve to her mother, Alicia and Jane. Soon they sat down for dinner. Keith offered a toast. "To Mrs. Pedersen, the best cook in town."

Bryan raised his glass. "And, to Norma and Harold for inviting us."

Alicia took a bite, then dabbed her lips with her napkin. "Mrs. Pedersen, I'd like this recipe. I definitely need cooking lessons before I invite you to dinner."

"I'll give you the recipe." Mom said, "Now tell me, how is your bridge game coming along? Are you using the cheat sheet I gave you?"

"It's been a great help. Thanks." Alicia smiled.

Jane added, "Mrs. Pedersen, you taught Alicia the Blackwood convention. The other day, we used it to ask for aces and made a small slam. The guys were sure shocked."

"We let you win so you wouldn't give up on the game. Right, Keith?" Bryan said.

Steve smiled. Since he hadn't said much, Norma asked him, "Do you like card games?"

"I do." Steve nodded. "I also play a little bridge."

Mom's eyes lit up. "We have people for two tables. Why not a game after dinner?"

Norma sipped her chardonnay. It was good to see the gleam in her mother's eyes. Although a native of Cedarville, she must

Chapter Ten

feel somewhat isolated like a newcomer. She couldn't drive anymore, and all her friends were either too old to visit, or had died. A round of the game she loved would lift her spirits.

Harold winked at Steve. "We invited you because Mom gave us an ultimatum that she wouldn't cook unless we play bridge. Without you, seven of us had to take turns at one table or poor dummy hopped from one table to the other. So, Norma had you investigated and found out you are a master player."

"Master Player?" Steve laughed.

During the card game, Norma got a chance to play and chat with all her guests. Before the evening ended they all decided to get together once a month for dinner and bridge.

CHAPTER ELEVEN

BRYAN

Despite his initial hesitation about accepting a position at Cascade Products, Bryan loved his job and liked his coworkers. Now that he and Jane were in the same town, they could be together several times every week and he knew Jane expected him to propose to her. Seeing the interactions of Harold and Norma, and Keith and Alicia, also made him think of marriage. However, his work often took him to the corporate office in Springfield or meetings with customers in Houston. The trips took the pressure off, of making an immediate commitment.

At the start of summer vacation, when Jane went to California for a teaching workshop, Bryan spent sleepless nights thinking about her. He wanted her and needed her. How long could he expect her to wait around? She waited for him to return from Vietnam, and while he finished his MBA. He decided to buy a ring before Jane got tired of him and found another man.

He called Alicia, "Hi, I need your help to choose a ring for Jane."

"Oh, Bryan, it's about time!" Alicia squealed. "I can meet you at Frederic Jewelers this afternoon. Why don't you ask Norma

Chapter Eleven

too? She knows more about jewelry."

"Okay, I'll do that. See you then."

At the jewelers, they found a dizzying array of rings. Some that Bryan liked were overly priced. Norma pointed. "Bryan, look at this." She asked the jeweler. "Could I see that one."

The diamond solitaire was a decent size and the price was reasonable. Approving looks from Norma and Alicia made the decision easy.

When they left the store, Norma asked, "So, when are you going to give it to her?"

Bryan chewed his lip. "Haven't decided. I'm waiting for the right time and place."

"Come on, Bryan." Norma patted his shoulder. "You have the ring, you have your girl. What are you waiting for? There's a nice restaurant in Anacortes where Harold proposed to me." A smile crossed Norma's face. "Of course, that was fifteen years ago."

Alicia said, "Jane loves the Diablo Lake area. They have great tours during summer."

"Good suggestions. And thanks for helping me with the ring."

* * *

When Jane returned, Bryan was ready with his surprise. He told her he had tickets for the Diablo Dam Tour. He hid the ring box and the tickets inside an envelope under the passenger seat of his car. As they drove toward the dam, Bryan thought of how Jane had stood by him. It was his turn to show his love for her. When they got closer to the visitor center, the majestic, snow-clad Cascade peaks gave Bryan a secure feeling about his future with Jane. He squeezed her hand.

After parking the car, Bryan checked his pockets. "What did I do with the tour tickets? They're not in my pocket. Were they on the seat? Must have fallen under."

Jane bent down. "I can feel something here." She brought out an envelope.

"Yeah, that's it." Bryan took the tickets out and slid the box in Jane's lap. "Open it."

Inside the box, Bryan had written: PLEASE MARRY ME.

Jane stared at the note. "Oh, dear God. Bryan, you planned this?"

He put his arm around her shoulder. "Will you marry me?"

Her eyes glistened. "Yes, Bryan. I love you."

Bryan slipped the ring on Jane's finger and kissed her.

He got out of the car, opened the door to the passenger side, extended his hand and helped Jane out. He slipped his arm around her, as they strolled to the visitor center.

* * *

At the office, Bryan opened the customer correspondence and tried to concentrate on his work. Carl Meyer came to the cubicle. "Bryan, do you have a passport?"

"Yes, I do." Bryan nodded. He had renewed his passport because after his MBA he wanted to travel to London and Scotland, but without any job prospects, the trip hadn't materialized.

Meyer sat down across from him. "There's a sales meeting in Stavanger, Norway. Then they'll be running tests on winches and fairleads on the oil rig in the North Sea. Do you think you can go?"

It was more an order than a question. "Sure, when?"

"The meeting is Tuesday, so you'd have to leave Sunday." Meyer stood to leave. "It'll be a good experience for you. I'll explain the details this afternoon."

Bryan tapped his pencil on the desk. Going to Europe might

Chapter Eleven

be good. But the timing stank. He and Jane had made plans to go to Victoria, British Columbia, over the weekend. Jane would get upset if he canceled that. He called her and asked her to meet him for dinner to explain the change of plans.

Bryan met Jane for dinner and taking her hand in his, he said, "I have to go to Stavanger, Norway this Sunday. We can't go to Victoria."

Jane pulled her hand away. "You were not that keen on going to Victoria anyway."

"Do you think I planned this? Meyer told me to go." Bryan controlled his rising voice.

"You mean to tell me you have a business meeting Sunday?" Jane frowned.

Bryan stared at Jane. Is this how she'd react to his business trips or change of plans? He leaned forward on his chair. "The meeting is on Tuesday and I have to reach there by Monday evening. The other project manager got sick, so my boss asked me. It was an order, actually. He also told me to go to an oil rig in the North Sea where they're testing our equipment."

Jane's face softened. "We'll take the trip when you come back, Love." She caressed her ring. "You have only two days to do your laundry and pack. I'll help you."

Back at his apartment, Jane helped him fold his clothes and pack his bag. She took out a small bottle of Tylenol and a packet of Pepto Bismol from her purse. "Better keep these with you for headache and stomach upset."

"Oh, I won't need that!" Seeing Jane's face full of concern, Bryan kissed her. "Maybe I should keep the pills. They don't take much room." His love for her grew at that minute.

* * *

Bryan met Sam Bachman, the salesman from Houston, in London, before they took the plane for Stavanger. After nine hours on plane, Bryan wanted to sleep during the connecting flight, but the turbulence and Bachman's chatter didn't let him catch a wink.

When they arrived in Stavanger on Monday, Bachman took him to dinner and ordered Bordeaux to go with their Chateaubriand. Bryan took a sip of his wine, glad he didn't have to pay for this. Unlike the engineers, this salesman seemed to have an obscene expense account.

The next morning Bryan took a shower and had two cups of strong coffee to keep him alert for the meeting at Lundgren Shipyard for the towing winches and fairleads that the shipyard had ordered. The coffee worked. Bryan didn't yawn once during his discussions with the chief engineer, Lars Bremer.

After the meeting, Bremer introduced Bryan to Jack Herbert, superintendent of the American barge LD201. Herbert told him, "The helicopter isn't available, so we'll take the service vessel which is leaving at one. Meet me here after lunch."

Later, after they boarded the service vessel, Herbert took him to the lower-level stateroom, which had two beds. "Feel free to rest here or walk on the deck. It'll take seven hours to reach the rig." Herbert put his briefcase on one of the beds.

"I think I'll walk around a bit." Bryan decided if he stayed awake, he would adjust to the time difference and sleep better at night.

While strolling on the deck, Bryan saw twenty-foot long pipes secured with rope in the pipe rack, along with boxes of canned food, produce, pasta and cleaning supplies. The monotonous waves and light breeze made him sleepy. Thinking it wouldn't hurt to take a short nap, he returned to the stateroom.

Bryan knocked, called, "Jack" and waited a moment. Assuming the superintendent had gone out, he opened the door. Herbert

Chapter Eleven

sat upright on his bed, his open briefcase overflowing with packs of hundred-dollar bills. He slammed the lid of the briefcase close. "Bonuses for our crew for beating their contract goals."

The man didn't look secretive. At least the money wasn't going to bribe elected officials but to the workers on the rig. Bryan swallowed to stop a chuckle. The superintendent was swimming in offshore accounts—literally.

Bryan yawned. "Jack, if it doesn't inconvenience you, I'll take a nap."

"Sure. Go ahead." He nodded.

Bryan had slept a few hours when Herbert awakened him for dinner. Soon after dinner, they reached the drilling rig. Bryan looked up at the giant rig, so huge compared to this service vessel. He saw a basket, consisting of a solid rubber donut with a net, suspended by six ropes attached to the outer rim and joined at the top by a crane hook. Four workers threw their bags on the net covering the donut-like hole, climbed and stood on the basket edge. While the basket transported the men, Bryan watched nervously and waited for Herbert. Was he still counting his money? The superintendent came out, dragging his bag and holding his briefcase. He threw his bag inside the basket but held on to his briefcase. Bryan deposited his bag and briefcase in the net so he could hold on to the rope with both hands. They climbed on the rim of the basket and grasped the ropes. As the basket swayed, Bryan looked below at the waves crashing against the vessel. They must have been at least a hundred feet in air. His grip tightened on the rope and he leaned inward, hoping the crane operator wouldn't make a wrong move. Herbert held the rope with only one hand and protected his cash-filled briefcase with the other.

The crane delivered them to the drilling rig with a thud. Bryan let out his breath. Though not on a solid ground, Bryan felt a relief as he stood on the football-size, brightly-lit rig. While the service vessel tottered in the choppy sea, the rig stood still, defying harsh winds and strong waves.

"Bryan!" Hearing a familiar voice, Bryan turned and saw Bob Gardner, the service assistant from Cascade. Bob wiped his face with his coverall sleeve. "I knew you were coming, so I waited here. Come on, I'll take you down to our stateroom."

In the passage, Bob showed Bryan the shower and toilet facilities, then stopped in front of a door. "Here's our room."

Bryan stepped inside and set his bag in a corner. Two of the four bunk beds were already occupied. Bob circled his hand over his paunch and sat down on the lower bed. "Well, I've been sleeping down here. There's not much room between the ceiling and the upper bunk for me."

"No problem, I'll sleep on the top."

After washing up, Bryan climbed onto his bed. Meyer had told him that engineers were usually provided separate rooms. On this barge he was stuck with three roommates. Well, he won't be here too long. He closed his eyes and quickly drifted off to sleep.

A thundering noise jolted Bryan awake. It felt like Vietnam, with helicopters overhead and mines exploding around him. Startled, he sat up. His head thumped on the ceiling and threw him back on the bed. The room spun and perspiration covered his body. He shivered and closed his eyes. Everything turned black.

"Bryan, wake up, man."

Who was calling him? An army buddy? Bryan's head throbbed. He turned to his side and saw Bob. Bryan asked, "Did we get hit?"

"What?" Bob stared at him. "Oh boy, you bumped your head real good. You've got a goose egg on your forehead."

Bryan recalled the series of booms. "Did you hear the

Chapter Eleven

explosions last night?"

"Explosions?" Bob frowned. "You must have heard the rumpus when the service vessel dropped a load of pipes on the deck above us."

Bryan climbed down, sat on Bob's bed, and massaged his head.

"Let's go to the nurse in the first aid center. He'll give you something."

Bryan gingerly touched the bump on his forehead. "I'll just take a couple of Tylenols and I'll be fine." Only now could he appreciate Jane's thoughtfulness. He would call her and thank her for packing the medicine for him.

Over breakfast, he asked Bob, "When do we start testing?"

"Do you think I would let you sleep till nine if we were testing?" Bob laughed. "I went up on deck early to check the schedule, and found out there have been some delays. Because it's their problem that's caused the delay, we can go to the rec room. Otherwise, when work is going on, if the superintendent sees us watching television or playing cards, he calls Cascade to complain."

In the rec room, some men were playing poker. "Want to play?" a man asked Bryan.

Seeing the ante of hundred-dollar bills, Bryan shook his head. "Too rich for my blood." He remembered the bonus money Jack Herbert carried. Would the workers gamble that too?

As they walked out Bob said, "I should have warned you about their high stake gambling. They play when their shift ends and they play when a storm stops their work, or the supply vessel is delayed. They gamble away their wages. But they have to entertain themselves. Can you imagine living like nomads, six months away from home?"

"Must be hard." He couldn't live such an unsettled life. Bryan wanted to have a home to go to. He had the urge to call Jane. "How do we make a call from here?"

"I guess you're too young to remember the phones where you spoke and listened from the same unit. It's that way with these phones. But it's midnight back home."

"I'll call in the evening when it's early morning there." He would ask Jane to set a wedding date before the end of the year.

CHAPTER TWELVE

STEVE

Steve settled in the airplane seat and looked at the rain-soaked runway. He turned to Keith, sitting next to him. "I can't wait for the real sunshine in Sao Paulo instead of this liquid one."

Keith smiled and nodded.

Brazpetro, a Brazilian oil company liked the design presented by Cascade for a set of four semisubmersible rigs, but wanted part of the manufacturing done in their country. They had suggested Brazil Manufacturing Fabrique (BMF) and had requested an engineer and a quality control person to meet with the staff to discuss the handling of drawings and manufacturing.

After the plane took off, Steve asked the stewardess for a glass of wine. When she delivered it, his eyes followed the petite, chestnut-haired woman. He turned to Keith, sitting next to him. "What a beauty."

Keith whispered, "She has a ring on her finger. You should have listened to Jane."

Steve shrugged. Last week, at Bryan and Jane's wedding, Jane had said she would throw her bouquet to any woman Steve liked. "You guys are challenging my bachelorhood, but I'm not ready to be tied down," Steve had said.

When they arrived in Rio de Janeiro, Hans Schneider, Cascade's South American representative, met them outside customs. He walked them to the Varig Airlines counter for their next flight to Sao Paulo. Steve saw the fog outside and wondered about the next flight. One hour went by, then another. Steve yawned. After eighteen hours of plane rides and layovers from Seattle and Miami, all he wanted was to reach Sao Paulo and sleep. The agent at the desk put up a sign: ALL FLIGHTS CANCELLED DUE TO LOW VISIBILITY.

Schneider checked his watch. "We get taxi now. We can be in Sao by evening. Right?"

Keith stood. "We better do that so we can make tomorrow's meeting."

Steve nodded. Not that his opinion mattered. He dragged his tired feet and his luggage as he followed Hans and Keith out of the airport. Schneider, a German, who had lived in Brazil for thirty years, was fluent in Portuguese. He hailed a taxi. From the words Steve heard, he knew Hans was asking if the taxi was air-conditioned. The taxi driver said, *"Sim."*

"Let's go." Schneider waved for them to get in the car as he and the driver put their luggage in the trunk.

By noon, as they traveled through the forest, the fog had lifted and the sun made the January heat unbearable. Schneider talked to the driver, who fiddled with some knobs in vain. Schneider looked back and shook his head at Steve and Keith in the rear seat. "The air conditioner is not working. Open the windows."

Steve rolled down his window and savored the fresh country air and the aroma of mango orchards and banana plantations as they drove.

After four hours they stopped at a roadside café. Schneider looked at the menu. "I recommend Feijoada. It's like your

Chapter Twelve

American chili, but has sausage, pork and beef chunks with vegetables and black beans. It's better at smaller places like these. I'm going to order it."

"I'll have it," Steve said.

"I want to eat light today. I'll have this rice dish." Keith pointed at the menu.

Toward the end of the meal, Schneider mopped the remainder of the stew with his bread. "Mmm. Keith, you don't know what you're missing." He turned to Steve. "Right?"

"Delicious." Steve took the last bite and gulped the rest of his beer.

In the evening, they reached the Hotel Meridian. Alone in his room, Steve took a shower, his first in two days. He watched the English language news on television and combed his curly necklength hair—his pre-sleep ritual. The sweet smell of pineapple and mangoes in the fruit basket on the table and the sight of cerveja, the Brazilian Brahma beer, in the mini-bar tempted him. He picked up the knife, peeled and sliced a mango, and opened a bottle of beer. A perfect finale to an exhausting trip.

In the middle of the night, a violent stomach cramp jolted Steve from sleep. He sat up and burped. Vinegary juices rose up in the back of his throat. He ran to the bathroom. Momentarily relieved, he returned, slumped on the bed and groaned. Was it the mangoes or the black bean stew?

Between trips to the sink and toilet, Steve dozed on and off. After daybreak, he heard a knock and staggered to the door.

"Seven o' clock. You not ready yet?" Schneider barked.

The demanding tone churned Steve's already queasy stomach. "I'm sick. I, like, can't go too far from the bathroom."

"You look pale. You need a doctor." Keith turned to Schneider. "Can we ask the receptionist to send for one?"

"Sure, they can do that." Schneider nodded. "I'll take Keith to

BMF. You rest. Ya."

Steve returned to his bed and closed his eyes. He slept until the ringing telephone woke him. He fumbled for the receiver on his bedside table. "Hello."

"Mr. McGill?"

Steve cleared his throat. "Yes?"

"Sorry, you're not feeling well, sir. You requested a doctor. He's here for his rounds. Shall I send him to your room? Room 522, right?"

"Please. Thanks." Steve replayed the woman's melodious and soothing voice in his mind. With a voice like that, she had to be beautiful.

The doctor came, examined him, and gave him some pills and liquid for rehydration. By five in the evening, his nausea had subsided. His trips to the toilet were less urgent. He decided to change his clothes and go meet the woman with the sweetest voice in the world.

He strolled through the lobby to the reception counter. Of the four women behind the counter, none matched his image or the voice of the caller. He approached one of them. "Did you call a doctor for me this morning?"

"No, sir. It must be someone from the morning shift."

Steve relaxed; glad this older lady wasn't the one who had called. That lyrical voice still rang clearly in his mind. "Is it possible to find out who called? I'd like to thank her."

"Sorry, sir. I don't know."

Frustrated and tired, Steve returned to his room. When the phone rang, he grabbed it, hoping it was the mystery woman. But it was Keith. "Hi, did the doctor come? How are you feeling?"

"Yes, he did. And I'm much better."

"BMF people are taking us to dinner. If you feel like joining us, we can pick you up."

Chapter Twelve

Steve massaged his stomach. "No, I don't want to take any chances. I'll order consommé and crackers here."

"That's probably a good idea. I'll stop by your room in the morning."

"Enjoy your dinner." Steve put the receiver down. He turned on the television and stared at the selection of fruits and the refrigerator with beer. No. Better not repeat yesterday's folly.

* * *

Steve felt better the next day and was able to go with Keith and Hans to BMF. For the next five days, whenever he left the hotel, he tried to listen to the receptionists. But no luck. With Schneider rushing them to breakfast and work, Steve didn't have a spare minute to search for the woman with the lovely voice. He and Keith had already completed the assessment of BMF, and Steve had prepared a rough draft of a contract to take back to Cedarville. He still had his unfinished personal business. He longed to match a face to that beautiful voice, but couldn't delay his return on that account.

Following Keith and Schneider through the lobby, carry-on luggage in hand, Steve heard the melodious tone. That voice! He turned and saw an olive skinned woman in a white and purple polka dot dress talking on the phone. Yes! Definitely the right voice. Oh, so sweet. Steve rushed to the receptionist's counter.

She finished her phone call and looked up. "May I be of help?"

Her brown eyes made Steve's pulse throb. He put his bag down and leaned against the counter. "Six days ago, did you, like, call a doctor for me? Room 522."

"I did." Her gold earrings danced as she nodded.

Steve pulled out his business card and handed it to her. "I'm Steve McGill. I wanted to thank you, but couldn't find you."

"How are you feeling now?"

"I'm fine. I'm returning to the United States today. Could I get your name and address so I can send you a proper thank you?"

She smiled. "I was just doing my job."

"Well, thank you." Steve held out his hand. She shook it politely. He felt a current of energy transfer from her. Besides her melodious voice, she had soft hands and a beautiful face. If Cascade approved the contract, he might come back again and get to know her.

Hearing the car horn, Steve gave her a big smile and rushed out. "I hope I can see you again on my next trip."

As he trotted to join his companions in the taxi, the receptionist's sweet voice and accent echoed in his mind. He imagined caressing her olive skin and kissing her full lips. He turned and looked through the taxi's back window, cursing Schneider for rushing him just when he'd met his dream girl. He didn't even get a chance to ask her name.

* * *

Back in Cedarville, Steve and his boss, Roger Hart, the director of manufacturing, met Keith and Carl Meyer, the director of engineering, to discuss the contract for Brazil Machine Fabrique.

Meyer's eyes moved from Keith to Steve. "Brazpetro has recommended this company, but what do you think? Were they able to communicate? Were they able to read the manuals?"

"We were satisfied with their quality control measures." Steve's pulse quickened, remembering the woman with a beautiful accent and flawless English. "For manuals and operating instructions, if we need a translator for Portuguese, we could hire one of the receptionists at the hotel. Some speak very good English."

Keith kicked him under the table. Steve sat up straight. He

Chapter Twelve

had confided to Keith about his search for this woman, but it was foolish of him to suggest that a hotel receptionist could translate technical manuals.

"They know enough English to interpret the blueprints and instructions," Keith said.

"Still, will they follow our manufacturing standards?" Roger Hart asked.

Steve handed the photographs of the company's equipment to the two men. "The factory has a good foundry and manufacturing machines. But since our winches are a new line for them, they requested that someone from Cascade be present during the initial production."

Hart nodded. "They've agreed to pay. So we'll rotate our guys for a year. Steve, since you already made some contacts, you should go first."

Steve nearly whooped with joy. He'll get to know the beautiful girl.

* * *

At the Hotel Meridian in Sao Paulo, Steve looked for the woman whose melodious voice and olive skinned face had inhabited his dreams for the past month. He scanned the reception desk and listened attentively whenever he walked through the lobby. Every day he made it a point to get downstairs early in the morning and late at night. A few times, he came from work to check the reception desk during lunch, but his dream girl was nowhere to be found. How could he search for an elusive woman whose name he didn't know? Steve smashed his fist into his palm. Darn, why hadn't he at least asked her name?

He heard someone in the lobby say that a receptionist who spoke good English had moved to Rio. Could it be her?

At the manufacturing plant, while reviewing the quality control report with Fernando Vargas, the young man said, "Everything close from tomorrow to Shrove Tuesday. I'm going to Rio. Want to come for Carnaval?"

"Rio?" Steve looked up. "I'd like that. Do you think we can get a hotel at this late date?"

"No hotel. I go to my parents. You stay with me."

"Thanks. But I don't want to impose." It would be odd staying with Fernando.

"I take friends home many times. I phone my parents. You come with me. Tomorrow at three we leave from bus depot here."

"Thanks." He wanted to go to Rio. Why not now?

* * *

At the Vargas home, remembering the greeting for women he had read in the travel guide, Steve kissed Mrs. Vargas's right cheek and then the left. Although Fernando's parents and four teenage siblings didn't speak English, they welcomed him with smiles and served him a delicious meal of grilled chicken, beans and corn cake. Steve was quite full after the meal but when they offered purple berries with crushed ice and honey, he just couldn't refuse. The sorbet was perfect on this hot evening.

The next day, Steve took the Vargas family to lunch. Later he and Fernando got on the bus to Pao de Acucar, the famous Sugarloaf Mountain. In the evening, they went to Corcovado Mountain. At the summit, the sky turned pink with the glow of sunset. Steve saw the lights of Rio de Janeiro below. The statue of Cristo Redentor sparkled above. Though born into a Catholic family, Steve hadn't gone to church during his adult life. Now, this magnificent statue stirred something within him. He closed his eyes and said a prayer to find the beautiful woman he had been

Chapter Twelve

searching.

The next day, at breakfast, Fernando told Steve, "I meet my college friends in afternoon. You come with me or take museum tour?"

Steve sipped his coffee. It probably would be better to go out on his own instead of being with a bunch of rowdy Brazilian men chattering in Portuguese. He chuckled. He thought Fernando and his friends were young and rowdy. At home he was called "The Wild Hippie," but in Brazil he needed to maintain his official image. "I'll visit the museum."

"We go to Centro together. My friends come there at two. The museum open two to six on Sunday. They have English guides."

When they arrived at the museum, Fernando told the man at the desk that Steve needed an English language guide. The man pointed to five tourists waiting in a corner. "English tour."

"Don't worry about me. You go." Steve waved Fernando.

When his host left, Steve joined the tourists. From behind him, he heard someone, "Hello, I'm Vera DeSoto, your guide."

The sweet voice! Steve gasped. A thrill ran through him. He turned. It was her—the same tender face, brown eyes, dangling earrings. A green and yellow bow fanned out from her ponytail.

She smiled. "Gentlemen, in addition to the 800 paintings and sculptures, we'll see folk art and other exhibits. But before we start, I'd like to know your names and the country you are visiting from."

One man, who acted like a group leader, spoke up. "I'm Andrew, five of us are from Australia." He pointed to his companions, who took their turns introducing themselves.

Steve couldn't pay much attention to what the tourists were saying. When they stopped, Vera turned to him.

Steve gathered his courage and opened his mouth. "I'm Steve McGill. From the United States, I met you once in Sao Paulo. I didn't know you had moved."

"Yes. You look familiar." Vera smiled. "I took this job because my family is here. And I get more practice with my English."

Family? Was she married? Steve glanced at Vera's left hand and was relieved to see no ring. He hoped she was talking about her parents and siblings. He followed the tour group through the classic paintings, statues, and Indian and African folk art. Several times when he looked away from the exhibits, his eyes met Vera's. Was she interested in him? He had to plan his next move soon.

After the tour, Steve lingered. "Would you like to have some coffee?"

Vera checked her watch. "The museum closes in a few minutes. I can go then."

Seeing Fernando waiting outside, Steve went to the steps. "I met a friend and I'm going to the café with her. You go ahead with your movie plans. I'll take a cab to your house."

"Don't go alone in taxi. Take bus. I give you bus number. Remember?"

"I remember. Don't worry."

Fernando ran across the street toward the partying crowd and colorful masks. Steve turned back and saw Vera. "Where would you like to go?" he asked.

"There is a nice café around the corner. Next to Teatro Municipal," Vera said.

Inside, after they settled in their seats, Steve said, "When I came back to Sao, I was hoping to see you. But I didn't know your name, so I couldn't ask anyone about you."

Vera's brown eyes narrowed. "What a coincidence that you came to the museum just when I was giving a tour. I still have your card."

"Really?" Steve leaned forward on the table.

It was more than a coincidence. His prayers had been

Chapter Twelve

answered. The best way to get her to open up, he decided, was to give his background. He told her about his parents and sister in Chicago, his job at Cascade, and his visit to Rio with Fernando. "How about your family?"

"My parents and brother. We all live together."

He nodded with a smile. So she wasn't married. But did she have a boyfriend?

Vera asked, "You look surprised. Were you expecting more siblings?"

"Oh, no. I'm just so glad we are here together." Steve thought of all different ways he could make the evening last longer. "If you have time, we can have a leisurely dinner. You'll have to tell me what to order."

Vera turned her eyes to the menu. "Do you like shrimp?"

"I love it." Food meant nothing as long as he ate it with Vera.

"You must try vatapa—shrimp in a coconut sauce. The recipe came from Africa."

They ate and talked and sipped their coffee until the matronly waitress in her flowing white muumuu came to tell them the café was about to close. There was so much to tell, so much to ask, but time was flying.

When they strolled toward the bus stop, Steve saw a long line that snaked all the way to the sidewalk. He took Vera's arm. "Fernando told me not to take a cab, but since you know the streets, they won't cheat us."

Vera's eyes twinkled. "Yes, I know the route. And I know how to watch their meters."

Sitting next to Vera in the cab, Steve wanted to put his arm around her, but didn't want to do anything rash. His day was getting better and better. "Are you working tomorrow?"

Vera shook her head. "The museum is closed on Mondays."

"If you're free, maybe you can give me a tour of the city."

"Sure. Would you like to listen to Samba music? They are all practicing for Carnaval. Most tourists love to see the masks."

Steve had seen enough of the people on the street with their bright-yellow and green sequined costumes, and blue and white masks, but he would do anything to be with her. "I'd love to."

"Okay then. I'll meet you at the steps of the museum tomorrow."

When they got out of the cab, Steve kissed Vera's cheeks. Fernando had told him that if a person is interested romantically, he should kiss the right cheek a second time. With his hand still on her shoulder, he kissed her cheek again and Vera's face turned to his lips.

* * *

When he returned to Cedarville, Steve went to work, played bridge at Norma's, and continued his routine. Still, he dreamt about Vera at night and thought of her constantly during the day. He couldn't wait to go back to Brazil. His boss had set up a schedule so each of the three quality control man would be in Sao Paulo for three weeks at a time. Even so, he would be in Sao Paulo and Vera in Rio.

Steve looked out the window of his apartment and gazed at a butterfly on the pink flowers and green leaves of the rhododendron. It fluttered as elegantly on the flowers as Vera's green and pink bow that had graced her ponytail.

The song on the radio by the Partridge Family echoed his sentiments. "I think I love you." He danced by himself and said out loud, "Not think, I know I love you."

He flopped on the couch. He and his friends in Chicago had believed in free love—date as many girls as possible. Why commit to a girl just to fit in with the crowd in Cedarville? Besides, none

Chapter Twelve

of the local women had captured his heart.

But Vera was unique. Even before he met her, she had taken over his heart and mind. After he left Brazil, he wrote to her and she had replied. He picked up her letter from under his pillow and read it again. It was no substitute for touching her, holding her, and listening to her melodious voice. He bolted to the phone. He had to talk to her now.

* * *

How quickly a year had passed. Steve arrived at the Rio de Janeiro airport, his stopover to see Vera before going to the manufacturing plant in Sao Paulo. The work was progressing well, and yet, he hoped the project would last longer. Unless something delayed it, the production would be over in the next three months. How would he see Vera after that? He sighed and retrieved his luggage.

He spotted Vera near the entrance. Crossing the room in a few long strides, he took her in his arms.

After checking into the hotel and having dinner, Steve and Vera walked hand in hand on the quiet footpath under the indigo sky. He kissed her. "I might get to come back once, at the most twice before December. How will I see you after that?"

Vera took a step back and held his hand. "I knew you were here for a job and were not going to stay after its completion. I ask myself why I gave my heart to you."

Steve tried to joke. "I guess that's why it's called falling in love. It has been quite a fall for both of us." He squeezed her hand. "Can you get some time off and come with me?"

Vera gazed at him with her probing brown eyes. "It's not that easy to get a U.S. visa."

Steve caressed her hand. If he wanted to be with her, he had to marry her. Was he ready to settle down? He swallowed hard. "Do you think you could leave your family and move so far away?"

Vera sighed. "I don't know what to say. If I never get to see you again, I'll be miserable. If I leave my parents and go with you, I'll miss them."

"Have you talked to your parents?"

"I told them I love you. They said they want my happiness. They know that even if I stay in Brazil, my job or marriage could take me to another town. And the few times they saw you, they liked you."

Steve smoothed his hand over hers. Did she mean she would move to Cedarville and that it was okay with her parents? Was she expecting a marriage proposal? He had not thought about that, but Alicia and Jane had warned him that no woman would wait indefinitely. "You mean, like, if I ask you to marry me . . ."

Her dazzling smile melted his heart. "My parents are traditional, and they would like it if you asked my father's permission first."

Oh, no. Not only had he proposed, sort of, he had to ask permission from Vera's father. Steve's toes curled inside his shoes. He'd come this far, he'd have to gather his courage and take the next step. "Next week when I come back from Sao Paulo, I'll talk to your parents."

Vera rested her head on his chest. "I love you."

"I love you too." The words tumbled out of Steve's mouth. It was happening so fast, but he couldn't lose Vera. He would do whatever he must.

* * *

After he returned to Cedarville, before going to work, Steve called his parents. "Hi, Mom, I just got back from Brazil last night but it was too late to call you. I have some news."

Chapter Twelve

"Stevie dear, are you okay?"

"I'm better than okay. I've found the girl of my dreams, and I proposed to her."

"Great, dear. Who is she? Do I know her? Have you told us about her?"

"Yes, Vera DeSoto. I told you I met her in Brazil."

"Brazil? You said something about a girl there, but I didn't know it was serious." His mother sighed. "I can't believe you proposed to her without talking to us."

"Mom, I've known Vera for over a year now. She's sweet and kind and she loves me. And I love her."

"Oh, Stevie. You're so trusting of everyone. Are you sure she's not using you? I've heard so many stories of foreigners marrying just to come to America."

"Vera is not like that, Mom," Steve snapped. He didn't want to lose his temper. Why did she have to be so negative? "I'm going to work now. Talk to you later."

Steve slammed the phone and stormed out to the car. God, his mother was cynical. By saying that Vera was marrying him for a visa, she implied that Vera couldn't love him otherwise. He started his car. Well, what his parents thought wasn't important to him anymore.

At the office, he showed off the tiepin Vera had given him. His coworkers congratulated him on their engagement, though Steve wasn't sure if they, too, were thinking like his mother. He went to his boss to review the final production schedule of the Sao Paulo company and told him about his engagement.

Roger Hart said, "I have your best interest in mind, Steve. I hope you're aware that sometimes people from other cultures can't adjust here. Remember what happened to Jeremy?"

Steve's chest tightened. Jeremy, who often went on repair jobs to Singapore, had married a woman from there. Last year, his wife left him for an old friend from Singapore who lived in California. But then, Jeremy was a jerk. Who knew what really caused that breakup?

Questions nibbled at Steve. Was he rushing into marriage? Had Vera talked him into it? No. He was the one who had pursued her. He strode to the engineering department to tell Bryan and Keith about his engagement. He went to Keith's cubicle.

"Congratulations." Keith shook his hand vigorously. "So, when is the big day?"

The tightness in Steve's chest eased as he talked to his friend. Keith's parents had come from Japanese and Black cultures. Their marriage must have gone through many hardships, and they were still together. Though his friend had talked about his childhood difficulties of not belonging to any community, Keith now had good friends and was happily married. He and Alicia were so sweet together. What a strange combination that marriage was—Oriental-Black with Dutch. Steve chewed his lip. At least he and Vera had more in common. Vera's parents were planning a big Catholic wedding. Although he hadn't gone to church in years, Steve wouldn't have to worry about having to convert to a different religion for the ceremony.

Suddenly Steve noticed Keith's questioning look.

"Oh, the date. It'll probably be November. I'm going back for the final phase of production, and I'll combine the time with Thanksgiving vacation." He fingered his tiepin.

Later, Bryan, Norma and Harold sounded genuinely happy to hear his news. Throughout the day he tried to forget about his mother's words and his boss's warnings. Instead, he pictured Vera's radiant eyes and smiling face. He knew his friends would welcome her.

After work, as Steve opened the door to his apartment, he heard the phone ringing. He ran to answer it.

Chapter Twelve

"Stevie, my boy." His father's voice boomed over the line.

"Hi, Dad." Now what? Would he have to listen to another lecture?

"Your mom told me the good news. We hope we can meet the lucky lady soon."

"Well, she's still in Brazil. I'll apply for her visa after we get married."

"When are you planning the wedding?"

"When I go in November I'm thinking we'll get a marriage certificate, so I can file her papers." He didn't want to tell them about the church wedding her parents had planned. "It's only a formality. Nothing big. You and Mom are welcome to come, but I'm thinking when she gets her American visa, first thing I'll do is bring her to Chicago."

"We'll look forward to that. We'll have a reception here."

"That would be nice, Dad." Steve put the receiver in its cradle and twisted his mouth into a wry smile. His father was just trying to appease him. In the past, such incidents might have turned into a shouting match, but age had mellowed the old man. Although Dad had a temper, he often tried to make compromises between Mom's rigidity and Steve's ideas. In the last few years, Steve had learned to control his own reactions too.

Anyway, this call, this half compromise, made him feel better. He tried to think from his parents' perspective. How would he feel if his friends or cousins left him out of their wedding? He promised himself to smooth things over before the marriage. He would try not to antagonize them. Then it would be easier for them to accept Vera.

CHAPTER THIRTEEN

KEITH

At the Cedarville Community Center, while Alicia and Jane arranged flower vases on the tables to welcome Steve and his Brazilian bride, Keith tacked green crepe paper onto the wall.

Harold stepped back and surveyed the hall. "Looks good." He jangled his car keys. "I'm going home to change and bring the lovebirds."

Elegant bunches of blue and white Dutch irises from Alicia's parents' garden at the center of each table reminded Keith of his own wedding almost four years earlier. How beautiful Alicia had looked when they held each other's hand and exchanged vows. He tiptoed across the room behind her and kissed her neck. Her silken hair brushed his cheek.

"Daddy!" Two-year old Kerry ran up to him, wrapping a length of crepe paper around her neck. "Look at my garland."

"Hi, honey." Keith picked her up and strolled toward Jane.

He gave Jane a quick hug then meandered around the tables to Norma in the kitchen. He made it to the kitchen, his daughter still in his arm. "Norma, you have done a great job."

Steve's boss had offered to bring the cake, and the friends had catered the food. Still, organizing the surprise party had fallen on

Chapter Thirteen

Norma, Alicia and Jane. Steve had married Vera in November in Brazil, but it had taken five months for Vera to get her U.S. visa. Finally, last week, Steve met her in Chicago, introduced her to his family and then brought her home to Cedarville.

"I hope we can pull off this surprise. Harold will have to make up a story and get them here." Norma brushed her hand against her yellow polyester dress.

"I'm sure your husband will manage that." Keith smiled.

Alicia handed Keith a banner and several tacks. "Sweetheart, can you put this up?" She took Kerry from his arms. "Come. Let's watch Daddy."

Keith gazed at his wife and his daughter. The little girl looked at him with wide eyes. Then, with a jolt, he remembered that tomorrow was Mother's Day. Alicia had already sent cards to her mother and his, but with all the deadlines at work, he had forgotten to buy a gift for his wife. Before going home to shower and change, he'd have to sneak out to the store for flowers.

He pinned the silver and gold banner on the entrance door and stepped back to look at it. CONGRATULATIONS STEVE AND VERA. The banner rustled with a gust of wind. Keith pushed a few more tacks into it.

"I shall return." He threw a kiss toward Alicia and Kerry, and left.

An hour later, when Keith came back to the hall, laughter and chatter filled the air with the Cascade employees and their spouses. Hearing a car horn—Harold's signal—Keith turned off the lights and ducked behind the door.

He heard Steve. "Are you sure Norma asked you to pick her up here?"

Harold's voice boomed. "Of course. Gosh, it's dark. Steve, can you turn on the lights?"

Lights flooded the room and everyone shouted, "Surprise!"

Vera's hand flew to her mouth. With olive skin, brown eyes, and a pink ribbon in her hair, she looked beautiful. Although Keith had heard about her, this was the first time he had seen her. No wonder Steve had fallen for her.

Steve blinked his blue eyes and pointed to Harold. "Oh, you sneaky devil, you."

Roger Hart, Steve's boss, shook his hand. "Congratulations." Then he turned to Vera. "Welcome to Cedarville."

Keith put out his hand to shake his friend's, hoping Steve wouldn't be reminded of what Hart had said about foreigners getting married just to get a visa. "Congratulations and welcome."

"Thanks." Steve wrapped an arm around Vera's shoulders. "Darling, this is my good friend Keith. He was the first one to know about my search for you." He turned to the guests. "Thank you all for giving a warm welcome to Vera."

The guests took their turns greeting them, Vera dabbed her eyes. "I don't know how to thank you."

"Well, we'll figure that out later." Norma hugged the petite woman.

* * *

A week later, at Norma's house after dinner, Keith helped Olga Pedersen with bridge tallies and cards. Steve said, "Thanks, guys, for a great surprise."

Bryan patted Jane's back. "Thank the gals. They did all the work."

"Thank you." Vera turned to Jane, then Alicia and Norma. "I was really worried about coming so far and not having any family or friends. But you all make me feel welcome." She hugged Norma's mother. "Mrs. Pedersen, you have been especially good to me."

Chapter Thirteen

"You can always come here and visit me." Olga took Vera's hand in hers.

Steve rested his chin on Vera's shoulder. "Mrs. Pedersen, how about being her bridge teacher?"

"I'd love to." The elderly woman smiled, her eyes crinkled.

Keith picked up the bridge tallies. Olga was his partner, and Alicia was Steve's. Steve grabbed another chair and straddled it, letting Vera take his seat. "You play my cards."

Mrs. Pedersen explained the game to Vera, while Steve twisted his wife's ponytail, whispered in her ear, and played with her dangling earrings. Keith wondered if Vera could concentrate on the game. It sure distracted him.

The players at table two had finished their first four hands and were discussing the Watergate break-in. Bryan, Harold, and Norma, staunch Republicans, were critical of the investigations. Jane a moderate, was quiet this evening. Keith's eyes met Alicia's. She put her calming hand on his, as if signaling him to ignore the discussion. If Steve had not been so occupied with his wife's hair or earrings, Keith knew he would have said something. He wondered what Vera's political leanings were. Or did she care at all about American politics?

Finally, when it was time to change partners, Keith stood to go to the other table. "Steve, let Vera and Mrs. Pedersen play as a team now. You go sit on the chair across from her."

Bryan winked. "Hey, Steve, no more hanky-panky. Let the expert teach your wife. You know that Mrs. Pedersen taught the fine points of bridge to Jane and Alicia."

* * *

On a sweltering August afternoon, Keith sat on a crew boat on the way to the ETM barge in the Gulf of Mexico. Jason, a service assistant from Cascade, stretched out his feet showing off his new cowboy boots. "What do you think of these babies? I bought them in Houston when you were at the sales meeting."

Keith glared at the pointed toes of the black boots. He had nothing against this rookie's shopping spree, but wearing them now was just plain stupid. "Those smooth soles will get slippery. You better change to your work boots." Keith scrubbed a hand down his jaw.

"I will, as soon as we get to the semisubmersible." Jason said.

On most of his trips to the oil rigs, Keith had taken the helicopter. This time, he would have to either go up on the crane basket, or climb the rope ladder from this crew boat. In the distance, against evening sky, he saw the orange glow of the blowout prevention flare. It looked bigger than usual. A lot bigger. He remembered the BOP flare as twenty feet at the most, but this one was shooting out to sea more than a hundred feet. Could the oil rig be sitting on a massive gas pocket?

The boat operator announced, "When we get to the barge, grab the rope ladder and climb up to the deck. Once you're on the ladder, keep moving. Others will be close behind. The crew will deliver your luggage."

"Is this the way you always board?" Jason's eyes grew wide.

Keith shook his head. "No. This is first time for me too."

He looked at the oil rig, stable in the rough waters. But the service boat bobbed and swayed and often slammed the side of the rig with the waves. The crew from the boat took turns climbing up the ladder. To Keith's relief, whenever the boat collided with the rig, the men had already reached the highest rung, out of harm's way.

"Okay, you go, I'll follow," Keith told Jason.

Jason jumped on to the swinging rope-ladder. After he had gone up two rungs, Keith planted his feet on the first ladder. The

Chapter Thirteen

rookie stopped. Keith looked down at the crashing waves, and the boat heaving below. If he didn't get going soon, the boat would certainly chop off his legs. "Come on, Jason. Move. Quick."

Jason lifted his leg, but his foot slipped. "I can't move. My foot hurts."

Those damn cowboy boots! Seeing the boat sway toward the rig, Keith pushed up, ramming Jason's butt with his head forcing him up. A man on the deck pulled Jason over the side. Keith scrambled up the remainder of the rope. He stood to regain his breath, taking in the salty, seaweed smell. Whew, that was close.

On the deck, Jason massaged his boot. "Dang. My ankle!"

Keith ground his teeth, heart hammering. "I told you not to wear those boots. You're lucky you didn't slip and fall. You would have taken me with you."

The man who had helped Jason "lift off" from the ladder, said, "You can go to the nurse's station to get it checked."

Jason looked like a desperate child, reminding Keith of two-year old Kerry whenever she was hurt or scared. He told Jason, "Let's go get your ankle checked."

In the infirmary, the nurse examined Jason. "It looks like you've sprained it. I'll wrap an ace bandage and give you Motrin. If it worsens, when the helicopter comes, we can send you to Houston for an X-ray."

"Thank you. I hope I won't need that." Jason smiled as he limped out of the room.

After leaving the infirmary, as they walked to the barge manager's office for registration, Keith saw the blazing, horizontal flare, whooshing noisily. It was not only bigger, but also louder, increasing the surrounding temperature and making the August heat unbearable.

At the office, Keith and Jason introduced themselves to the manager.

"I'm Dennis Haugen." Shaking Keith's hand, the man explained, "As you can see, we've encountered a gas pocket. We're hoping it burns off before any bubble forms."

Keith recalled the whooshing, dancing flames. Instead of oil, they had hit gas and were diverting it up the pipe and burning it. A film from his astronomy class about black holes devouring stars flickered through his mind. If a huge gas bubble created a pocket and rose up from the ocean floor, this barge could collapse into a marine black hole. Though nervous, Keith managed to say, "I'm sure by tomorrow it will be under control for us to replace the gears."

As they were leaving, the barge manager said, "Dinner is being served in the galley right now."

At the buffet, as Keith went with Jason through an array of spaghetti, salads, bread, and fried chicken, he remembered the delicious meals on the Italian barge two months earlier. What royal treatment that was! The rig manager had offered him Scotch in his office, then asked him to join his table for dinner. Keith's mouth watered, thinking of the cannelloni, baked trout, tomato salad, and tiramisu he had enjoyed on the Italian ship. Food aside, the Italians treated the visiting engineers really well.

He told Jason, "Let's eat quickly and rest up for tomorrow."

After dinner Keith went to his room, got ready for bed and started reading Newsweek. At least he had his own stateroom and could rest. His eyes got heavy and he drifted off to sleep.

A siren wail jolted him awake. He dashed out to the main deck in his pajamas and was accosted by humid, hot air. He had heard the emergency evacuation spiel several times, but like the routine "in case of emergency" demonstrations on airplanes, he had stopped paying attention to them. He followed a group to Deck C. The bright, orange flame that roared in the background, made Keith's pulse pound.

Chapter Thirteen

The security officer handed him a life preserver. He put it on and looked for Jason, but couldn't recognize him amid all the orange-clad men. Someone jumped into the rescue capsule attached to the deck and signaled others to follow. Keith wondered if he should wait for Jason, but following the emergency procedures, he went behind the men in front so as not to clog the way for others. He slumped onto a seat, giving respite to his trembling legs. The bench seat was covered from one end to the other with men. At least it was cushioned. Metal clanged as the top of the capsule swung down, sealing them inside. Lights flicked on and Keith felt the vessel being lowered.

As the engine droned and the capsule groped its way into the dark thrashing sea, Keith asked the man sitting next to him, "Where are we going?"

"My guess is we'll roam within a twenty-mile radius for a few hours. If there's no blowout, we'll go back to the rig. But if the ETM rig collapses, either another drilling barge or the Coast Guard will rescue us."

Rescue? Already feeling claustrophobic in this small, crowded place, Keith gulped. He knew the capsule had sensors and the oil rig could locate it via its satellite system, but if the rig collapsed and no other rig or Coast Guard found them, what then? They probably couldn't open the sealed latch and would suffocate and die. Even with thirty people in there, he felt alone. What would Alicia and Kerry do without him? And his parents? He shouldn't have snapped at his mother. He should have played ball with Kerry when she asked.

Keith thought of Jason. The man next to him appeared to be part of the crew who knew the emergency procedures pretty well. Although his mouth was dry, Keith managed to ask, "Do you think everyone evacuated?"

"Yeah. Everyone, except the rig manager, supervisor and

tool-pusher. There are eight capsules and we have a small crew. No more than 130." The man brushed a hand over the stubble on his chin. "If there is any chance of the bubble surfacing, the tool-pusher will release brakes of all but two winches, to move the rig away. The supervisor must be busy turning off the power and waiting for the tool-pusher to decide if they should leave too. We've been evacuated once. Most probably, before we know it, they'll call to say that we can go back."

The man talked as if this were just a fire drill. Keith closed his eyes. The static noise of a walkie-talkie alerted him. He heard the announcement, "I just got the message. It is safe to return to the ETM barge."

"Well, that's good." Keith cleared his throat. He gave a restrained smile to the person next to him and checked his watch. They had been out for one hour, but it felt like four.

Could he risk going back to that rig again? He had no choice. He was tired and at least he could sleep in a proper bed there. He wished someone would check the fatigue-limits for humans, like they did for machines and metals.

Upon reaching the exploration rig, Keith peeked in Jason's room. Relieved that he and his three roommates had returned safely, Keith went to his own stateroom.

In the morning, after a sleep punctuated by nightmares of fire and drowning, Keith awoke with a headache. He gulped a Tylenol, and went to the galley for breakfast. He loaded a plate with eggs and toast, and filled a cup of coffee. Spotting Jason alone in a corner, he joined him and asked, "You okay?"

Jason bit into his toast. "My first trip, and I sprain my ankle trying to get on the rig, then I take a cruise in the capsule."

Sensing Jason's fear beneath the angry tone, Keith tried to reassure him, "A crewman in the capsule told me that it's like a fire drill. He was confident nothing would happen." Keith didn't

Chapter Thirteen

want to admit that he, too, was shaken from the experience. Just a few months earlier, a barge had collapsed in a storm. "Look at the bright side. We don't have to work till the crew gets everything back to normal."

Jason swallowed. "What're we going to do in the middle of the sea?"

"We can go to the rec room. They have television, Ping-Pong, cards, and other games. I warn you though, don't ever play poker with the crew here. They play high stakes, sometimes wagering their paychecks. How about a game of Ping-Pong?"

Jason shook his head. "Can't play."

Keith recalled Jason's limp from last evening. "Is your ankle still hurting?"

"Yeah. Now this is hurting too." Jason rubbed his shoulder. "I think I pulled a muscle when I slipped on the rope ladder."

Keith sipped his coffee and tried to think of something nice to say. Was Jason blaming him for pushing him up the rope? But it was Jason's own fault that he hurt his shoulder and ankle. Still, Keith felt responsible for him. "Let's have the nurse check your shoulder."

"I saw him here this morning and talked to him about it. He said, it's probably a muscle sprain, and the Motrin he had given for my ankle will help this too. He said I should rest."

Keith stood and stretched his arms. "Well then, you rest. I'll go watch the news."

"Wait, I'll come watch TV with you." Jason followed him.

In the recreation room, the Ping-Pong players, their paddles in hands, and the poker players, still holding their cards, had their eyes on the television, listening to President Nixon's resignation speech. Keith and Jason sat on the sofa and listened as the president listed his accomplishments in battling inflation, opening trade with China, negotiating a treaty with the Soviet Union and so on.

He said he was resigning so that the Congress and government could get back to taking care of the country instead of wasting time on the Watergate investigations. Keith shook his head. The president only resigned after his taped conversations discussing the Watergate cover-up came out. Would he have left office otherwise?

In the middle of the sea, they were trying to get over the shock of the possible rig-collapse, yet everything stopped for Nixon's speech. Keith wondered, had there been some casualties, would it have preempted the resignation speech?

Keith took a deep breath. He had often tried to convince himself that working on the oil rigs was as safe as driving in Seattle. After all, people died all the time from heart attacks, cancer, and car accidents. Alicia had often pleaded with him to find another job. One where he wouldn't have to travel so much and life would be more predictable. Especially on these trouble-shooting jobs, he got just a few hours' notice before leaving. But in this recession, while other companies were laying off workers, Cascade was hiring. Shortage of oil and the OPEC embargo had been good for their industry. And he loved his work. The engineers and draftsmen in the office respected him and appreciated the way he explained design concepts to them. Besides, Alicia didn't want to leave Cedarville.

Keith stood to go to his room to relax and read *The Gulag Archipelago* "Jason, if things are in working order by evening, we'll replace the gearbox tonight, so let's try to rest now."

They spent the whole day waiting for their work to begin. After dinner, the barge engineer finally called to say they were ready for the job. Keith put on his coveralls and boots, then met Jason and other service men at the northeast corner of the deck.

Jason stood on the ledge, unbolted the inspection cover and removed it. Keith peered into the hole with a flashlight. The light

Chapter Thirteen

shone on oil and shiny steel filings. He used a magnet to confirm that the shiny particles were indeed metal. He sighed. More work had to be done before they put in the new parts. He told Jason, "Better clean up the shavings and oil first, otherwise the gear teeth will wear out again."

Jason jumped down from the ledge. "Shit. My ankle!" He hobbled and came back up.

Keith looked at the other service men. "Could one of you go in and clean up?"

A man said, "Our manager told us not to interfere with your work, since it is Cascade's responsibility."

"But we'll help you from outside." Another offered, "I'll get some rags for you."

"What the heck. I'll crawl inside." Keith handed the flashlight to Jason. "Can you hold this for me?"

Jason took the flashlight. "Sorry, Keith, I know I should be doing this."

Keith squeezed inside the eighteen-by-twenty-four-inch inspection hole. Kneeling, he took a rag that someone handed him. Fortunately, the space inside was large enough so he didn't feel claustrophobic. Unfortunately, it meant he had to clean up a larger area on his knees, since the headroom was barely three feet. When a rag got covered with sludge, he raised his arm and handed the slimy rag to Jason, who gave him a clean one. Finally, two hours and twenty-six rags later, he crawled back out onto the deck, straightened his cramped legs, and smelled fresh ocean air instead of nauseating petroleum.

Jason turned off the flashlight. "I'll go through the checklist before we start."

"You do that." Keith nodded. "I'll call Bryan and give him our progress report."

He went to the barge engineer's office to make his call. As

usual, he was supposed to call his boss and give an update on the job. Bryan, his friend, had become the director of engineering when their old boss, Carl Meyer, retired. Keith dialed the number.

Bryan answered, "Hi there. Since you didn't call yesterday, I figured there were more delays."

"We had a problem with gas pocket. We had to evacuate the barge."

"Is everyone all right?" Bryan asked.

"Yeah, we're all fine. It could have been serious, but it also proves that they are well-prepared for emergencies." Keith needed to utter those words aloud to reassure himself.

"So, what's the situation now?"

"Now that I cleaned up the oil and shavings from the gear box, we'll replace the parts and do testing. I expect things to go smoothly."

"Why did you have to clean? Is Jason okay?" Bryan asked.

"He sprained his ankle. I'll explain later."

"Great work, buddy. I bet you can't wait to come home. Hey, we missed you this Saturday. Your wife and Vera organized a great baby shower for Jane."

Keith couldn't be there to help Alicia host the shower and to enjoy the men's evening out with friends. "Were you able to keep your mouth shut and keep it a surprise for Jane?

"Of course." Bryan laughed. "She thought we were getting together for cards."

"I wish I had been there. I better go see if Jason is ready."

Bryan said, "As soon as this gearbox job is done, you and Jason come home. No detours this time. See you soon."

"Bye." Keith hung up and went back to the deck.

With the increasing work at the office, maybe he could send one of the other engineers to sea next time. He would call Alicia after the job was completed. Keith had learned not to give her

Chapter Thirteen

a return date before he was sure of it. Once he had told her he would be there the next day. Then a glitch delayed the sea trials by a whole week, and Alicia started to cry on the phone.

* * *

March winds howled, and rain pounded on the window, but Keith, comfortable and warm inside the Cascade office meeting room, wasn't bothered. But listening to the salesman's design ideas made Keith grit his teeth. He stared at Alfred Hall, who had a habit of promising the customers more than engineering could deliver.

Keith pointed out the stricter safety guidelines the Norwegian agency, Det Norske Veritas, had mandated for offshore drilling equipment. "DNV gave me these guidelines when I visited their office in Houston. Surely you've read the files I circulated last month."

The salesman flipped through the pages of the American Bureau of Shipping Guidelines. "ABS would allow the brakes the way I'm proposing."

Keith's grip on his pencil tightened. "Al, ABS is just starting to set up maritime rules. At present, all they say is, 'It should be a robust design.' Maybe that's okay for your sketches, but it won't work for my calculations."

An angry knot formed on Bryan's brow. "Keith, can't you make a compromise?"

"Well, if you decide on a design that DNV won't approve, who'll push it through?" Before Keith could say more, the telephone rang.

Bryan answered, then handed it to Keith. "It's Jim, for you."

Keith stood. "This may take a while. I'll take it in my office."

He stormed out of the room. The Cascade engineer's call

from the LT 270 semisubmersible could mean news of more problems with their equipment on the rig, but Keith was relieved to get away from the meeting. He realized he needed to be open to other ideas, but whenever Alfred suggested something, Keith lost his patience. And Bryan? These days he sided with the salesman and told Keith to play with other concepts. But when there were deadlines to meet and backlogs of orders, why should he waste his time on unrealistic ideas? He slumped into his chair.

Keith picked up the phone. "Hi, Jim, what's up?"

"I'm calling from Rotterdam. One of the mud pumps didn't work, so the barge manager decided to turn around and get it fixed at the plant here."

Relieved it wasn't their design, Keith let out a breath. "At least it wasn't our product."

"The company in Rotterdam is replacing a new pump." Jim groaned. "But the barge manager is panicking. He ordered everyone to get their department managers here for sea trials."

Keith could sense the frustration in the engineer's voice. He was well aware of delays on the rigs. Sea trials involved several parts manufactured by various companies. It was easy to lose patience by the time they tested them, turn by turn. Keith tried to calm him, "Jim, you've been there for fifteen days. Let me talk to Bryan and see if we can send someone to replace you."

"Keith, the barge manager insisted that for the trial of Cascade winches, you have to be present. He asked specifically for you."

"I'll call you in an hour." Keith tapped his pencil.

He couldn't go now. He was needed at home, especially now that Alicia was expecting their second child. Normally, she and her mother took turns taking care of Kerry, but from February to April, they were both busy with the tulip photographs and gift shop at her parents' Devries Gardens.

The past month, Alicia had been in a lousy mood. Maybe it

Chapter Thirteen

was the pregnancy, maybe the extra work at the gardens, and three-year-old Kerry's tantrums. Last Saturday, Keith had a deadline and Alicia was working, so he brought Kerry to the office, where she quietly colored in her coloring book. Keith occasionally looked up from his calculations and saw Kerry pursing her lips and twisting her head in the direction her crayons were taking on the paper. He was tempted to go hug her, but stayed in his chair. The engineers and draftsmen who came to Keith's office, joked with Kerry, "Hi, boss." She looked up and gave her charming smile.

Although Keith didn't want to deal with Bryan after this morning's arguments, he had no choice. He went to Bryan's office and relayed Jim's message.

"The barge manager has asked for you to be there for sea trials." Bryan smiled and pointed to the framed sign on the wall: RULE NO. 1. THE CUSTOMER IS ALWAYS RIGHT. RULE NO. 2. SEE RULE NO. 1.

It dawned on Keith that he had not gone to sea since his last trip in August of 1974. A seven-month record! He wouldn't mind getting away from office politics. Perhaps when he returned, Bryan and Alfred would come to their senses about the new proposal.

But Alicia? Although the baby wasn't due for a month, Keith hoped she wouldn't get one of her crying spells, when she heard about the trip. His parents had offered to come and help them with the baby. He might have to ask them to come now. Before going home and breaking the news to his wife, Keith asked Norma to call the travel agent to book a flight to Rotterdam. He was sure the winches could be tested quickly. He'd be home in a week.

* * *

March winds howled, but now instead of comfortably sitting inside his Cascade office watching the rain splash against the window, Keith stood on the deck of the semisubmersible exploration rig. They were moving toward Ecofisk oil field, so named because of its equidistance from the British, Danish, and Norwegian coasts. With no landmarks or road signs, watching the gray clouds and endless white-capped waves bored him. He yawned. Better catch up on sleep before they began testing. Once the sea trial started, while crew members worked twelve-hour shifts, Keith would have to be present to note the readings of rope pull, whether it took ten hours or twenty.

The next morning when he went for breakfast, he couldn't figure out their location but he knew it was not Ecofisk.

"There's a severe storm predicted," the barge engineer told him, "we have to wait here till it passes."

"Any idea how long it will last?"

The barge engineer wrapped his hands around his coffee mug. "Sometimes it passes in a few days, sometimes it lasts for weeks. We'll wait and watch."

The whole day Keith waited for the storm to subside, watching eighty-foot waves leaping one on top of the other. He was too far above the deck for the crashing whitecaps to drench him, but salt-laden heavy mist and frigid wind stung his face. Fortunately, the semisubmersible, with its columns connected to the large underwater displacement hulls, reduced the wave-force and stood firm. Surely no storm could topple a larger-than-a-football-field giant that could displace 17,000 tons of water. Feeling reassured, Keith retired to his cabin for the night.

Hearing a thud, Keith swung his legs over the edge of the bed and turned on the flashlight. The cabinet by his feet swayed and tilted toward his bed. With the next jolt, it straightened itself, then started seesawing. Another roll, and part of it fell where Keith's

Chapter Thirteen

feet had been. He jerked out of bed. He had trouble keeping his footing.

Usually, the rig was so stable they could play pool and Ping-Pong, and draw straight lines when explaining designs to service assistants. Now the football-sized rig seemed as fragile as a canoe bobbing on the choppy sea. Keith braced himself against the wall as he staggered out to the maintenance room. Two men came and wedged the cabinet between the bed and the wall.

One day passed, and then another. Then a week, and another. Keith called Alicia every other day, but had to bite his tongue whenever she asked about his return date. Why couldn't she understand that he had no answer to her question and no control over this unforeseen situation? After all, he wasn't on a cruise ship.

He paced, watching the black clouds hovering above and the dark sea below, its waves rising higher and higher. He kept his mind occupied by reading, watching television and the crewmen's poker games. He wondered how many paychecks these men had gambled away by now. He wished he could just get on a helicopter and leave.

Finally, after he had read two novels and watched several reruns of "The Rockford Files" and "Colombo" the storms subsided. The semisubmersible reached Ecofisk and the crew flooded the pontoons to lower the rig to its normal height. When the anchors were laid, and the winches tested perfectly on the first try, Keith felt as if a huge burden had been lifted off his back.

When Keith jumped on the helicopter, he had been away from home for twenty-four days. He would make it home before the baby arrived.

* * *

Even after three days in Cedarville, Keith still felt a swaying sensation while standing on the ground. He had gone to bed early, and was fast asleep when he felt something poking his ribs. Something tumbling in his cabin? He sat up. Alicia stood beside him. "Sweetheart, let's go to the hospital."

Keith opened his eyes. "Oh, thank goodness, I'm home. I thought I was…."

"We have to go to the hospital. Now," Alicia cut him off.

Something had poked him, but it didn't hurt him. Keith turned in his bed. "It's not bad."

"Not bad? My pains are ten minutes apart. You don't know how it feels. You don't have to go through this."

Keith's eyes focused on his wife's protruding stomach. "You're having the baby now?" He jumped out of bed, picked up her packed bag, ran down the hall, and knocked on the guest bedroom. Fortunately, his parents were with them so they didn't have to drag Kerry out at night. "Mom, Dad, we're leaving for the hospital."

At the hospital, Alicia wouldn't talk to him. When he squeezed her hand, she didn't squeeze back. When Kerry was born, Keith had held Alicia's hand and kissed her in between her labor pains. Now she didn't want any of that.

He left the room to get some coffee. Still dizzy after the long stay on the rig, Keith rubbed his eyes. Babies had a way of choosing nights to make their grand entrances. Poor obstetricians!

After a while, he peeked through the door. The doctor was giving Alicia an injection. Beads of perspiration covered her forehead. Keith's jaw tensed. He had been feeling sorry for himself because his wife didn't respond to his caring touch. How much pain must she be in? He went over and wiped her forehead, then took her hand in his.

Kayla Wilson was born in the early morning hours of April 12, 1975. Keith put his arms around his wife and their newborn.

Chapter Thirteen

Soon the nurse took the baby away for a checkup.

Alicia gave him a weak smile. "Sweetheart, why don't you go home?" She closed her eyes.

He gently placed his hand over her closed eyes. "You rest now. I'll come back later with Kerry, Mom and Dad."

When Keith got back to the hospital in the afternoon, he stopped to gaze at the newborns through the window. He lifted Kerry up to see her baby sister. She pressed her nose to the glass. Keith turned to his parents. His father's face beamed and his mother's eyes brimmed with joy.

He hugged Kerry. "Let's go see Mommy."

CHAPTER FOURTEEN

NORMA

Dressed for the office Christmas party, Norma set the table for her mother and children, then sat with them as they ate dinner. She brushed her hand over her purple skirt. How times had changed. Eric was already sixteen, a junior in high school. Anne, her baby, was getting a few babysitting jobs now. Today, she was going to take care of Steve and Vera's infant son. While her children were growing independent, her mother was becoming more dependent on her. Most of her mom's friends had either died or moved away to be closer to their families. That along with health problems had slowed Mom down. The only thing Mom looked forward to, was the once-a-month bridge game with the Staffords, Wilsons, and McGills.

Harold called from the bedroom, "Honey, call Vera. What's taking them so long?"

Steve and Vera had asked Anne to babysit their four-month old. Since Anne had never taken care of an infant, Norma suggested they bring Xavier to the house so Norma's mother could be with Anne and the baby. Steve's family, as well as Vera's were far away, so Mom had become little Xavier's grandmother, too.

Chapter Fourteen

Norma dialed the phone and heard Vera's "Hello."

"Hi, are you leaving now?"

"I don't know. Steve went out half an hour ago." Despair edged Vera's tone.

"Where?"

"I don't know." Vera's voice broke. "He got angry and left."

"Don't worry, we'll be right over." Norma put the phone in its cradle.

When Norma and Harold arrived at the McGill home and knocked, Vera said the door was open. They went in. Vera, dressed in a black satin skirt with a yellow and black blouse, sat at the kitchen table, her head resting in her palms. The baby slept peacefully in his infant seat. Norma put her hand on Vera's shoulder. How selfish of Steve to go out leaving his wife and son. Norma clutched her purse. She and Harold had gone through rough times, but never had he walked out during an argument.

Harold paced the floor and looked out the door a few times. "Let's go to the party. If Steve wants to come, he knows where to find us."

Norma shook her head. How could Harold suggest this? But sitting here and waiting wasn't helping anyone either. She looked at Vera. "Would you like to go with us?"

"I guess so." Vera dabbed her eyes, smearing the mascara.

Norma whispered, "Go check your makeup before we leave."

Vera plodded to her room. Norma sighed. The poor woman had every reason to be depressed. Last fall, she had lost her part-time job at the Cedarville Community College due to budget cuts. She often told Norma how much she loved teaching classes there in conversational Portuguese and Brazilian art. At that time she had said she was relieved she wouldn't have to teach immediately after the baby arrived. Then the baby was born, and it seems so did the problems between the McGills.

Norma wrung her hands hoping Steve and Vera would survive rough times in their marriage as she and Harold had in the last twenty years. For the McGills, it was only the third year of marriage, and problems had overtaken their lives.

When the baby was fed and changed, they took him to Anne and Mom, before going to the Christmas party.

At the restaurant, Harold warned the others not to ask Vera about Steve. Seeing her just pick at her food, her face grim, Norma suggested to Harold that they take Vera home after dinner.

After picking up Xavier, they drove the baby and Vera to their home. When they opened the door, Norma saw Steve on the couch, his feet on the coffee table, staring at the blaring television. Vera took the baby to his room.

Harold slid next to Steve. "You jerk, how could you do this to your wife?"

Steve's face turned red. "Nag, nag, nag, all the time. Then she starts crying. What am I supposed to do?"

Norma couldn't keep quiet. "So you leave her and get drunk? Give her a break. She's just had a baby. I was very depressed after Anne's birth. It happens to new mothers. And she is so far from her family." She stopped when Vera came in.

Harold stood. "You missed a good party. We've got to go." He bent over Steve and hissed, "Grow up!"

* * *

Where had seven months gone after Christmas? At the office, Norma dabbed the sweat from her face with a hanky. This was an unusually warm August in moderate Western Washington. It certainly didn't fit the billboard in downtown that said, "Find out when summer is and take that day off." The hot day had extended through the whole month.

Chapter Fourteen

She started the fan on her desk. The papers under the paperweight fluttered in their place but a few isolated ones floated down. "Drat, how did I miss those?" She grabbed them and slid them underneath the files.

"Oh, oh. Norma is cursing." Steve's voice came from behind her.

Seeing Steve, Vera and their baby, Norma grinned. "Well, you caught me."

The one-year old whimpered in Vera's arms. She said, "He's just had his shots."

Norma cooed, "Oh dear, Xavier." The little one responded with a smile.

"Got to get back to work." Steve kissed his wife and son and rushed toward his office.

Norma was relieved to see that since the Christmas party disaster, the McGills were getting along better. Vera had recently started translating the operating manuals for the winches that were sold to a company in Brazil, into Portuguese. A little work seemed to have improved her spirits.

Vera jiggled Xavier on her hip. "I thought I'd check if there is something else that needs doing."

Norma dug under a paperweight and took out a folder. "Roger Hart left this file. I was going to bring it over to you this weekend and visit."

"Thank you." Vera turned to leave. "Stop by with your mom."

"I'll do that. Mom loves to visit with you and Xavier." Norma waved. "'Bye."

As Norma returned to her cubicle, she spotted Keith and the young employee, Melissa Smythe, moving her drafting table to the back. She frowned. What was going on now? Wasn't this new draftsman or drafter, the unisex term they'd adopted, satisfied with any place assigned to her? What she really needed to do was change her wardrobe. Norma glared at Melissa's low cut floral print blouse and orange miniskirt.

Norma shook her head. If any of the secretaries she supervised ever dressed like Melissa, they would definitely get a lecture on work-appropriate attire. But Melissa wasn't a secretary, so Norma had no authority over her.

All twenty-two draftsmen turned to watch the commotion caused by moving the drafting table. Perspiration glistened on Keith's dark forehead. After getting Melissa settled, he picked up a chair and took it to the middle of the hall under the ceiling fan. He sat and talked with a draftsman.

Bryan, who was returning from the director's meeting, stopped next to Norma and watched the drafters in the hall. Melissa's pencil fell on the floor and when she bent to get it her plump thighs bulged beneath the hem of her short skirt.

Bryan rolled his eyes and glanced at Norma. "We need to talk about this situation. Why don't you come to my office?"

Norma followed him. As they passed Melissa who was leaning over her drafting board, Norma saw her well-endowed cleavage peeking from her low-cut blouse. No wonder the men ogled her. Granted, it was hot in the building, but that was no excuse for such clothes.

Bryan called to Keith, "Can you come to my office after you're done?"

"Sure, I'm through here." Keith stood.

As soon as Norma and Keith entered Bryan's office and sat down, he closed the door. He asked Keith, "What's with moving Melissa's table again?"

Keith scratched his forehead. "When she was assigned a middle table she complained that some of the draftsmen stared at her. Once I saw Ron hanging too close to her and had to almost drag him away."

Chapter Fourteen

"I know." Bryan nodded. "Ron has this annoying habit of getting too close to people when he talks. He doesn't mean anything. Even I have to back off from him."

"I explained that to Melissa. I thought if I moved her to the front, the draftsmen wouldn't have to pass her table when they needed to talk to me or the project engineers." Keith laughed. "But then they could see her from behind. I noticed some of them ogling her back."

"More like her backside, when she bends over." Bryan chuckled, and tapped his pencil on the table. "The productivity of some draftsmen has definitely dropped since we hired Melissa."

"She's a good worker. She's thorough and picks up new concepts quickly." Keith leaned forward. "Besides, we can't afford to let go of another woman drafter."

Norma pursed her lips. The woman who was given a layoff because of incompetence, had filed a sex-discrimination suit against the company. Norma agreed in principle with the Equal Rights Amendment, but that woman was abusing the new law. Anyway, what to do about Melissa? Norma felt sorry for this twenty-two-year old girl with her short bangs and glasses. She wasn't that attractive. Most of the women in the office were prettier, but Melissa was causing quite a sensation with her proactive clothes.

Bryan chewed on his pencil. "We're caught between a rock and a hard place. If Melissa gets upset, she might file a sexual harassment suit. We can tell the men to keep their distance from her, but we can't bluntly order them not to look at her. Can we?"

"I've spoken with them and asked them to treat Melissa with respect. I'm trying to avoid alienating my team." Keith asked, "Norma, you have experience in supervising women. Can you talk to her about some kind of dress etiquette?"

"Well, I'll try. But I'm not her supervisor. She may think I'm interfering."

"How about you ask her to your weekly lunch?" Bryan suggested, "Maybe take her a few times with other secretaries, then after she feels comfortable with you, casually discuss it."

Keith nodded. "That sounds good."

Norma returned to her desk, making up different dialogues for approaching Melissa. Easy for them to say, but not that easy for her.

* * *

Norma was in a good mood. Summer heat had given way to a pleasant fall, and the dark winter months were still far away. Her teenagers were back in school, busy with classes and either playing or watching football.

Since her talk with Bryan and Keith, Norma had included Melissa in the secretaries' once-a-week lunch. Though today would be Melissa's fifth lunch, Norma hadn't broached the subject of clothes yet. First, she wanted the girl to feel comfortable with her. Since the other secretaries were busy today, she and Melissa went to lunch by themselves.

At the restaurant after their food arrived, Norma asked, "So, how's work going?"

"I love this job. Keith is a good boss. Some drafters and engineers are helpful, but I have trouble with others." Melissa reached across the table for the salt, displaying her cleavage.

"What kind of trouble?"

"They just keep staring at me. Yesterday, this guy, you know, Ron, looked down my tank top the whole time he talked to me. I told Keith and he said he would speak to Ron."

"Men will be men." Norma took a bite of her sandwich. "Since we work in a predominantly male office, we must be careful how we dress. That way if a situation arises where they are harassing, we can't be blamed for encouraging them."

When Norma returned to her desk, she was pleased with herself for handling the conversation tactfully. She would know tomorrow whether Melissa took her not-so-subtle hint. The ringing phone broke into her thoughts.

"Mom!" Eric's voice sounded shaky. "Come home right now."

"What happened?" Norma's grip tightened on the phone.

"Grandma fell on the kitchen floor. She can't move."

"Call the ambulance. I'm coming." Norma's heart raced faster than her trembling legs as she ran to Harold's office.

* * *

Sitting at the hospital bedside, Norma touched her mother's burning forehead. The hip-surgery after the fall was supposed to be simple. How did the infection set in? She rested her head on her mother's bed and whispered, "Mom, please wake up. Please give me a chance to show how much I love you."

Guilt consumed Norma. She hadn't looked after her mother as well as she should have. Sure, Mom lived with them, but whenever she cried or talked about her loneliness, Norma ignored her. She could blame her busy schedule, work, children, husband, but she should have taken more time for her mother.

Harold pressed Norma's shoulder. "Honey, I'll stay with Mom. Why don't you go home and rest for a while."

"I want to be here when the doctor comes." Norma took her mother's hand, which curled around her finger.

Hearing her mother's rasps, Norma sat upright with alarm. She pressed the call button. Her hands shook as she waited for someone to come and help. She stood. "Harold, do something. Get the nurse."

When Harold returned with a nurse, the woman shouted something and an army of hospital staff came in with carts and equipment. The doctor put the stethoscope on her mother's chest. In spite of the commotion in the room and in her heart, Norma could only hear silence.

After what seemed like an eternity, the doctor said, "I'm very sorry."

"But the surgeon said the operation had gone well." Norma balled her hands into fists. "You must call him."

Harold said, "Honey, what he's saying is that Mom is gone."

"No, it can't be," Norma screamed.

Harold put his hands on Norma's shoulders. With her face on his chest, she sobbed.

A nurse brought her a chair. After a while, the nurse returned and handed Harold a plastic bag. "I have collected Mrs. Pedersen's items."

"Thanks." Harold took the plastic bag from the nurse.

Later, in the evening at her home, friends and family tried to dissect the cause of Olga Pedersen's death. Harold said, "One doctor said there could have been a blood clot after the surgery. Another said probably the infection took her life."

Norma clutched her sodden hanky. Did it really matter whether it was the clot or an infection? Was one agent of death superior to the other? Mom was gone and Norma had not done enough for her. The more people tried to tell her how good a daughter she was, the more miserable Norma became.

After everyone left, Norma went to her mother's empty room. Closing the door behind her, she sat on Mom's bed and opened the nightstand drawer. She saw a childhood drawing of stick figures she had drawn of her and her mother. At the bottom it said, "I love you Mommy." After all these years, Mom had kept that picture in her drawer, close to her. Norma covered her eyes

Chapter Fourteen

with her palms and sobbed. Oh, why couldn't she tell Mom she loved her the way she used to do as a child. She sighed, dabbed her eyes, and gazed at the photograph on the wall of her parents with Eric and Anne. The kids looked so secure and happy with their grandparents. Norma silently thanked her mother for looking after the children. Her teenagers must be missing their grandmother too. It was wrong for her to sit and feel sorry for herself. Norma rose from the bed to go comfort Eric and Anne.

CHAPTER FIFTEEN

BRYAN

Bryan went to get coffee for himself and saw Norma, her elbows on her desk supporting her face. It was her first day at work after her mother's death. Bryan made an extra cup of coffee, sat down by her, and handed her the cup.

"Thanks, I needed this. It's just that every time the phone rings, it reminds of when Eric called to say Mom had fallen."

Not knowing how to respond, Bryan nodded. "Your mom was dear to us. I miss her too." Bryan put a hand on Norma's shoulder and tried to lighten her mood. "Your gals tried to keep your desk clean, but the files kept piling up. See how important you are?"

Norma smiled. Just then Keith strode toward them and hugged Norma. "We missed you here." He handed a few papers to Bryan. "Melissa's performance review. I've given her a copy. I'm off now."

"See you when you return." Bryan waved to Keith, who was headed to Galveston and then on to an exploration rig in the Gulf. Bryan gulped his coffee and stood to leave. "Norma, if you feel overwhelmed, go home and rest. Don't worry, work can wait."

He crossed the hall and stopped by Melissa's desk. "Can you

Chapter Fifteen

come to my office so we can go over your performance review?"

"I'll get my copy and be right there."

When Melissa came in and sat across from him, Bryan said, "Keith rated you highly as far as work goes. You are thorough, punctual, and are willing to work overtime when needed."

"Thank you." She pushed her eyeglasses up on her nose, then opened her mouth, but didn't say anything.

"Let's move on. It seems you have a tough time working in a team."

Melissa leaned her elbows on the desk. "The drafters just don't share things with me, so I have to go to the engineers for answers. Besides, I work on different projects than they do."

"Well, since you complained about some of the draftsmen, we tried to give you separate projects. Still, there are times when people have to take on each other's responsibilities. It seems you haven't been receptive to that." Bryan checked the paper in his hand.

He looked up and saw tears glistening in Melissa's eyes. She blinked rapidly and her face turned red. Oh, no. She was about to cry. Concerned that others would witness her meltdown, Bryan stood to close the door, but hesitated. It could be misconstrued.

Melissa covered her eyes with her hand. Bryan went to her side and put a hand on her shoulder. Suddenly, she turned her head to his waist and sobbed. He froze. Jane was due any minute to join him for lunch. What if she walked in now?

Stepping back, Bryan patted Melissa's shoulder. "With experience and a little effort, you and the other drafters will be able to work better together."

Melissa wiped her eyes. "I'm sorry."

Bryan heard Jane talking to Norma in the hall. He examined the front of his damp and wrinkled shirt. Maybe he could cover it with his tie. Darn! This thin tie wasn't much help.

Jane stood at the door, "Am I interrupting?"

"Come in, love," Bryan said, "Jane, you've met Melissa."

Jane smiled. "Yes, hello."

When Melissa left, Bryan looked at Jane from the corner of his eye. Would she question him about his wrinkled shirt or Melissa's tear-stained face?

* * *

As the Air France plane sped across the Atlantic, Bryan closed his eyes, trying to get some sleep, but Jane's accusations flooded his mind. Ever since she had seen Melissa in his office, she accused him, "You flirt with everyone. How do you think I feel when you ignore me and comfort other women?"

He had already told her about Melissa's problems with the draftsmen or drafters. He joked, "Why would I choose that little twerp? There are prettier girls in the office."

Instead of a smile he had expected, the remark brought a deluge of tears. What the hell was all that about? She wasn't jealous or suspicious before Jennifer was born. His friends had told him that women became moody after the birth of a baby, but that never happened to Jane when Brad was born. Bryan rubbed his chin. How long would he have to put up with this crap before she returned to her normal self? For now, Bryan needed to concentrate on the sales meeting in Paris.

At the Charles de Gaulle airport, Bryan came out of the customs, and saw Sam Bachman, the salesman from Houston, waving to him. Bryan sighed. Sam must be tired too after the long trip, but would probably drag them straight to the Cascade sales office. The French salesman for Cascade, Pierre Douquette, had a habit of arranging meetings as soon as they arrived.

"Hi, Sam." Bryan shook his hand as he fought a yawn. "I'm

pooped."

"Me too," Sam agreed. "I already talked to Pierre. He has scheduled the customer meeting at ten tomorrow. Let's take a cab to the hotel."

"Good." Bryan let out a breath. "Finally, Pierre timed it right. We can catch up on sleep and it will give us a chance to go over the winch proposal before presenting it."

When they arrived at the hotel, Sam suggested, "Instead of sleeping now, it's better to have an early dinner and get proper rest at night. Why don't you freshen up and come to my room so we can review the proposal before dinner."

"I'll be back in half an hour." Bryan took his bag to his room.

After a quick shower, Bryan gulped the last drops of the strong coffee he had ordered from room service, and left for Sam's room.

"Come in." Sam pointed to the coffee table and two chairs by the window. "Let's sit there." He brought his briefcase and opened it. Dirty underwear and smelly socks tumbled out. "Damn. The nerve of that woman. I'm up to here with Laura." Sam put his hand to his neck. "Did she have to stuff this in here? God, she's sick."

Bryan rubbed his unshaven stubble. It would have been embarrassing if Sam had taken the briefcase to the sales meeting. No matter how angry Jane got with him, she would never pull a stunt like that. He asked, "Sam, you want to call the laundry service?"

Sam threw the dirty clothes on the floor and reached for the papers in his briefcase. "Oh, Laura pulled this surprise to get even with me. I've packed clean clothes. I'll be fine."

As they discussed the design proposal, Bryan's mind kept going back to Sam's predicament. What did the poor guy do to cause his wife's wrath? Was he cheating on her?

The next morning, at the Cascade sales office, Pierre briefed them about the customer requirements. Sam told Bryan, "Don't be too detailed. And do not, I repeat, do not talk costs."

Pierre laughed. "I'll kick Bryan if he starts rambling numbers."

Bryan argued, "I think customers need to know whether their particular demands will make a difference in the performance, or whether the extra weight or size will be compatible with other equipment on the barge. Moreover, it adds to the engineering hours, so extra cost must be mentioned."

"For now, focus on getting the order. Details can be worked out later." Sam flopped his feet on an empty chair.

Bryan shrugged. Easier for the salesmen to promise than it is for the engineers to deliver. His eyes fell on Sam's shoes resting on a chair. A spot of his skin peeked out of his black sock. "Sam, there's a hole in your sock!"

Sam turned his ankle and poked at the torn sock. "Right you are."

Bryan momentarily stopped and clutched his pen. He didn't need to embarrass Sam more after yesterday's briefcase incident.

Sam grabbed the pen from Bryan. "Is it black?" Without waiting for a reply, he scribbled on a piece of paper. "Aha, it is." He reached down and colored his skin through the hole in his black sock. "There."

"Good job." Bryan clapped. Neither dirty clothes nor a torn sock dampened Sam's cheerful attitude. And here Bryan was upset with Jane, because she was in a lousy mood recently. The more he thought about it, the more he appreciated his wife. They had their ups and downs—and there were lots of downs right now—but she was a good wife, and a very good mother to Brad and Jennifer. He couldn't wait to go home and take her in his arms.

* * *

Bryan turned off the alarm and drew Jane close to him. It was

Chapter Fifteen

restful to sleep in his own bed with his wife beside him. "I love you." He promised himself to say this often from now on.

Jane nestled against him "What happened to make you so mushy?"

"Poor Sam Bachman." Bryan laughed, recalling Sam's dirty laundry. "I'll tell you the story later."

Bryan kissed Jane, stretched and stood to get ready for the office. After breakfast, while he sat rocking Jennifer in his arms, Brad came running and climbed on his chair. Bryan patted his son. "Daddy needs to go to work. When I come back, we'll go for ice cream."

Later at the office, as he buried his head in reports, Keith knocked on the open door. Bryan waved for him to come in. Keith handed him a file. "Here are the wind turbine calculations."

"Take a seat. Let's go over this together before my meeting with Mr. Jenkins." Bryan opened the file. He couldn't believe how someone's crude wind turbine with old helicopter blades could be turned into a sophisticated design. With 191 feet height, 165 feet rotor diameter, and rotor speed of 41 rpm, this design would produce 3,000 kilowatts in 40 mile-per-hour winds. "So, how did you like working on this project?"

Keith smiled showing his bright, white teeth against his dark face. "I loved this challenge. I hope we get more wind turbine orders. It's less polluting and safer." Keith paused. "Hey, did you hear what happened on DPT 11 rig in the Gulf?"

"Something went wrong again?" Bryan raised his brows.

"We fixed the drum. But while Jason and I were waiting at the heliport deck, he was blown backwards by the chopper blast."

"Oh, no. Is he okay?"

Keith nodded. "Jason of the cowboy-boots-on-the-rig fame, managed to stand up, walk and take the flight home with me. I told him to get a checkup. The X-ray was clear, but his back still hurts. I suggested he take it easy for a few days."

"I'll give him a call. Thanks for the update."

After Keith left, Bryan spoke with the injured man. Then he recalled the news of some oil rigs collapsing or fires causing injuries and deaths. Fortunately, in his ten years at Cascade, the servicemen and engineers had avoided casualties. Perhaps wind turbines, though expensive, were a safer way to produce energy. And who knows, twenty years from now at the turn of the century, wind turbine might become better and more efficient. He had a meeting with the president, Ronald Jenkins, and marketing manager Chris Atlee and would definitely push for more wind turbine orders.

In the president's office, after Bryan presented the new design, the marketing manager, Atlee moved to the edge of his chair. "More and more companies are getting interested in wind power. In fact, engineering should start working on other turbine proposals."

The president took off his eyeglasses and chewed on the earpiece. "I wanted to give you heads up on the company status. Eagle Energy has made an offer to buy our Cascade division from Springfield Steel. They're still working on the details, so don't announce it yet."

Chris Atlee asked, "So what does it mean for us?"

"They've promised to keep the same benefits and policies. But they want to concentrate on deck machinery equipment, which is ninety-percent of our business anyway. Springfield Steel is not selling the wind turbine project." The president leaned back in his chair. "In any case, I've decided to go back with Springfield in Illinois."

When they came out of the office, Chris told Bryan, "All businesses say they'll keep the same policies, but I'm not sure about this one. Otherwise, why would Jenkins leave?"

Chapter Fifteen

"Well, we'll hope for the best. I wish we could have kept the wind turbine. Everyone in my team is enthusiastic about the project." Bryan walked back to his office.

* * *

Bryan glanced out into the gloomy afternoon at the pelting rain on his office window. In two months, so much had changed, and yet so much remained the same. He was still director of engineering, working with the same group of people. But the memos and reports had a different heading. New stationery with green "Eagle Energy Cascade division" emblem had replaced the blue "Cascade Springfield Steel." In the shop the painters had repainted the old soothing blue logo an ugly green.

However, for Bryan, the major headache was the new president who interfered with each and every project. Often, he would pick a director or manager and grill him. Fortunately, he picked one person at a time and would transfer his wrath to a different man after a few weeks. Everyone in the office joked about being the chosen one and consoled each other that the "Axe" would fall on someone else soon.

Suddenly the alarm on Bryan's wristwatch beeped. He had set it so he wouldn't be late for a meeting that the new president, Rodney Axel of Houston, had called for him and director of sales. The new president found fault with everything, so why give him more reason to bitch?

Bryan knocked on the open door of Rodney Axel's office. The man raised his brows. "Come in." No smile. No greeting.

As soon as Sam joined them, the president started. "I looked at the annual budget and engineering schedule for next month. You've been spending too much for the OTC." He asked Bryan, "Why do you have to take all five engineering managers there?"

The Oil Technology Conference in the Houston Astrodome in May was one of the highlights of the engineering and sales departments. Bryan sat on the edge of his chair. "The engineers display our products, man our booths, and meet customers." Hadn't Axel ever gone to OTC and seen the Cascade booth shaped like an oil rig?

Axel's square jaw moved from side to side. "Our salesmen in Houston can do the job."

"OTC is a good place to introduce engineers to customers." Bryan leaned on the desk. "This is where the customers dream up new projects. It gives the engineers some idea of other equipment on the rigs. They can also see what the competitors are doing."

"Then rotate them every year. Why should you waste all those engineering hours for this?" Axel turned to Sam. "What's this? Smoked salmon flown to Houston? And double expenses for promotional materials?"

Sam said, "The salmon is for the reception that Cascade, Eagle Energy—that's you—will be hosting for customers. And the extra expense is because we had to put in a rush order for brochures, pencils, pads and candies with our new logo. We couldn't give out the ones with Cascade Springfield Steel logo."

The rain on the window seemed to hammer in Bryan's head. What would the president think of the girls at the booth they hired every year to distribute the promotional materials?

"Since OTC is only a month away, I'll let it pass this time." Axel pounded the pen on his desk. "Next year I want this budget cut by fifty percent."

Bryan nodded. They always booked the rooms a year in advance, before they returned from the conference. OTC was the only opportunity for his engineering team to get together and let loose a little. At least they'd enjoy this one last year.

When Bryan came out of the office, Steve gave him a quizzical

Chapter Fifteen

look. "So, did the Axe fall on both of you?"

"We need to straighten this Axe," Sam muttered, "Are you next in line, Steve?"

"Fortunately, I'm leaving for Montreal for the casting job."

Bryan laughed. "You sure are eager to run away."

CHAPTER SIXTEEN

STEVE

At the hotel in Montreal, Steve checked his briefcase to make sure he had the specifications for the castings. Because of a huge backlog of orders, Cascade had decided to "farm out" the manufacturing of castings at other plants. Steve had investigated several facilities within the United States, in Canada and Korea. Over the phone, Jacque Gaulthier from Montreal had given a good bid, so after some consideration, Steve and his boss decided to give them the first chance. Last night, Jacque had called at the hotel and told Steve he would meet him at the café across the street and take him to the plant.

Steve went to the café and ate crepe. From the window, he saw a picture of a bare-breasted beauty on the billboard across the street and sheepishly looked around to see if others had noticed his stares. To his relief, they kept on eating and chatting in French. He wanted to explore the anatomy of the woman once again, but thinking of his wife and sons, forced his attention away from the picture.

A tall red-haired man appeared at the doorway just as Steve took the last bite of his crepe. "Hello, I'm Jacque Gaulthier."

Chapter Sixteen

Steve stood and shook his hand. "I'm Steve McGill."

On the way to the plant in Jacque's car, Steve said, "Boy, am I glad you're here. Yesterday, I took the subway to go eat and was completely lost. Why don't they have signs in English just like Vancouver?"

"We're French province."

Steve shook his head. It didn't make any sense that the rest of English-speaking Canada, in order to accommodate the minority French, tried to be bilingual but this little province refused to use English. "I'm concerned about the casting job."

"Why?" Jacque asked. "I'll show you the plant. We have a good facility."

"I think language might become a problem."

"Most people at work know English," Jacque assured him.

When they arrived at the plant, Jacque showed him the foundry and machinery, then took him to the office and introduced him to a large, goateed man. "This is our manager, Monsieur Henrique Drury."

Steve shook the man's hand. Drury spoke in English. "I'll call the plant supervisor and the quality control man to meet you." He picked up the phone and talked in French.

Two men entered the office and sat across from Steve. Jacque introduced them. "This is Fabien and this is Ivonne."

"Hello, I'm Steve McGill." Steve shook their hands, then gave the contract to Drury, who set it on the table.

Drury and the other three men ignored the paper and launched into an animated discussion in French. The manager stroked his beard. His round face looked rounder as he puffed his mouth.

Steve's eyes roamed from one man to the other. He asked, "Jacque, is there a problem?"

"No." He shook his head without looking at Steve.

The chatter continued even after Steve tapped his pen at the contract to remind them of his presence. He put the papers in his briefcase and walked out the door. When he was halfway down the hall, he heard footsteps, then Jacque's voice. "Steve, what's the matter?"

"Well, you assured me that language wouldn't be a problem. But it is."

"We were explaining the terms to the men from the shop. We'll sign the contract."

"That's bull." Steve took out the contract from his briefcase, tore it into pieces, and stuffed the paper in his pocket. "You just lost a three-million-dollar job." He stomped out of the building and hailed a cab.

In the cab, Steve crumpled the torn contract in his pocket. What had he done? Why couldn't he keep his temper in control? Even if he could convince his boss, Roger Hart, that it was best not to give business to these people, what would the new president, Rodney Axel say?

But the nerve of those people! In other countries, including France, business people attempted to speak some English. Even when he was in Brazil, they had tried to accommodate. Before these French-speaking people tattled on him, he'd have to call Roger from the hotel and explain what happened. And as soon as he reached Cedarville, he'd send a telex to Daesoo Industries in Korea to discuss the job. He unclenched his fist.

* * *

Ten days after stomping out of the Montreal meeting, Steve was in Pusan, South Korea. Woo Sung Chae, a short stout man picked him up at the airport and drove him to Daesoo Shipyard. He introduced Steve to the plant workers, then showed him the

Chapter Sixteen

manufacturing facility. It had been four hours since he had left the airport, and Steve's bladder was about to burst. He looked around for a men's room. "Do you have a restroom?"

"Yes," Woo Sung replied, and continued the tour of the plant.

He asked another man and got a nod. But no one directed him to the men's room. Were they trying to keep it a secret? He tapped Woo Sung's shoulder. "I've got to go to the toilet. Now!"

"Oh. Sorry. Good toilet far away in office."

"Take me to your shipyard toilet."

Steve followed Woo Sung. When he opened the door, he stopped, seeing nothing but a hole in the concrete floor. He didn't have the time to aim properly and inadvertently sprayed the walls. At least his pants were okay.

Later, after talking with the management and touring the shop, Steve was confident the Korean company would do a good job. Since they were competent, polite, and spoke broken English, he wasn't going to hold the lack of good bathroom at the plant against them. During the production phase, other men from Cascade would have to visit, but there were proper facilities in the office for them to use.

From Pusan, Steve flew to Tokyo and took the train to Kobe to visit Matsua Manufacturing, which had bought drawings and calculations of winches and fairleads from Cascade, and wanted to discuss the production process.

Mr. Hiriyashi, who had visited their office in Cedarville, met him at the train station. In his navy-blue suit and gray tie, the Japanese was quite a contrast to the Korean, Woo Sung Chae.

In the cab on the way to the hotel, Mr. Hiriyashi asked, "McGill-san, if not tired, want to play pachinko?"

"How do you play that?"

"I teach you. Good game."

It wasn't quite dinnertime yet and Steve couldn't take a nap this late in the day. "Okay."

Steve soon got into the rhythm of Pachinko, a vertical pinball machine. He pressed the button to eject a small stainless steel ball and watched it hit various targets.

Before dinner, Steve told Mr. Hiriyashi, "I'll eat any food, but no raw food or sushi." He had tried shabu shabu, pieces of beef or fish to be dipped in hot broth. His host had said the food got cooked by the time it took a person to say shabu shabu twice. He didn't care much for that.

"McGill-san, I take you good tempenyaki."

Ignoring several restaurants on the street, Hiriyashi set a brisk pace as Steve trailed behind. Finally, panting, they entered a building. The red carpet, pictures of Mount Fuji, orchids, and the aroma of fried tempura made Steve's mouth water. He followed the beautiful hostess, her kimono elegantly draped around her. When she led them to the low table, his stomach contracted. After all that walk, now he'd have to sit in a lotus position to eat. How would he juggle eating and sitting at the same time? To Steve's relief, he saw that the seats had a pit underneath for legs. It was just like sitting on a chair. He let out his breath in relief.

Steve enjoyed his *Sake* while the cook performed food-and-knife juggling at their table and cooked their dinner. When he served the beef and shrimps he had just cooked, Steve whispered to Hiriyashi, "Can I get a fork?"

The host spoke in rapid-fire Japanese to a waiter, who shook his head. Steve didn't need translation. No forks. His stomach rumbled.

"I teach you." Hiryashi picked up one chopstick and held it. "Like a pen." Then he took the other one and held it between his index and middle finger. "Bring thumb chopstick to finger and pick up the food."

Steve picked up the shrimp between his two chopsticks. That

Chapter Sixteen

was easy. He put it in his mouth and savored the taste. Now he could go home and brag about his new eating skills.

While walking to the hotel, Hiriyashi asked, "McGill-san, good food?"

"Great. But my feet are killing me."

"Killing you?"

"I mean, my legs are hurting. I'm tired."

"You want massage? Next to hotel. Very good. I pay."

"That sounds good."

At the massage parlor, Hiriyashi talked to a woman in Kimono, who led Steve down the hallway to another woman in a low cut top and short shorts. Steve followed her to a room with a massage table and a couch. She poured warmed *Sake* for him. When he finished the wine, she gestured for him to remove his clothes, her beautiful hands helping him in the process. Mild instrumental music, unrecognizable to Steve's ear, played in the background.

While he lay on his stomach, he felt her hands kneading his back. Often her soft thighs rubbed against his. The oil she applied to his skin filled the room with jasmine fragrance. Then she asked him to turn over. As she massaged his arms, chest and stomach, he saw her loose blouse slipping from her shoulders. She leaned over his chest to massage his other arm, her smooth skin rubbed against his chest. He glanced over and saw her bare back resting on him. When did she take off her blouse? The touch electrified him from his feet to his tongue. Still leaning on him, she massaged his thighs, then pulled him up and led him to the couch.

An hour later, when Steve returned to the hotel, guilt stung him as if ants were crawling all over his body. "Damn, Hiriyashi, why did you make me drink and do this?"

His clenched his fist until his fingernails began to dig into his palms. What would he say to his wife? Vera complained about his ogling and flirting but never had he cheated on his wife. In his eight-year marriage, whenever he got mad at Vera, he dashed off to a bar just to drink and dance. And now he wasn't even mad at her. He would immediately call her in Brazil, where she and the kids were visiting her parents. He would tell Vera how much he loved her.

* * *

Back in Cedarville, Steve's conscience burned with the memory of the erotic massage. He would try to forget about it and plunge into his work. He went to the shop.

He walked past Andy, a new hire, who asked, "Steve, what should I do for spec compliance?" He gave Steve a copy of the drawing.

Steve looked at it, then bent down and picked up a dial indicator to show him the technique. "Critical dimensions are pitch diameter and bore. Also measure the width."

"Thanks," Andy responded.

Several hours later, just before five, when Steve returned to his desk, he saw a complaint letter from the machine shop supervisor. He was being "written up" for interfering with union work. Steve banged his fist on his desk. "That's crazy."

He marched to his boss with the letter. "Roger, look at this."

"I got a copy too." Roger pointed to a paper. "These are the union rules."

"I was only showing Andy how to measure. I used to work in the shop before."

"You're in management now. They just gave you a warning this time, so be careful."

Steve chewed his lip. When he first started work, there were no watertight compartments for labor and management. Many of the managers had started their careers in the plant. That

Chapter Sixteen

experience had come in handy during the union strike last year when engineers and manufacturing personnel had kept the production going.

Well, he wasn't going to fret about this. He had enough personal issues to handle.

After work, Steve drove to the Skagit Bar. As he nursed his drink, he heard a man, "That jerk. If he had kept quiet, he would have saved his marriage."

Steve massaged the bridge of his nose. That's what he would do. Keep quiet and be extra nice to Vera when she returned from Brazil this Saturday. Once she was in his arms, he would never stray again.

CHAPTER SEVENTEEN

NORMA

Norma set two decks of cards on each table for their monthly bridge game. While her husband and friends were chatting, she went to the kitchen to check the lasagna. She called "Okay, dinner is ready."

When everyone sat down at the table, Harold asked, "You know about our state lotto that just started? Want to buy tickets?"

Jane set her wine glass down. "The proceeds from the lotto are supposed to go toward education and teachers' salaries."

Bryan chuckled. "In that case we better play the lotto to insure your job. Especially since we're not certain what's going on with the new management at Cascade."

"Let's pick six numbers between one and forty." Harold turned to Keith. "What numbers would you choose?"

"Probably our birth dates, and our daughters' birth dates." Keith put his hand on Alicia's. She smiled and nodded.

Harold set his fork on the plate. "You need six numbers if you're playing one row, twelve for both rows of the ticket."

"What would you think about a collective lottery?" Norma scanned everyone's reactions. When she didn't see any shaking heads, she continued, "We could buy one each time we play bridge."

Jane rested her hand on her cheek. "We could play the same twelve numbers every time for both rows. How about everyone's birth dates, and our wedding dates?"

Vera clapped. "Great idea. We could all put in a dollar when we play."

"A dollar per couple would be four dollars every month, enough to play the lotto every week for a year," Norma said.

Keith scratched his chin. "Actually, we need thirteen dollars for fifty-two weeks."

Harold cuffed Keith's shoulder. "Don't be too picky. Let's start with a dollar per couple per month to cover four Saturdays. We'll skip the few fifth Saturdays."

"I think that's a good idea," Steve agreed.

"Are we all for it then?" Harold asked.

"We're in." Vera held Steve's hand and raised it.

"Let's do it." Alicia patted Keith's arm.

The men nodded and smiled.

After dinner, Norma picked up the casserole dish. "Well, if everyone wants to play lotto, while we do the dishes, maybe the men can go get a ticket."

"Okay, let's go." Steve stood.

Jane collected the plates. "Guys! Do you remember our birthdays and anniversaries?"

"Of course. Let me think." Harold combed his hair with his fingers.

"Well, maybe we should write them down." Bryan picked up a pen and the paper napkin from the table. "Norma, shoot."

Since she remembered everyone's special day, Norma dictated to Bryan. "Birth dates—21, 11, 3, 4, 8, 30, 5, 2. And anniversary dates—27, 29, 24, 6."

After the men left and the women settled in the living room,

Vera said, "Now, let's talk about how we'll spend our winnings."

"Ha, ha." Jane laughed. "Have you played at a casino? Just have fun and assume that the money we play will go to schools."

Alicia leaned back on her chair. "Just for fun let's call this lottery something."

"I've never heard of giving a lottery any name, but often a group of players call themselves something, for example The Bridge Players' Lottery." Jane picked up the cards and shuffled them.

"Or, Cascade Lottery Players." Vera looked at Norma. "What do you think?"

Norma liked both names. Their friendship had evolved because of the men's work at Cascade and their spouses' interest in bridge. It could grow stronger with this one more common bond. "When we win, we'll call our group Cascade Bridge Lottery Winners."

* * *

From her kitchen window, Norma looked at the red and orange leaves on her maple tree. She cleared the breakfast dishes, then slumped on a chair. This was the first Saturday since her children had left. Although Anne was at the nearby university in Bellingham, Eric was 2000 miles away in Chicago. Now that he was a working man, he wouldn't get long summer vacations to visit home.

In the summer, the house had been lively with Eric's boom box and Anne's television shows. Even when the children visited friends or went to the movies, Norma knew they would return home. She went to their rooms and opened the drapes, but the sunlight filtering through the windows couldn't fill the void within her. The silence in the rooms seemed to scream.

Chapter Seventeen

She returned to the kitchen where Harold sat on a chair, his face buried in the newspaper. Deliberately making a screeching sound with the chair, Norma sagged on it.

Harold put his paper down and leaned across the table. "Honey, it's a nice day, why don't we drive Mr. Asahi, Rich and Little Joe up Highway 20 into the Cascades?"

"That would be nice." Norma jumped at the chance to get out of the lonely house.

Harold phoned the three Matsua Ship Building Company engineers who had come from Japan to familiarize themselves with the deck machinery designed by Cascade, to be built in Kobe. Two of them went by nicknames the Cascade engineers had given them. One was called Rich, because of his fancy, jeweled watch, another Little Joe after the Bonanza character. The third, Mr. Asahi, rejected any nickname. Norma had promised to take them sightseeing, so why not today?

Harold hung up the kitchen phone. "Okay, they said they'd love to go. Get ready."

On the way to Diablo Dam, Norma looked out her passenger side window at the Skagit River meandering along Highway 20. She wished she and her children, like the road and the river, could stay on parallel paths. Then she could at least keep an eye on them, even if she couldn't change their course.

Memories of driving with her children on this road, bordered by tall cedars and alders filled Norma's mind. She turned her face to the back seat and told her Japanese guests, "When my son was three years old, and we drove this road. I said, 'beautiful!' and Harold said, 'wow.' Then any time we stopped at a scenic view, Eric said 'wow.'"

The three men smiled. Norma wasn't sure if they realized she had been talking about the absence of her children, which was a nagging presence in her mind.

During the boat trip on Diablo Lake, Harold asked, "Is it beautiful?"

Little Joe nodded. "Wow, like your son say."

"Yes." Norma smiled. "Thanks."

They took the tour of the generating facility for Seattle City Light, then stopped for lunch. The way Little Joe and Rich ate the ham and cheese sandwiches that Norma had packed made her feel good. But she wasn't sure about Asahi. He seemed like a snob. He insisted they call him Mr. Asahi. Well, Little Joe and Rich appeared to be enjoying themselves, and if the third, stiff man didn't like the picnic food, tough.

Later, as they drove past a road sign for White Rock, Mr. Asahi said, "My name mean White Rock. In America, you call me White Rock."

"Okay, White Rock," Harold replied.

It seemed Mr. Asahi was warming up to American ways. Norma's heart filled with gratitude for the Japanese men who had distracted her mind from her loneliness.

* * *

A month had gone by, and now, in the office lobby, Norma inhaled the aroma from a crockpot of clam chowder, then set the other dishes on the table: fresh crab, chicken Kiev, baked beans, potato salad, and corn muffins. A large cake proclaimed, Goodbye—Sayonara. Her throat constricted. Her friends would leave tomorrow. For two months, Norma had made sure they were comfortable at work, just as she had done for her children at home before they left.

Rich came to Norma. "What po luck?"

"Potluck is when everyone brings a favorite food or special dish, and we eat together."

Chapter Seventeen

White Rock strode to her and bowed. "You and Harold visit to me and my family. We show you Japan."

"I wish I could." There was no way the company would send a secretary on business. And she couldn't imagine Harold, the accountant, going to Japan or any other fancy place. "I'll write letters to all three of you."

Little Joe filled his plate. "Norma, po-luck lucky? Like lottery?"

"I'm not sure." Norma thought of the weekly ticket she had been buying for their bridge group. Their chances of winning were about as much as her ever going to Japan or Joe finding a fortune in the lucky pot. She pursed her lips. No sense in dreaming.

* * *

Norma finished writing her Christmas cards but just couldn't get in the mood to decorate the house. At Thanksgiving, Eric had brought his girlfriend and announced that he would spend Christmas with her family this year. Then Anne called to ask if she could go to Colorado with her roommate. As much as Norma wanted her daughter home for holidays, she couldn't stop her from taking this opportunity to ski at Vail.

"We'll have Anne and her roommate here on the twenty-third, to celebrate Christmas, and then drive them to the airport." Good old Harold had found a solution. "I think we should go away someplace. You want to go to Minnesota?"

Although she was getting along better with Harold's brother and his wife, the thought of flying to that icebox in winter made Norma shiver. "I'd rather go there in summer."

"How about Hawaii?" Harold asked.

"Let's not think about traveling. We need to mail the package to your brother and to Eric. And we must get the tree and put up the lights." Even if Anne was only going to be home for a day, the house had to have Christmas decorations.

The next day, in the car on the way home from work, Harold reached over and patted Norma's hand. "Guess what! We get to go to Japan for Christmas."

"What? Are you kidding?"

"Honest, honey, Axel just told me to go. The Matsua Chief Financial Officer sent a telex asking someone from Cascade to come so they can go over a final list of items and the contract before they make the payment." Harold tapped his fingers on the steering wheel. "Both Bobby and Axel have to attend a meeting on December 29 in Houston, so they couldn't go."

Norma frowned. "So, they're making you spend your Christmas away from home?"

"Wait! Didn't I say WE—you and me? I told Axel I would only go if I could take you along. Axel agreed as long as it didn't cost extra. Instead of one business class, I told the travel agent to get two coach tickets." Harold had a big grin on his face. "We can take Anne and her friend to the airport, park and catch our flight."

Norma clenched and unclenched her fists. She had never been away from home for the holidays. It would be a little strange, but her children wouldn't be home, and she did want to visit Little Joe, Rich, and White Rock, who had left almost two years ago. They had been asking her and Harold to visit them. Harold had never taken business trips overseas. This would be nice for him. Norma gazed at her husband. He was the highest accountant at Cascade. Sure he could handle the job. She sat up straight in the car. "We're going to Japan!"

* * *

As they came out of customs at Narita airport, Norma saw

Chapter Seventeen

someone waving through the window in the waiting area. She wasn't expecting anyone. She turned to pick up her bag.

Harold elbowed her. "Honey, look, Little Joe is here."

Norma peered through the tinted glass again. Yes! Their friend had come from Kobe. She strode toward him, dragging her bag. Little Joe ran and hugged her. Norma's heart soared like the 747 that had brought them to Tokyo. With Little Joe to guide them, the trip from Narita Airport to the train station and then on the Bullet to Kobe would be less stressful.

As soon as they settled on the cushioned bucket seats in the train, Little Joe said, "Rich come to Kobe station. He take us to Mr. Asahi for dinner."

"Will we get to see your family?" Norma yawned and strained to keep her eyes open.

"Yes. My wife and sons. And Rich's family." Little Joe nodded with a smile.

Norma had seen pictures of Little Joe's infant son and his wife. While the men talked, Norma closed her eyes. The light sway of the train made her drowsy, and she drifted off to sleep.

"We're in Kobe." Norma heard Little Joe's voice.

Rich met them at the station. Once inside the car, Norma took out a small mirror from her purse and scowled, looking at her haggard face. She quickly put on her lipstick, and hoped her glasses would disguise her puffy eyes.

Mr. Asahi welcomed them at the door. Harold shook his hand. "Mr. Asahi, good to see you again."

"No Mr. Asahi. White Rock. Remember?" He bowed to Norma, then turned and introduced his wife, daughter, and other guests.

Norma sat on the couch by Mr. Asahi's daughter Katsumi who spoke decent English. "Sorry for the informal outfit." Norma brushed her hand over her sweater. "Your mother and the women look elegant in their kimonos."

Katsumi ran her hand over her own jeans. "But, see, I have pants on."

Rich pointed to the table laden with breads, shrimp, chicken, salad, and cake. "Remember po-luck? We have po-luck."

"What? No sushi or tempura?" Harold raised his eyebrows.

Katsumi explained, "My father said tomorrow Mr. Hiriyashi is having a traditional dinner for you. So we decided to have Western food today. For Christmas."

Norma patted the teenager's back. "Harold was joking. We're glad to have this special Christmas meal with you." She gave a big smile to the women.

The next day while Harold was at Matsua Shipbuilding Company, Katsumi took Norma to visit Buddhist temples. In the evening, the young girl dropped Norma off at the restaurant entrance where she was supposed to meet Harold and the Matsua financial officers.

Norma entered the Pagoda-shaped restaurant and stood in a corner on the red carpet, nervously searching for familiar faces. Soothing music filled the lobby. She saw Harold, his head almost a foot above the crowd. He came forward, put his arm around her and turned to the company president. "Mr. Hiriyashi, my wife Norma."

The man, although in a high position, bowed to her. Not knowing what to do, she bowed also. As they took their seats on the high-back chairs with lotus-designed tapestry, two women, dressed in black skirts and jackets, said "hello," to her from across the dark lacquered table. Harold introduced them as financial officers at Matsua. Norma returned their smiles. Suddenly her eyes froze at the sight of chopsticks. Occasionally in Chinese restaurants in Cedarville Harold would eat with chopsticks. But whenever Norma tried, the food would just slip off the sticks.

Chapter Seventeen

Here she was, with Harold on one side of her and Mr. Asahi on the other, and the Matsua dignitaries around the table watching her. What could she do?

When the miso soup came in a cup, along with a spoon, Norma thought of keeping the spoon, but the porcelain spoon wouldn't pick solid food. After the soup, the main dish arrived, and Mr. Asahi produced a set of silverware from his pocket for her.

"Thanks a million," Norma whispered. She would never forget White Rock's thoughtfulness.

After a delicious dinner Norma and Harold thanked everyone and returned to their hotel. Early, the next morning, the ringing phone jolted Norma awake. She remembered that Harold had requested a wake-up call so he could talk to Axel and Bobby in Houston. Because of the time difference, he couldn't call yesterday and had to get up with an alarm.

Harold picked up the receiver and thanked the receptionist. He yawned and stood, then dialed the telephone. Norma curled on her side and heard Harold, "Good morning, sorry, afternoon, Axel. I wanted you and Bobby to know that our meeting went well. Everything is in order and Matsua gave me a letter of credit for Cascade."

After a pause, probably in response to Axel, Harold said, "We're leaving for Tokyo today and then tomorrow, 30th, will leave for Seattle, arriving there the same morning."

Keeping the receiver close to his ear, Harold sat down on the bed and raised his brows. "Okay, I'll change the tickets."

He replaced the receiver, leaned over and kissed Norma. "We can leisurely do our sightseeing in Tokyo for two days. Can't go home before the first."

"What?" Norma sat up straight.

"Here's the deal." Harold grinned. "Bobby figured the Matsua payment should be deferred because the company has made too much profit this year. If I don't reach Cedarville before the end of the year, the letter of credit can't be deposited. Then it will be counted as next year's income."

Norma asked, "Why couldn't you hold on to it and deposit it after the first?"

"I'd be asked why I didn't deposit the credit letter for two days. Now we need to change our tickets. Why don't we call Katsumi and find out what we can do in Tokyo."

"She, Little Joe and everyone had said we must see the Imperial Palace and visit the Kabuki Theater." Norma scratched her chin. "I still don't get this business deal though."

* * *

Crisp autumn leaves crunched under Norma's heels as she walked from the parking lot to her office. What a difference a year had made. In December 1985, she and Harold had to delay their return from Japan just so the company accounts wouldn't show too much profit. Now, as they approached the end of another year, they were reducing their workforce. She would have to give pink slips to two of her secretaries. How would she tell Donna and Stacey that they have to leave?

The offshore exploration that had boomed after the Arab Oil Embargo in the seventies had slowed down with the oil glut of the eighties. Still, other companies in the same field were surviving or diversifying. Cascade had invested in other products in the past. But the previous owners took the windmill project to Springfield. Norma shook her head. Eagle just didn't manage things well.

Norma picked up the memos and went to the copy machine, where Bryan, Steve and Harold were talking. "Hi, Norma." Bryan nodded, then turned to Harold, "Did you know that Eagle was going to buy Texas Steel?"

Harold shook his head. "The headquarters don't tell us what they're doing."

"How could they acquire a new company and then file for Chapter 11?" Bryan asked. "Now, Norma, would you buy a car or new furniture if you were about to lose your job?"

Before Norma could answer, Steve jumped in, "Your President Reagan is doing the same thing. Well, all three of you voted for him. Twice. He cut taxes and increased spending. Now the whole country is in bankruptcy, not just Eagle."

"Eagle isn't in bankruptcy." Harold shook his head. "It has filed for Chapter 11 in order to reorganize and defer loan payments to the creditors. We'll still get our salaries."

Norma wrung her hands. She often disagreed with the political views of the McGills, but she couldn't fault Steve for his outburst. Leaving the men to discuss the Eagle Energy problems, Norma went to make copies of the memo, then returned to her desk and sagged on her chair.

***

Throughout the year, Norma attended farewell parties for the employees who were leaving. Of the 843 employees only 120 remained. Eagle Energy had decided they could shift the manufacturing to Houston, so the equipment and machines from the Cascade shop were up for sale. Norma reached in her desk drawer and took out the picture of her grandfather. What would he think of all this? What would her father think?

She glanced up and saw Steve approaching her desk. "Norma, I've good news and bad news. The personnel office got a telex from Springfield Steel. They have an opening for a manufacturing manager. I'm going for an interview. If they offer me a job, they'll credit my years of service with Cascade—the years when Springfield owned it before Eagle took over."

Norma nodded. "Springfield was a great parent company. We were doing so well under their management. But Vera loves Cedarville. I hope you can find something here."

"They took the manufacturing to Houston, so what do they expect me to do here?" Steve scratched his forehead. "Anyway, it's only an interview."

"Good luck with whatever you decide." Norma forced a smile.

Her stomach burned at the thought of losing her friends. More than twenty years ago when Mr. Clemens's family business, Cascade Products was bought by Springfield Steel, Norma worried about the change. But the company expanded, and she made good friends in the new Cascade. Then when Eagle Energy bought it, she thought the change might bring progress, but just in a few years, the new management made a mess of everything.

When the layoffs started last year, Norma had hoped they'd rehire the ex-employees when the situation improved. When would this turmoil end?

* * *

Norma decorated the chocolate cake, but couldn't come up with the right words to put on it. "Good bye" or "Farewell" just didn't sound right. She swallowed the lump in her throat and wrote in the icing: "Good Luck Dear Friends." She set the cake aside and prepared pasta and salad for dinner. She wanted to make something special, but couldn't. The thought that Cascade Products was closing, and her close friends would be moving away, drained her.

When her friends arrived, Norma couldn't pretend it was just a normal monthly dinner and bridge evening. They all raised

Chapter Seventeen

their wineglasses and toasted to their friendship. After dinner, they settled down for a game of bridge. As Norma shuffled the playing cards, she kept thinking this might be the last time they'll play together. Keith had decided to move with Eagle Energy to Houston. Bryan had found a job in Seattle with Boeing, and Steve was moving to Illinois with the old parent company, Springfield Steel.

When her partner Steve, and opponents, Keith and Vera said, "pass," Norma threw her cards down. "I pass too." She had fifteen points, but she just couldn't concentrate on the game.

Vera was not her usual vocal self. Her mascara had run and her eyes looked puffy. Norma drew her into the conversation. "Vera, how was Springfield?"

"Too cold." Vera blew her nose.

"And Houston was already hot in April. It'll be boiling soon." Alicia turned to the other table of players. "Bryan and Jane, you're lucky. You don't have to move too far."

Jane said, "It might be easy for Bryan, but I'm giving up my teaching position. I don't know what I'll find in the Seattle School District."

"It is hard on all of you." Norma sighed. "I'll miss you all so." She didn't want to mention that after the last boxes were off to Houston, she and Harold would be forced to retire.

"Alicia and Jane have their families here so they'll visit, and maybe even move back someday. With my family in Brazil, and Steve's in Chicago, I don't know if I'll see you again." Vera's voice cracked.

Norma's heart burned for her friend. "We're your family. You must come and visit us." She patted Vera's back. "You know you're welcome anytime."

"Table Two, you haven't dealt your cards yet?" Bryan asked.

"No one is in the mood." Norma threw down her cards. "Let's

have coffee and talk."

Norma went to the kitchen and others shuffled to the dining table. While Harold served the coffee, Norma brought out the cake.

"Oh, Norma. Where will we find friends like you and Harold?" Keith hugged her.

A chorus of assent followed from the group. They all took turns hugging her.

"If only we'd won the lottery, we wouldn't have to leave." Vera bit her lip.

"We'll all keep wondering what might have happened if we had continued playing the lottery." Jane sipped her coffee.

"Well, we could send Norma our money, if she agrees to buy the tickets." Steve turned to Norma, "Would that be okay?"

"Of course." She couldn't refuse this request from her friends.

"It's a deal." Bryan shook Norma's hand. "We can send you twelve dollars with our Christmas card. I hope we'll be in touch at least once a year."

"Are you kidding? We'll talk to you more often than that. And if we win, we can take a cruise together." Harold raised his coffee cup.

They all raised their cups and clinked them.

* * *

A sense of melancholy settled over Norma. She walked around the empty engineering office and cubicles, collecting drawings and files. There was nothing to do but get the engineering documents in order and pack the files to be sent to the Houston office.

Eagle Energy had sent their "expert" Terry Smith, to make sure everything important was filed and shipped. The mustached-man hustled around the office barking out orders.

Chapter Seventeen

The technicians and secretaries had been laid off, so he ordered Norma to find temporary help to get things done. She hired two high school girls and her old secretary, Donna.

Donna was going through a rough divorce, and was always on the verge of tears, so Norma put her in the conference room to sort the drawings by herself, away from the "expert." About mid-morning, seeing Terry march into the conference room, Norma jumped to her feet and followed him.

He stood in front of the table, glaring at Donna. "What are these files?"

Donna looked up from the files, but didn't say anything. The man turned to Norma who was standing at the door. "Does she know what she's doing?"

"Yes, Terry, she has done this many times. She's separating the drawings just the way the engineers have been organizing them—by numbers and dates."

Smith fumed and stomped out to where the two young girls were working. Now what was he up to? With a determined stride, Norma went after him. Amber, who was typing the data into the computer, paused to glance at the file.

Smith sneered. "Can't you type without looking?"

Amber looked down and bit her lip. The man turned his glare at Krista, who was arranging microfilms. He towered over her desk. The girl's hands trembled. She stood and bolted toward the hall.

Smith asked, "Break time already?"

Krista came back to her chair, her eyes glistening. When Terry left, Norma gritted her teeth, and muttered, "Jerk." She hugged both the girls. "You're doing just fine. I'll talk to him."

The man had all three temps crying before eleven.

When Smith passed by her desk, Norma called to him, "Terry, if you have a minute, I'd like to speak with you." He turned and came to her. She kept her voice low. "The temps need time to get acquainted with the job. Intimidating them will only delay things."

"I'm responsible for taking everything to Houston. I have to know what they're doing."

"If you have any questions, ask me. We'll enclose a list of all the items in each box and we'll make a separate copy for you." Norma was surprised how she'd found the courage to confront this Texan. What could he do? Fire her? She chuckled.

* * *

On the last day at the office, Norma checked the numbered and labeled boxes against the list to give to Terry. As the boxes were being loaded in the company truck, the few remaining employees came out to watch. Harold joined her.

Norma clutched her handkerchief. When her parents died, she had felt the void. When her children left for college and work, it brought more emptiness inside, which intensified when her friends left Cedarville. Now her work, Cascade Products was gone. The FOR SALE sign hung on the building. Furniture, machinery, everything would be gone.

The Eagle Energy truck rolled out of the parking lot leaving nothing but fumes and swirling dust. Norma blinked back her tears.

THE SCATTERED YEARS
(1988-1994)

CHAPTER EIGHTEEN

KEITH

Keith deposited his golf clubs in the trunk, slid into the car and started driving. Eight months in Houston had evaporated like the Texas winter. He couldn't have played golf in January in Cedarville, yet when he looked at the sunlight that peeked through the boughs of the sycamore tree, he couldn't believe he actually missed the gray Cedarville clouds. Playing golf wasn't the same without Bryan, Harold and Steve.

When Keith had moved to Houston with his family in late spring, to his relief, Alicia and the girls hadn't complained. At first, they kept busy selecting wallpaper, furniture for the extra bedroom, and enjoying the community swimming pool. But in September, when Kerry went back to Cedarville to stay with Alicia's parents for her last two years of high school, Kayla whined and asked why she couldn't be closer to her friends. Three months dragged by. Then, at Christmas, Kerry came home with Keith's parents and everyone's disposition improved.

Keith tapped the steering wheel. Now that Christmas holidays were over and his older daughter and his parents were back in Western Washington, the family's enthusiasm had collapsed like an old balloon. He parked the car in the garage and strode to the porch, where jasmine smell permeated the air. He picked a few fragrant white flowers, went straight into the kitchen and held his palm in front of Alicia.

"What a wonderful scent!" She looked up from the sink where she was peeling potatoes.

"How was your day?" Keith asked.

"Nothing special." Alicia's eyes looked moist.

Keith drew her close to him. His wife cried so easily these days. He knew she missed her family and Kerry. And it didn't help that she hadn't received any positive response for her photography. Thinking that talking to their older daughter would cheer up Alicia, Keith suggested, "Let's call Kerry and see how she's doing."

"Kayla and I talked to her a while ago." Alicia said, "Mom called. She was wondering if we could visit them during Kayla's spring break. Besides seeing Kerry, I could help Mom and Dad at tulip time."

"That's a good idea. Why don't you book your tickets?" Spring break was six weeks away, but Keith hoped looking forward to the visit would improve Alicia's mood.

* * *

Keith settled in his chair at the office to review some calculations. Not even a week into spring, Houston was already hot. Alicia and Kayla were probably enjoying the mild weather and family and friends in Cedarville. Hearing a knock, Keith looked to the open door. An engineer from his department stood there. Keith waved him in. "Hi, Greg, let me call Matt and Jerry too, so I can explain the details and make schedules for you."

Greg sat down on a chair across from Keith. "Charlie asked

Chapter Eighteen

Jerry and Matt to work on the cranes."

"Why would he do that?" Keith threw up his hands. Another interruption from Charlie Webster. The crane division manager seemed to have it in for him. "I better see what I can do."

Though the engineers and draftsmen had to be shared among different departments, Keith wondered why they would move his engineers when he had a tight deadline. He stormed to Charlie's office. When a draftsman told him he had gone to the president's office, Keith marched there. He knocked on the door, and hearing Axel's "Yes," went in.

Axel asked, "Hello, Keith, how is the winch progressing?"

"I estimated the engineering hours and requested three engineers for the initial phase of the Singapore project. It was agreed at the last meeting that I would get them. I just found out they've been moved to the crane division."

Axel propped his elbows on the desk. "I thought you could manage with one engineer and a few draftsmen. You said, you could use the old Cascade drawings with a few changes."

"We just can't copy and change an old design. I need to make modifications to suit the customer, and we have promised Singapore we'd deliver by May. You approved that timeline. I can't meet the deadline unless I have the engineers and draftsmen."

Axel turned to Charlie. "Can you spare two from your project?"

"Guess I'll have to." Charlie grinned. "We have to make sure Keith gets what he wants."

Sensing sarcasm in Charlie's voice, Keith raised his eyebrows. "Charlie, you know as well as I do that we can't afford to lose the Singapore job."

"Yeah. A drawing with your signature is good for the company." Charlie leaned back in his chair, hands behind his head and muttered, "It'll satisfy the quota."

Quota! Affirmative Action! Keith's face turned hot with rushing blood. He restrained from raising his voice. "I got my master's and this job before the Equal Rights Amendment came into effect. I'm a manager because of my job performance, not to satisfy any damn quota."

Axel rose from his chair and stepped toward Keith. "I have known you for five years. Everyone at Cascade told me you are very competent and fast. Charlie didn't mean that you are here only because of Affirmative Action."

"Of course." Charlie nodded. "But now that we have to follow ERA requirements it will look good to have a minority in charge."

"Many companies hire minorities to satisfy quotas." Axel leaned his heavy hip against the desk. "Then if the employees can't do their jobs, they're let go. I know you couldn't have survived at Cascade for so many years if you weren't a good engineer. You were there when I came to Cedarville five years ago. How long did you work there? Nine, ten years?"

"Since '71." Keith calculated in his mind. "Sixteen years."

"See, you're a pro." Axel turned to Charlie. "Go over the list of engineers and draftsmen Keith needs."

Keith tried to ease the tense muscles in his neck as he glanced at the list. "I had already talked with Greg, Matt and Jerry. They're familiar with the deck machinery."

"I'll send them to your office," Charlie said.

"Thanks." Keith stood, turned on his heel and left.

In his spacious office, Keith slumped into the chair. The mahogany desk and the brass nameplate with his title blurred as his satisfaction of accomplishments dulled. Did everyone think the ERA got him where he was? He wished he could get out of this place. But where else could he go? He could check with Steve about the Springfield Steel job. Their management was good when they owned Cascade, and he would get credit for his eleven years with them before Eagle took over. But they weren't into offshore products anymore. All Keith had done for seventeen years was designing and trouble-shooting for deck machinery.

He swiveled his chair toward the file cabinet to retrieve the winch design he was supposed to modify. He had a job to do. No point in brooding over some stupid remark.

CHAPTER NINETEEN

STEVE

Brown snow crunched under Steve's boots as he walked from his office to the parking lot. Almost two years had passed since they moved to Springfield, but Vera hadn't gotten used to calling this town her home. Their sons were just as reluctant to adjust to the school. Steve sighed. It was April, but instead of daffodils and tulips, all he could see were icicles hanging from the bare twigs, awnings, and rain gutters. The only positive factor was the job—he had one, he liked it, and it paid well.

He kicked a clump of dirty snow thinking of the week before they moved from Cedarville. Steve had had a few drinks and had blurted out about his visit to the massage parlor in Japan. Vera sat there—no crying, no tantrums. Her coldness made his heart freeze. He had begged her forgiveness and said he would do anything to save their marriage.

Now she drank every day, cried about every little thing, and accused him of wooing other women. He had thought of taking her someplace romantic in hopes of rekindling their love. However, on this Easter weekend, they would be going to his parents in Chicago. He hoped Vera was packed. These days, she seemed to deliberately delay their visits to Chicago.

Chapter Nineteen

Steve went into the house and kissed Vera. She wasn't ready for the trip, and he smelled Scotch on her breath. She said, "I'll go up and pack."

Steve sighed, poured himself some Scotch and turned on the television.

After a while, Xavier came to him and asked, "Dad, when are we going?"

His son stood with a questioning look, while young Ryan played marbles nearby.

Steve checked his watch. If they left now and stopped for dinner on the way, they wouldn't reach his parents' home before ten. He looked out at the steadily falling snow. "Maybe we should leave in the morning. I'll call Grandpa and tell him."

Xavier called, "Mom, we're not going until tomorrow. Can we eat now?"

Vera came down and hurried to the kitchen. "Gosh, I didn't realize it was getting so late. I'll warm up the spaghetti, and make some salad. Driving in daytime will be better in this weather."

After a while, Steve ambled to the kitchen where Vera was standing by the stove. He bent to inhale the spicy aroma and put his arms around her. "How about some Merlot?"

"Sure." She didn't look up at him.

He poured the wine. Only after a few drinks could they love each other the way they used to.

* * *

Steve, Vera and their sons spent a quiet Saturday with his parents. When his sister and her family arrived on Sunday morning, Steve wished he could hurry his return. While waiting for Easter dinner, Steve buried his head in the newspaper and listened to his father and his brother-in-law, Bob, talk about their stock investments.

He had not told them that he had bought mutual funds with his IRA rollover money when he started back at Springfield, and after a few months came the crash of October 1987. Then on the advice of his accountant, he had sold those stocks at a loss to get tax benefits. If he told his father that, Daddy would have yelled, "Haven't you heard to buy low and sell high? When are you going to learn?"

Well, for Steve it had been buy high and sell low. A few months back, when he had saved enough and the market improved, he bought more mutual funds at a higher price.

His niece came running into living room and whispered in her father's ear. Bob raised a brow. "The boys have opened a bottle of beer." He glared at Steve. "My son has never touched alcohol before."

"Neither has mine." Steve returned the glare and jumped to his feet.

He dashed downstairs to the basement with his father and his brother-in-law. In the family room, Xavier and his cousin, Mike, were passing a bottle of beer between them. The veins in Steve's temples throbbed. He grabbed his son's arm and forced him to the sofa. "What do you think you're doing?"

Xavier stared at him wide-eyed. Nine-year old Ryan's eyes darted from Steve to Xavier.

Bob asked his father-in-law, "Grandpa, has my son ever gotten into your booze?"

"It's the first time this happened." Steve heard his father's voice through an angry fog.

Were they both implying that twelve-year old Xavier initiated the drinking? Steve frowned. "Xavier is two years younger than Mike. He wouldn't have come up with the idea of raiding Grandpa's liquor cabinet."

Steve stood, took Ryan's and Xavier's hands in each of his and

Chapter Nineteen

led them to the guest bedroom. Xavier wriggled out of Steve's grasp. "Dad, Mike opened the bottle and gave it to me to taste."

"You gulped that beer on your own. We're leaving right after dinner. Make sure you're packed. I'll call you when it's time to eat." Steve slammed the door.

On his way down, Steve smelled the Dublin Coddle—ham, sausage, carrot, onions and oatmeal casserole. It was his favorite dish, but today the smell nauseated him.

He peeked in the kitchen and heard his mother, "Thanks, Mary, for bringing your Dad's favorite brown soda bread. You're a good cook." She turned to Vera who was slicing cucumbers. "Vera, here, let Mary show you how to cut the cucumber into three sections."

Seeing his wife's thinly pressed lips, Steve gritted his teeth. Vera had often said, "There's a saying in Brazil, 'In a house with a smart daughter, there is no room for a daughter-in-law.' No matter how hard I try, I'll never be as perfect as Mary in the eyes of your mother."

Steve called Vera, "Darling, can you come upstairs?"

He wanted to take her in his arms. He had not realized until now, how many little things had resulted in cumulative resentment inside her. His mother praised Mary and put Vera down, not just in cooking, but even child rearing. And now they were putting down Xavier. Easter, Christmas, Thanksgiving, the family reunions were stressful.

When they lived in Cedarville, they couldn't come to Chicago for all the holidays, which had worked out well. At least this Thanksgiving they wouldn't have to come. Norma had called last week and invited them to stay with them. She had said Keith and Alicia were going to be in Cedarville visiting their families, and so would Bryan and Jane. Perhaps they could all get together for dinner the day after Thanksgiving.

After Easter dinner, Steve let go of his anger and hugged his parents. His mother kissed the boys on their foreheads and turned to Vera. "It's always good to have you all here."

Mary hugged Vera. "Thanks for your help."

Steve forced a smile and waved good-bye. The menacing snow had stopped, but gloomy clouds still hung over Chicago.

CHAPTER TWENTY

NORMA

Rain pelted the dining room windows, but it didn't bother Norma. She scanned the smiling faces of her guests and family around the Thanksgiving table. An Asian poem she had read long ago, echoed through her mind, "Sometimes, on dark monsoon nights, lost travelers can find their way back home."

That's exactly how she felt today. After more than two years, Steve, Vera and their boys were having Thanksgiving dinner with them in Cedarville. Tomorrow, they would all get together with Keith, Alicia, Bryan and Jane for dinner and bridge. While her friends were adjusting to their new locations, Norma had to adjust right here without them. She felt uprooted without leaving. This week, for a short time, she could recapture the old days.

Norma wished her son, Erik, who was now married and working in Chicago, could have come home. At least her daughter was with them. Norma gazed at Anne, who had accomplished so much and still managed to keep her little-girl charm. Already an electrical engineer in Bellingham, Washington, she had the career that Norma had yearned for long ago but couldn't pursue. Norma smoothed Anne's silky, reddish-brown hair and asked her to say grace.

After they filled their plates with turkey, stuffing, mashed potatoes, gravy, yams, and salad, Harold poured Merlot into the wineglasses.

Anne rose from her chair. "Xavier and Ryan, I'll get milk for us."

Norma thanked Anne with her eyes. Her twenty-seven-year old, who used to baby sit the McGill boys, had opted for milk because she had heard of Xavier's beer tasting adventure. Vera, on the other hand, seemed to drink more than ever. Couldn't she see what influence that had on her sons? But Norma wasn't going to preach to her guests about child rearing.

After dinner, leaving the rest of the group to watch football, Norma and Vera went into the kitchen to clean up. Vera poured herself another glass of wine. Norma pursed her lips. "Are you okay, Vera?"

Tears trickled down Vera's cheeks. "Oh, Norma, I wish we lived nearby so I could talk to you. So much has happened."

Norma embraced her. "I know you're having a tough time. Steve told us."

"He did?" Vera looked up. "So you know that he cheated on me. If not for the boys, I would have gone back to Brazil."

Norma knew that sometimes Steve had walked out on Vera during their arguments to go to a bar, flirted with other girls, danced and drank. But cheating? "Did he have an affair?"

"I don't know if you can call his crazy behavior in Japan an affair. But he definitely cheated." Vera slumped on the dinette chair in the kitchen.

Norma gasped. "He went to Japan before you left Cedarville. That was more than three years ago." She sat down beside Vera. "You never said anything."

Vera wiped her eyes. "He confessed just before we moved to Springfield. He says he loves me and is devoted to our marriage.

Chapter Twenty

People say forgive and forget. But that's hard."

Norma thought of those long-ago days in St. Paul, when she had been angry with Harold over his attention to his sister-in-law. Poor Vera, in addition to being uprooted and dealing with Steve's carping family, she had to face this blow. Norma patted Vera's hand. "If there's any way I can help you, let me know." Her heart burned for her friend.

"Just talking to you has helped." Vera stood and hugged Norma.

CHAPTER TWENTY ONE

BRYAN

Bryan glanced at Jane in the passenger seat, as he drove from Bellingham after dropping their son at the Western Washington University dorm. He wished Brad could have gone to the University of Washington in Seattle. He would miss him and his arbitration when teenager Jennifer threw tantrums, or Jane got upset.

Good thing they had planned to stop in Cedarville and visit with the Gunnersens after dropping Brad. Bryan couldn't have driven straight home with his mind fogged with the thought of the vacuum that his son's absence would create.

Norma welcomed them with hugs. "You both already miss Brad, I can see."

"You know, Brad is a mature young man. You parents need to grow up." Harold cuffed Bryan's shoulder and led them to the living room. "Do you want to see our grown up son?"

While Norma went to get coffee, Harold brought out the album from their visit to Eric and his wife in Chicago. "And we also went to Springfield to visit Steve and Vera." He turned the album page to show photographs of their friends. "Did you know

Chapter Twenty One

Steve is leaving Springfield and going to work for a small company in New Orleans?"

Bryan asked, "How come?"

Norma brought coffee and cookies and sat beside Jane. "Moving away from his parents and sister will be good for Vera and the boys. He said his boys are having drinking problems."

"Oh?" A picture of his daughter flashed in Bryan's mind. Jennifer was suspended from school when marijuana was found in her locker. Well, that was some time back. Bryan hoped she had learned her lesson now. He steered the conversation back to Steve's job change. "I hope he doesn't regret the move. Springfield Steel is a solid company with good management. If they hadn't sold Cascade to that darn Eagle, we would all still be working for Springfield Steel here." Nostalgia washed over him.

"I wish I could leave Seattle." Jane set her coffee mug on the side table. "At least Steve is thinking of his wife. I know she was so unhappy in Springfield."

Bryan frowned. What was with Jane? She had lived in Seattle before she found the job in Cedarville, and now she acted as if she couldn't stand the city.

"I loved working at Boeing before, but it's not the same anymore. Still, I'm tolerating it until I have ten years so I can get the Boeing pension and health benefits. Like it or not, we have to be in Seattle for now."

Jane chewed her lip. "You don't sub in Seattle schools where kids throw spit wads, wear earplugs during lectures, and switch desks and names just to confuse the substitute teacher."

"Well, you don't have to work if it's that bad," Bryan said.

Jane scowled. "And do what? Sit at home?"

Bryan gritted his teeth. This conversation often raised tempers and never brought solutions. "We'd better go now." He hugged Norma and shook Harold's hand. "Now that Brad is in your neighborhood, we might make more trips up this way."

During the drive home, the warm September evening and peaceful setting sun didn't bring any comfort to Bryan. He was sure letting go of her son was difficult for Jane too. But he couldn't bring himself to hold her hand and comfort her. He drove in silence.

When they got home, Bryan saw the flashing light of the answering machine. He pushed the play button. "Mr. and Mrs. Stafford, this is Principal Gosset. Jennifer has been detained at school for possessing a controlled substance. Please come as soon as you get this message."

It must be the influence of that Molly whoever. Bryan's face grew hot. He pounded his fist. "No more football games for her."

Jane gave him a scorching look. "It's your ultimatums that caused Jenn's problems in the first place. I told you we should go for family counseling. I suggested other disciplines but . . ."

"I don't need your lectures." Bryan snapped, "Are you coming to the school or not?"

Bryan stomped out of the house. Jane followed, slamming the door behind her.

* * *

Newspaper in hand, Bryan reclined in his chair in the living room. He was thankful that now that the school year was over, he wouldn't have to listen to Jane's complaints about her substituting job. And since September, Jennifer hadn't gotten into any more trouble after the marijuana incident. Best of all, Brad had come home for three weeks. His visit seemed to have a calming influence on the family.

But three weeks flew away with jet speed.

Soon, Jane took Brad to Bellingham for his summer courses.

Chapter Twenty One

She and Jennifer had planned to stay a few extra days with her parents there. Bryan came home from work to the lonely house, and poured himself a glass of wine. The house was calm, but he still couldn't overcome the inner turmoil. He couldn't point to any one thing that had caused his agitation.

Hearing the phone ring, he picked it up. Jane said, "Hi, we were just talking and Mom and Dad suggested that Jennifer should stay with them for the summer."

Bryan didn't know what to say. Jennifer wasn't the easiest teenager to deal with; still, she was his daughter, and he wanted to raise her. "Do they know about Jenn's problems?"

"They think a change of location will be good for her. Dad can get her a job too."

"Let me think about it. I'll call you later." Bryan slumped in his recliner. Having a job might make Jennifer responsible, and she would be away from her pothead friends in Seattle.

Bryan decided to talk to his daughter and called, "Hi, pumpkin, Mom said you want to stay in Bellingham."

"Yes, Dad, Grandpa can get me a salesclerk job for summer. Is that okay?"

"It's okay, but don't give your grandparents a hard time."

Later, when Jane returned, Bryan had expected to have some alone time with her, with both of the children away. But Jane kept busy with reading and writing letters. They were drifting farther apart. At least they weren't arguing about Jennifer.

* * *

Before the new school year began, Jane's parents suggested that Jennifer could finish the last two years of high school in Bellingham. "She likes it here, has made friends, and she'll be closer to Brad," Jane's mother said.

"We'll talk about that when we come." Bryan wanted to see for himself how Jennifer was adjusting and if she had changed her irresponsible ways.

On their next trip to Bellingham, Bryan told Jennifer, "We have to make sure you're not causing any problems for your grandparents."

Jane looked at her parents. "Mom, Dad, you'd let us know if she doesn't behave."

"Grandchildren are good company in old age. Especially someone as nice as Jenn," Jane's father patted Jennifer's back.

His daughter looked happy and she said she had worked regularly and had even saved some money from her earnings. It wouldn't hurt to try this arrangement temporarily. Keith's daughter had lived with Alicia's parents in Cedarville and appeared to be doing well. Staying with her grandparents might help Jennifer too.

* * *

Bryan set aside his project file at the office. He would tackle it tomorrow. It was time to go home—no matter how empty the house felt. The departure of both his children left a void. With no football games, PTA meetings, debate and drama club schedules to discuss, he and Jane didn't have much to talk about. She complained about her work. His job made him too dejected to complain.

As he sloshed through the rain to the parking lot, Bryan saw Carol Bishop, the bookkeeper, walking to the bus stop. Bryan had given her a ride a few times. "Carol, do you need a ride?"

She held her hand above her eyes and squinted. "Once more, my son needed the car."

"Your apartment is almost on the way. I'll take you there."

Chapter Twenty One

They walked together to the parking lot. Bryan held the passenger door open for her.

"Thanks." She sat and buckled her seat belt.

When they reached her apartment, Carol asked, "Would you like to come in for coffee?"

Bryan hesitated for a moment then nodded. Jane was in Bellingham for the day and he was alone anyway. The first few times he had given Carol a ride, she immediately left the car. Last time she asked him to come in but he was in a hurry to go home. This time, she had started talking about her teenage son who suffered from depression. He had to let her finish her story.

In the small apartment, Bryan settled on the olive sofa that sank under his weight.

Carol brought coffee mugs and a plate of cookies and sat next to him. "My son hasn't been himself ever since his dad left us." Her eyes glistened and her voice cracked.

Bryan put a comforting hand on hers. She gently withdrew it. Oops. He hadn't meant anything. He was a married man. "Our daughter is having some problems too. Now that she's with her grandparents, away from the Seattle crowd, we hope she's behaving."

On the way home, the swish-swish of the wipers matched the rhythm of Bryan's heart. How could he discuss his daughter's problem with a stranger? He never talked this way even with Jane. Well, Carol listened and didn't argue or judge him the way Jane did.

* * *

As months passed, it became a habit for Bryan to offer Carol a ride. He found himself looking forward to the evening commute. Today, Carol had cried on his shoulder while talking about her son.

When Bryan went home, Jane met him at the door. "Where have you been? I called your office, and no one answered. I got worried that you were in an accident."

"I'm fine. I gave Carol a ride."

"Does it take two hours?"

"Carol was talking about her son's depression, and I couldn't leave in the middle of it. Anyway, why did you call?"

Jane flung the *Seattle Times* on the coffee table. "There's a job opening for a business teacher in the Bellingham school district. I wanted to talk to you about it."

"Isn't that too far to commute?"

"If I get the job, and if you really want to make our marriage work, we could find a house in Everett. I can't rot in this Seattle School District forever. But, if I were to get an offer and you aren't willing to move, I'll stay with my parents. Now that you have a girlfriend, why should you care what I do."

"Stop! Carol is not my girlfriend." Blood rushed to Bryan's face. "Since when has giving ride to coworkers counted as an affair?"

He glared at Jane. Her shoulder-length auburn hair made her a beauty. Compared to her, Carol looked plain in her short hair, small stature and glasses. But if Jane was suspicious, he was going to let her think that way. He was tired of arguing and defending his actions to the paranoid teacher Jane. "Seems like you have made up your mind to leave. I won't stop you."

CHAPTER TWENTY TWO

KEITH

As the Boeing 737 landed at Sea-Tac airport and crawled toward the gate, Keith gathered his belongings ready to dash out. He had to get to his father at Tacoma General Hospital right away.

Finally, the plane stopped. Keith fidgeted in his seat as the slowpoke sitting in the aisle seat stood. Keith picked up his carry-on luggage and shuffled along behind other passengers. He hoped Bryan would be waiting for him. When he had called his friend about this unexpected trip, Bryan had offered to pick him up at the airport and drive him to the hospital. Weaving his way through the slow-moving crowd, Keith sprinted out to the arrival gate and saw Bryan's white Toyota. He threw his bag in the back seat and settled in the passenger seat. "Thanks buddy."

"No problem. I want to see your dad too."

At the hospital, Keith hugged his mother, then hurried to his father's bed. He took Dad's dark, calloused hand in his. It was so cold. The rhythmic drip of the IV brought to mind the conversation with his father. Two days ago, Dad had called and suggested that Keith and his family visit Tacoma during Kayla's spring break. With the problems at work and the unscheduled traveling he had to do, Keith just couldn't make plans for vacation. He had lashed out, "Dad, do you think I can take off anytime I want? I have other responsibilities."

Keith massaged his father's fingers. "Dad, get better soon. Alicia, Kayla and I are coming next month during spring break."

His father nodded with glistening eyes.

Bryan came over to the bed. "Mr. Wilson, I'll leave now. See you in a few days." He waved to Keith. "Call me if you need anything."

After Bryan left, Keith sank into a chair next to his mother. He wanted to tell his father he was sorry for snapping at him. But the words stuck in his throat. Just as he opened his mouth to apologize, a doctor entered the room.

The physician nodded to them. "Hello."

Mom stood. "Dr. Harris, this is our son, Keith."

The doctor shook his hand and turned toward the bed. "George, the angiogram shows eighty-percent blockage. We feel the best option for you is to have bypass surgery. If you agree, we can make arrangements and transfer you to Virginia Mason tomorrow."

"But, but," Keith stammered, "Isn't he too weak for surgery?"

"His condition has stabilized. The specialists in Seattle will take good care of him." Dr. Harris gave a reassuring smile. "I recommend the surgery and the sooner the better."

Seeing his mother's face, Keith felt the blood drain from his own. He turned toward his father's bed. "Dad, do you want to think about it?"

"Well, if I need surgery, why not get it over with."

The doctor nodded. "If you don't have this surgery, you'll continue to have angina attacks. The risk factors are low in such operations. I'll make arrangements to transfer you to Virginia Mason."

Chapter Twenty Two

After the doctor left, Keith went to the lobby and called Alicia.

"I'll get a flight tomorrow," Alicia said.

"I think you should come after I return. To help Mom, while Dad recuperates."

"Okay, sweetheart, take care of yourself. And give Dad a hug for me."

The next morning, Keith and his mother drove to Virginia Mason Hospital, where his father had been transferred. Dad was sitting up, watching the news on television. Mom patted his hand. "You're in a good mood."

Dad's black eyes crinkled. "Alicia and Kayla just called. And Kerry is coming over."

It didn't surprise Keith that his older daughter, a sophomore at the University of Washington, would come to see her grandfather before his surgery.

Keith wanted to tell his Dad that he was a good father, and he loved him. But with the nurses coming and going, this wasn't a good time.

His father looked up. "Miyoki, did I sign an organ donor card?"

Mom nodded. Even though Keith too had signed it, he didn't want to think about that now. "Dad, we have all signed it. Don't worry about that now."

Seeing Mom caress Dad's hand, Keith decided to give them some time alone and went out to the hall. He was pacing the floor when he saw Kerry coming. "This way!" He waved. She ran toward him. He met her halfway and hugged her.

They walked into the pre-op room. Kerry rushed to her grandfather and put her arms around his neck. "Grandpa, I love you."

Swallowing a lump in his throat, Keith followed Kerry's lead. "Dad, you're a great father and grandfather. I love you too." There!

His father smiled.

When the nurse came and wheeled his father away, Keith, his mother and daughter trailed behind. They stopped at the double door that swallowed the gurney and blocked them from following. The three of them returned to the waiting room. The doctor had said these operations were becoming routine, but Keith's anxiety rose as he recalled the list of risk factors in bypass surgeries.

He had to escape the room. "Let's go get some tea."

"I'll wait here." His mother grasped the armrest of the vinyl sofa. "You two go."

Keith glanced at his mother. Mom seemed to have aged in the last few months. Her black hair had more silver streaks than before; her forehead more wrinkles. "We'll be back quickly," he told her.

In the cafeteria, he asked Kerry, "Do you want a sandwich?"

Kerry nodded, so Keith picked up sandwiches. "One for you. Grandma and I'll share one." His mother hadn't eaten breakfast. He would have to force her to eat something.

He brought their lunch and tea to the waiting room. Watching his mother nibble at the edge of her sandwich, Keith swallowed his food with difficulty, washing it down with the tea. What could he say to distract Mom's worrying mind? He asked Kerry about her classes but couldn't concentrate on her reply. He idly flipped through a magazine.

"Here's the surgeon." His mother stood from her chair.

"Mom, relax. It's going to take at least three hours for surgery."

When the doctor came toward them, Keith stood too. The doctor shook his head. "I'm very sorry. His blood pressure dropped. We tried our best but couldn't revive him."

Something buzzed in Keith's ears. He hadn't heard it right. "What did you say?"

The somber-faced surgeon repeated, "We couldn't save him."

Chapter Twenty Two

"How? Why? He was fine before you took him in there." Keith knotted his fists.

His mother's face turned ashen. Kerry embraced her grandmother. Keith wanted to slam his fist into the wall. They didn't try hard enough. Was it because Dad was black? What was the percentage for failure? Just two percent? His father had become that statistic.

A nurse came up to them and took his mother's arm. "I'll take you to him so you can say your good-byes."

Keith wiped his sweaty palms on his pants, put one arm around his mother and the other around his daughter, and followed the nurse.

While making the funeral arrangements and comforting his mother and daughters, Keith didn't have time to grieve his father's death. Alicia and Kerry came from Houston, and Alicia took over the household responsibilities. Keith could block the thought of his loss while visiting with his friends and Alicia's parents who drove a hundred miles several times to be with him. When Jane came alone one evening, he suddenly realized she and Bryan were separated. He was losing friends and family to separation and death. It would never be the same again.

* * *

A week later, Keith returned to Houston with Kayla, a senior in high school, while Alicia stayed behind in Tacoma to help Mom. Away from his family and friends, the grief caused by his father's death grew deeper. He wished Alicia would return soon. And he wished he could be with his Cedarville friends.

Keith was struck by the contrast between his Cedarville friends and the self-centered Houston bunch. Only two engineers, assigned to his project, had expressed condolences. No flowers, no cards. Neither the coworkers nor President Rodney Axel said anything about his loss.

Keith sighed, stood to get a file from the cabinet and stumbled on a torn section of carpet. He lost his balance and reached for the chair. The wheels of the chair moved, making Keith fall forward. He twisted his knee. "Ouch" He managed to slide into his chair.

As he massaged his injured knee, the telephone rang. Keith banged his fist on the desk then picked up the receiver.

"Hi, Keith." He heard Paul Nelson's friendly voice.

Paul used to work at Cascade in Cedarville when Keith had first joined the company. Ten years ago, he had started working for American Marine in Houston. Just hearing Paul's voice made Keith feel better. "Paul, so good to hear your voice."

"I heard from Bryan about your Dad. Was it sudden? How are you holding up?"

"I'm managing as well as I can. Are you in town or traveling?" Keith asked.

"Actually, I'm near Hobby airport and have an appointment with a customer in an hour. You want to meet me at the Holiday Inn for lunch?"

That was close to Keith's office. "Great. I can be there in ten minutes. Thanks."

When Keith stood, the pain shot up in his injured knee. He picked up his sandwich bag, hobbled to the lounge, put his lunch in the refrigerator, and then limped to the parking lot.

At the Holiday Inn, Paul embraced him. "You've been in Houston for five years, and we haven't seen each other that often. This has to change. I'll tell Susan to set a dinner date."

"I can definitely use some old friends now." Keith said as he walked to the dining area.

"Hey, watch your words. Don't call me old." Paul raised his brow.

Chapter Twenty Two

"Come on, you know what I mean. I'm so tired of the jerks at Eagle." Keith told him about the company's nearsighted policies—not letting them hire temporary workers in spite of the big backlog, not investing in new designs for offshore drilling. "Besides, they are unfriendly and inconsiderate."

After the waitress took their orders, Paul leaned forward on the table. "How many times have I told you, you should come to American Marine? Their owners know how to manage a business."

Keith nodded. Paul, who was Director of Marketing and Sales at American Marine, had often suggested Keith join their engineering department. "Paul, it's not that easy. I have invested almost twenty-two years in the company. Whenever I bring up the subject of applying any place else, Alicia and Kayla say, why change jobs and give up the benefits of my years of service if we're going to be stuck in Houston."

"Well, you know what is best for you. In any case, we have to get together more often so Alicia starts liking Houston."

"That would be great." Keith smiled. It was good to see Paul again.

* * *

The swelling and pain in Keith's knee had continued for more than a week, so he had gone to his doctor, who sent him to an orthopedic surgeon. The surgeon said he needed an operation for a torn meniscus. Keith scheduled the surgery after Alicia returned home.

A week after the operation, Alicia drove him to work. Perched on his crutches, slowly and painfully, he limped to his office. When he reached his desk, he was panting. He sat, took out the ice pack he had brought, put it on his knee, and checked his correspondence. There was a memo from the shop that they were ready to test the winch he designed. Darn! He wouldn't be able to observe.

Keith phoned the shop manager. "Hi Tracy, I won't be able to observe the testing. I just had knee surgery. I talked to Greg and he'll be there."

"Yeah, he told me that. Take care of your knee."

"Hope all goes well with the testing. I'll check with you later. If there's any problem, call me and I'll be there." Keith put the phone down.

Although, groggy from the painkillers, Keith read the customer specifications for the new order he was working on. By afternoon, he was too tired, so he called Alicia to come pick him up. He reached for his crutches and hobbled to the hall. A few draftsmen gave him sympathetic smiles.

"Hope you feel better soon," one said.

"I hope so, too."

Rodney Axel, the Eagle president who was in the hall, came and patted Keith's shoulder. "Hi, Keith, glad you're up and around. Charlie and I want to go over scheduling with you. We need to send someone to Singapore. I know you won't be able to go, but let's meet to hash out the details."

"How about tomorrow?"

"That's fine. At eight?" Axel asked.

"Sir, the doctor has scheduled my first physical therapy tomorrow at eight."

"Well, can't you change that? Most physical therapy offices are open until late."

"I'll see what I can do." Keith staggered toward the parking lot, sweating and fuming. He couldn't believe that guy.

Alicia was waiting in the parking lot. When he settled in the car, he told her, "I'm going to call Paul about the possibility of a

Chapter Twenty Two

job with American Marine."

* * *

Keith had called the Director of Engineering at American Marine and had faxed his résumé. Within a week, he had been offered the position of Manager of Special Products.

After being at American Marines for just a few months, Keith loved the work environment and his job responsibilities. Paul was right. This company was well managed, and the people were friendly. While still new in the company, he was asked to represent the company at the Offshore Technology Conference in the Houston Astrodome.

In the American Marine booth at the Astrodome, Keith arranged the company brochures and put up the posters. He and his coworkers from Cascade used to come to Houston to attend this annual OTC conference in the first week of May. But when Axel took over, he had said it was a waste of money to send engineers. "Let the people in sales do their job."

Now, here he was, representing Eagle's competitor. Keith smiled. It was good to be back in action. He heard Paul speaking to someone. "We're working on several proposals for new winches and for refurbishing the old ones. Come on, I'll introduce you to our new product manager. You probably know Keith Wilson. He's working on a new concept for a combination-chain-wire winch."

He heard a familiar voice. "Keith Wilson from Cascade? Of course, I know him."

Seeing Paul with Benjamin Attley from Gulf Drillers, Keith scrambled to his feet. "Hi, Ben, I recognized your voice." Ben's company had been one of Cascade's valued customers.

Ben shook Keith's hand. "Where the devil have you been hiding all these years?"

"I've been right here in Houston for five years. With Eagle Energy, Cascade's parent company. Recently, I joined American Marine."

Ben looked at the posters and pictures, then picked up a brochure. "A new winch, huh?"

"Yeah, just an idea I'm working on."

"I'll have to tell the boss about it." Ben waved the brochure as he left.

In the afternoon, when it was quiet at his booth, Keith strolled over to the Cascade/Eagle Energy stall. When he used to come to the Astrodome from Cedarville, this oil-drilling-rig-shaped stall used to buzz with activity. Customers came to ask questions, girls in miniskirts handed out promotional materials, and engineers displayed their designs. The conference used to be a time to make contacts, promote their products, and enjoy with the coworkers. Now the old stall looked drab and uninteresting. Just one man from marketing and one from sales sat behind a counter with a few brochures and tall glasses of lemonade. What a contrast to Paul from American Marine, who consulted the engineers, prepared a list of responses to questions he expected from customers, and circulated around other booths.

Keith extended his hand. "Hi, Fred. Hi, Gene."

They both shook his hand. "Good to see you, Keith." Gene smiled.

"Yeah." Fred raised his brows. "So, you get to come here."

Keith squared his shoulders. "Actually, the owner, Chief Engineer, and Director of Sales, all asked me to be here to answer questions about the new combination winch I'm working on. Better go in case they need me."

He walked away muttering, "The same old cold fish!"

* * *

Chapter Twenty Two

Keith couldn't believe he had been working for American Marine almost for a year. Despite the fifty-minute commute each way, he didn't feel the stress he had felt at Eagle Energy. Things were settling down with his mother too. She occasionally visited Houston or her relatives in California. To Keith's relief, Kerry, a senior at the University of Washington, often checked on her grandmother. But soon she would go to New York for an internship in financial planning. Last year, Kayla graduated from high school and was now a student at Columbia University in New York. Maybe he and Alicia would get used to Houston.

After looking at houses in Sugarland, closer to his new job, Keith and Alicia drove home. Looking at the spectacular August moon that appeared to follow them to Clear Lake City, Keith let out a contented breath.

Keith glanced at Alicia. She was unusually quiet. Thinking she was worried about the girls, he tried to coax her into conversation. "Let's go to New York for Kayla's Parents' Day in October. Kerry will also be there by then. What would you like to see there?"

"I can't think of anything right now. We have to settle this housing thing—sell one, buy the other. I did it once when we moved from Cedarville. I don't want to go through it again."

Keith took the exit for Clear Lake city. "But I thought you agreed that we should find a house closer to my new job."

Alicia sighed. "Buying another house in Houston makes it so permanent. I thought if we moved again it would be back to Cedarville. I don't want to live here forever."

Keith's grip tightened on the steering wheel. "It's not my fault we had to leave Cedarville. We couldn't retire like Norma and Harold. I needed a job that would put two girls through college."

"Sorry I've never had a regular job and couldn't help you." Alicia's voice cracked.

"But sweetheart, you have helped. You designed catalogs and brochures for your parents' bulb garden and were paid for it. You're always working, raising the girls, taking care of your parents and mine, and you are beginning to get photography assignments."

Keith parked the car and glanced at his wife. Alicia had been dejected when she couldn't find any freelance jobs, but finally they were trickling her way. Still, that early enthusiasm that she had about decorating the house, inviting people over, and planning trips, seemed to be gone. Perhaps it was the empty-nest syndrome. Perhaps it was her age. He had read about menopausal symptoms. Whatever it was, he just didn't know how to deal with her changing moods.

The answering machine light was blinking when they entered the house. Alicia pressed the button and they heard her mother's voice. "Hi, honey, call me when you get back."

Alicia glanced at the clock. "It's only eight in Cedarville. I'll call right now."

Keith nodded, then went to the bedroom. While he was flipping through Newsweek, Alicia burst in. "Mom's having an operation."

Keith dropped the magazine. Oh, no. Another illness! Cancer? "What did she say?"

"That her Pap test didn't look right and the doctors ran some more tests and recommended a hysterectomy."

Keith rubbed his palms together. He tried to calm Alicia. "Bob, an engineer at work told me his wife had that too. I just read in Newsweek that many women in their late-fifties or early sixties need hysterectomies. Your mom is going to be fine."

Alicia glared at him. "Even if they found a football size tumor in her, you'd still say that what she has is a common thing."

"Don't twist my words." Keith tried to control his rising voice.

Chapter Twenty Two

Alicia stalked to the family room. Keith followed her and found her staring at the calendar. "When is the surgery?"

"Two weeks from tomorrow. I want to get there by Saturday, so I'll have a day with Mom before she goes in."

Keith put his arms on her shoulders. "I'll call the travel agent and get your ticket."

CHAPTER TWENTY THREE

NORMA

Norma hummed as she prepared shrimp with taco seasoning. Today she was getting together with old friends. Alicia was in Cedarville to be with her mother after her surgery, and this was the last week of vacation for Jane before school started, so Norma had invited both for lunch. Thinking of Vera who had moved to Portland because Steve had taken a new job there, Norma had called her to join them, and to stay for a few days with her and Harold.

Harold gulped his coffee. "Honey, you know, how long do I have to stay out?"

"You don't have to leave, but I doubt you want to be with a bunch of women." Norma laughed. "I thought you had planned on playing golf today anyway."

"Got it. You want me gone for at least five hours." He reached

Chapter Twenty Three

for the Aleve bottle.

Norma pursed her lips. His knees must be hurting. Still, he enjoyed golf, and the fresh air would be good for him. "Harold, if your knees bother you, just come home and join us."

"I'll be fine." Harold kissed her and went to the porch. He called back, "Vera is here."

Norma ran out and hugged her friend.

Harold waved to them. "I have orders to leave, you know. Bye."

Vera patted Harold's shoulder, then gave Norma a dozen yellow roses. "From the Portland Rose Garden." As they walked inside, Vera continued, "I've been itching to see you. And visiting with Alicia and Jane is a bonus. Thanks for inviting me."

"You must be thirsty after that four-hour drive." Norma handed her a glass of water.

She wondered if her friend still drank as much as she had a few years back when she had visited them. Before she could ask about Steve and the boys, she heard the doorbell and rushed to greet Jane and Alicia. Jane handed Norma the blueberry pie she had offered to bring.

Norma took it, then turned to Alicia, "It's good to know that your mom's surgery went well. How is she doing?"

"She's getting better." Alicia's brown hair fell over her forehead to the rim of her glasses. She didn't bother to push it back.

Alicia didn't look her usual cheerful self. Was it because of her concern about her mother? Memories of her own mother's hospitalization flooded Norma's mind. A few days back, Alicia had also said something about not being happy in Houston.

Vera came from the kitchen and greeted Jane and Alicia. They took turns hugging her.

Thinking that friends could relax during lunch and perhaps either forget their problems or share them, Norma said, "Hey, we can move to the dining table and talk while we eat."

She set the shrimp, salad bowl, refried beans, tacos, and salsa on the table and filled the tall glasses with iced tea.

At the table, Norma turned her attention to Jane, elegant in her sleeveless, floral print dress. She was the only divorcee here. Norma didn't want to make her uncomfortable by bringing up husbands, but asking about children should be safe. "How are Brad and Jen?"

"Brad is doing very well in college. He'll be an architect soon." Jane sipped her iced tea. "And Jen is Jen. A few problems with pot. But she's keeping up her grades."

Alicia broke off a piece of taco shell. "She's a smart girl. This marijuana thing is probably just a passing phase."

"That's my hope. By the way, have you met Bryan's paramour?" Jane sneered and made quotation mark signs when she used the word "paramour."

"Who?" Vera leaned forward.

"You mean Carol?" Alicia asked.

"No." Jane shook her head. "A hippie chick, Lisa."

Norma quietly chewed her food. After Carol left town last year, Bryan had brought a longhaired, cigarette-smoking blonde to Cedarville. She blurted out, "Bryan must be out of his mind."

Jane's face turned red. "I gave him an ultimatum. I won't send the children to visit him if that tramp is there. Jen told me that Bryan once lectured her about the sins of marijuana, while his girlfriend sat next to him, beer bottle in one hand and cigarette in the other. When Jen said that pot was no worse than alcohol or tobacco, and people used it as medicine, Bryan got mad. Don't you think my girl has a point?"

"Absolutely. I'll have to lure my boys with pot so they give up drinking." Vera's purple earrings dangled as she swirled ice in her glass.

Chapter Twenty Three

Not sure if Vera was joking, Norma tapped her fingers on the table. "You can't exchange one addiction for the other."

"You're right. At least alcohol is legal." Vera set her glass down.

"Not for teenagers." Jane's voice rose.

Norma had looked forward to a fun gathering, but it was turning sour. On the other hand, what were friends for if they couldn't discuss their problems?

Vera reached for a taco shell. "Alicia and Norma, you're fortunate your children haven't given you heartaches."

Alicia bit her lip. "You think it makes me happy that my girls chose their work and school in New York, my mother is sick here, and I'm in Houston alone?"

"What do you mean, alone? Isn't Keith there?" Jane raised her eyebrows.

"He travels a lot. I've barely made a few friends in the neighborhood, and now Keith wants to buy a house that's closer to his new job." Alicia's eyes glistened.

Norma crumpled the napkin in her hand. An afternoon with old friends was turning into an "I'm-more-miserable-than-you" contest.

Thankfully, Vera changed the subject. "Hey, let's think of something fun. Norma is still buying lottery tickets. We might win and we can all take a vacation together."

"Wouldn't that be great?" Jane put her arm around Alicia. "We'll come to Houston for a trip to Belize or Mexico."

"Or take a trip to Brazil," Vera added. "I'll give you a tour."

"It's a deal." Norma clapped, but doubted it would ever happen.

She had been buying lottery tickets for so long, it had become automatic. They had all given her the twelve dollars for this year. Next year, maybe she'd tell them not to bother. If they won, it still wouldn't recapture the old days they had enjoyed together.

Cascade Company was long gone, and everything around her and Harold had changed, making them strangers in their own town. Even a lottery win wouldn't bring Bryan and Jane back together. It wouldn't solve the drug or alcohol problems of the Stafford and McGill children. It wouldn't take away Alicia's loneliness in Houston. And it certainly wouldn't bring her own children back to Cedarville.

A NEW BEGINNING
(1994-2002)

CHAPTER TWENTY FOUR

NORMA

Norma awoke to the buzzing of the table saw coming from the garage. Harold just couldn't sleep in late. Whenever she asked him not to get up so early on a Sunday he reminded her that every day had been like a Sunday for the past seven years. Norma groaned, dragged herself out of bed, and trudged to the kitchen. She poured a cup of coffee Harold had made, put on her glasses, and picked up the *Cedarville Gazette*. After skimming the headlines, she turned to the second page to check the lotto numbers. Just like sleeping in late, it had become her Sunday-habit ever since she started buying the joint lottery ticket.

When her friends were in town two weeks ago, they had talked over lunch about what they would do if they won the lottery. While Vera, Jane and Alicia discussed going on a cruise or visiting South America, Norma had said, "After eleven years of buying, I think winning a lottery is like finding a needle in a haystack. Since you've already sent the money for this year, I'll get tickets until December, but no more after that." Realizing she sounded pessimistic, Norma had added, "We don't need to win a lottery to get together. Let's plan on meeting here once a year. We can take day trips to the islands or to Mount Baker."

The faces of her friends flashed before Norma. She sighed and returned to the Sunday paper. Sipping her coffee, Norma glanced at the winning numbers. Having played the same twelve numbers every week, looking for eight birth dates and the wedding dates of each couple had become a second nature to her. The first row had the birth dates of Jane, Alicia, Vera and Keith. Hmm. Then she saw her anniversary date. Were her eyes playing tricks? Oh my Gosh, next to hers was Bryan and Jane's anniversary date. She glanced at the newspaper—September 10, 1994. Yes, she was looking at the right day. Her heart fluttered.

She dashed into the bedroom, grabbed the ticket from her purse, and rushed back to the kitchen. Harold came in from the garage and peered at her. "Are you okay, honey?"

"I have to check the lotto numbers." Norma picked up the newspaper from the kitchen table and matched the numbers with the ticket in her hand. She blinked and read them again. Her voice trembled. "Harold, I, we…We won. The lottery."

Harold raised his brows. "What?"

"Here." She handed him the ticket and shoved the newspaper under his nose.

Harold's eyes moved from the lottery ticket to the newspaper, then to the ticket again. He read it aloud, "3, 4, 8, 11, 27, 29." He grinned. "Hot dog! You know, you're right." He kissed her and took her in his arms. "We won! We won!"

Norma's heart raced. She ran to the phone. "We need to tell everyone." She handed the receiver to Harold. "I can't talk. You do it."

"Who should we call first?" Harold asked, "How about Bryan?"

"That's good." Norma settled on a chair to gather her thoughts, her mind still turning cartwheels. "After you talk to Bryan, tell him to call Keith. I'll tell Alicia, Vera and Jane."

CHAPTER TWENTY FIVE

BRYAN

Sunday morning, groggy after a restless night and an unfinished dream, Bryan sat up in bed and rubbed his eyes. In the dream, he was inside a revolving door, while Jane, Carol, and Olivia stood in three corners. He wanted to reach out to Jane, but the door kept turning. He massaged his temples. It was the same in his waking life. Things kept revolving, going nowhere. He yawned and looked at the clock. No use trying to sleep, it was already nine.

He shuffled to the porch to get the newspaper. The sunlight stung his eyes. He dropped the paper by the recliner in the family room and went to the kitchen, poured a cup of old coffee and zapped it in the microwave.

Just as he settled with his cup, the telephone rang. He heard Harold's voice. "Hi, Bryan, are you sitting down?"

"What happened?" Bryan set the cup on the table and gripped the armrest of his recliner. "Is Jane okay? Norma okay?"

Harold laughed. "We're all fine. Do you have the newspaper?"

Bryan picked up the *Seattle Times* from the floor. "Yes."

"Oh, forget the paper. We did it, my friend."

"Did what?" Bryan asked.

"We have the winning lottery ticket. We've won twenty-four million dollars."

"You're kidding." Bryan sprang upright on the edge of the recliner. "Are you sure?"

"Of course. Norma checked and I double-checked. You know, I called you first."

"Wow!" Bryan thought of his ex-wife and lottery partner. "Will you tell Jane?"

"Norma will call her right away. We'll tell Alicia too. She's in town to help her mother who is recovering from surgery. You get busy and call Steve and Keith."

"Sure thing." Bryan drummed his fingers on the coffee table. "Harold, thank you. And give a hug to Norma to thank her. If she hadn't bought the tickets all these years, we wouldn't be having this day."

"I already gave her a big hug." Harold chuckled. "Bye."

Bryan reached for his cup, gulped his coffee and dialed Keith's number. "Hi, stranger."

"Hi Buddy, good to hear your voice."

Talking to Keith always cheered up Bryan. "You still hate Houston?"

"I miss you all." Keith sighed.

"Why don't you come back here?" Bryan teased.

"How can I come back without a job?" Keith said, "Besides, my new job here is great. American Marine treats me very well."

"You won't need a job." Bryan paused. "We've won the lottery. Twenty-four million!"

"Twenty...four...million?" Keith whistled. "Are you sure?"

"Positive. Harold just called. You and Alicia always wanted to come back here. Now you can, buddy."

"Wow!"

"Keith, can you come next week? We should all go together

Chapter Twenty Five

to claim the prize."

"I'll talk to Alicia in Cedarville right away and book my flight. I'll try to arrive next Friday before noon."

"Perfect. I'll take Friday off too. We'll do something together over the weekend."

"Thanks, Bryan. As soon as I know the flight number, I'll call you. See you soon."

Bryan replaced the receiver and called Steve.

The bright sunlight that had stung his eyes a few minutes earlier now warmed his heart. He wanted to call his friends, his mother, his children, and Jane. Especially Jane. This was a joint win, but instead of talking with her, he was going to let Norma tell her.

* * *

For several days, Bryan and Harold discussed how to collect their winnings—a lump sum or an annuity. Harold, who had been coordinating with everyone, said, "Bryan, you know, I warned the women that if we take the lump sum we'll only get a little over half. I think IRS will take about thirty-nine percent. Still, they want to get it all."

"Did Jane agree?"

"Yes, they all did, except for you and Keith," Harold replied.

Bryan had thought his fiscally-cautious ex-wife would prefer an annuity. "Well, in that case, majority wins. See you Friday."

Bryan really didn't have a strong preference about how they took their money. At work and in his routine, he didn't feel any different, but talking with Harold or Keith, he felt their joy over the lottery winning. He needed to talk with Jane. Bryan dialed her number.

Jane answered the phone. "Hi, I was thinking of you." Her

voice sounded warm and cheerful. "So, how does it feel to be a millionaire?"

Millionaire! Bryan's mind whirled. "Isn't it something? This is our common prize, so I wanted to confirm if you're okay with getting the lump sum."

"It makes more sense to get whatever we can. I spoke with Alicia, and she felt we can invest our money better than the government. It can also provide for the children's education, and you won't have to spend so much on them."

"With the lump sum, we'll still get twelve million after taxes. That would be around three million for each couple. Over a million each for you and me." Bryan flopped on the sofa. The joy of winning was also a reminder that he and Jane were not together to enjoy it.

"Even the divided win is a good size nest egg. By the way, Harold wanted to hire a limo to pick you up, get Keith at the airport, and then go to Olympia to get our winnings."

"In a limo?" Bryan chuckled. "Like the winners on television going to claim their prize."

"Alicia and I talked him and Norma out of that idea. I told Harold it would draw extra attention, and we need to act as normal as possible. I thought Steve and Vera would feel left out if we went by a limo while they drove their Ford from Portland."

"You're right." His ex was thoughtful at times.

"We finally agreed that I'll drive the van. We'll pick you up at eleven, then get Keith at the airport before heading to Olympia."

"Great. See you Friday. It was good to talk to you." Bryan put the phone down, his fingers twirling the cord. When and why had he and Jane stopped communicating this way?

* * *

Chapter Twenty Five

Friday morning, a grinning Bryan welcomed his lottery partners to his home in Seattle. Harold whooped as he climbed the steps to Bryan's door, Norma and Alicia following him. Bryan hugged them. His eyes met Jane's, who looked elegant in a navy blue pantsuit and shoulder-length auburn hair. Controlling an urge to embrace her, he simply said "Hello."

She smiled with a spark of warmth in her eyes.

They sat at the dining table and had coffee. Soon Harold announced, "You know, Keith's flight is going to arrive any minute. Let's get moving. Bryan, Where's your overnight bag?"

Bryan grabbed it from inside the door. Since, Alicia and Keith were staying with her parents, Harold and Norma had invited him, Steve and Vera, the three out-of-towners, to stay with them in Cedarville for the weekend. All eight friends had talked of going to Victoria to the Empress Hotel or to Orcas Island, but they had settled on a dinner at Chuckanut Manor, then playing bridge at the Gunnersens.

Bryan followed the group down the driveway. Jane got in the driver's seat of the Dodge Caravan and Alicia went to the back seat. Norma paused. "Bryan, you want to sit in front?"

"You go ahead, Norma." Bryan climbed in next to Harold. It was strange, being in the backseat of his old van that now belonged to Jane.

Hearing the women's chatter and Harold's exuberant laughter, Bryan's mind filled with joy. He watched Jane as she changed lanes without signaling, but he bit his tongue and looked the other way. It was a happy day. Why spoil it?

At the airport, Bryan saw Keith outside the baggage area. As soon as Jane stopped the van, Bryan jumped out to hug his friend. "Hi, buddy. Get in the back seat. Alicia is waiting."

Keith climbed inside and Bryan followed him. "Everyone settled?" Jane looked back, then started the van.

"Pinch me! Can you believe we won the lottery and I'm here?" Keith's white teeth gleamed against his dark skin.

Harold laughed. "You know, you better get used to the fact that we are millionaires."

Bryan turned toward the back seat and saw Keith's arm around Alicia's shoulder, their fingers entwined. He felt a jab of pain, wishing he could share his joy with Jane this way.

When they reached Olympia, Harold leaned forward. "Okay, Jane, take the next exit." He continued with his directions, "Turn right, then straight. Here's the old grocery store. That's it."

They pulled up to a building that looked like an old house. It didn't fit the picture in Bryan's mind of a fancy lottery office. No gates. No guards outside.

As Jane parked the van, Norma said, "Hey, Steve and Vera are already here."

They climbed out, and the women ran to the McGills. They hugged each other, giggling. The men shook hands, and they all walked inside. Bryan saw a desk in the middle with several steel file cabinets. Though Harold said it used to be an old grocery store, the place resembled a lawyer's office.

Norma approached the man behind the desk. "I'm Norma Gunnersen. I have the winning lottery ticket. We all bought it together." She handed him the ticket.

The man with thick glasses and brown crew cut hair stood and shook Norma's hand. "I'm Richard Glasser. Please have a seat." He pointed to a chair across from him. "Sign your ticket. I'll also need to see your Social Security card and driver's license or another picture ID."

Bryan watched quietly, the silence interrupted only by the rustling of papers. Norma signed the ticket and gave it to the man along with her identification cards.

Glasser examined them then looked at everyone standing

Chapter Twenty Five

behind Norma. "You're all co-winners?" Without waiting for their response, he opened a drawer and took out some papers. "You'll all need to fill out these forms. After Mrs. Gunnersen deposits this check in a bank, you can claim your share." At last, he gave Norma the check. "Congratulations."

CHAPTER TWENTY SIX

STEVE

While driving to Cedarville, Steve tapped a happy cadence on the steering wheel.

"This is a dream come true." Vera giggled. "Remember our old house on that hill? Darling, we must start looking at homes so Xavier and Ryan can begin their new school soon."

Darling! The word sounded so sweet. Vera hadn't called him that for at least seven years after he had blurted out about his Japan trip. With the move, their personal problems, and living near his parents and sister, she had been sulking and drinking more.

He reached for her hand and squeezed it. "We'll buy a house, but first thing today, we'll open our bank account, so we can deposit our winnings and settle here soon."

Their friends, who had to move when the company had closed, had relatives in the area, but he and Vera were the most excited about reestablishing roots in Cedarville. Steve had already decided to leave his job and move to Skagit Valley.

Soon, they arrived at the bank, and joined the others in the lobby. Harold told the teller, "I called earlier. We have an appointment with Joyce Altman."

Chapter Twenty Six

The manager ushered them into her office. Norma presented the check. The manager made out eight checks. While the couples filled their applications for their accounts, Steve glanced at Bryan and Jane, who were filling out separate forms. He put his arm around Vera, thankful that their marriage had lasted after several ups and downs.

When they came out of the bank, Harold said, "You know, it's time for celebration. See you at Chuckanut Manor."

As Steve entered the restaurant with Vera, he heard Bryan greet the owner. "Hello, Pat."

Pat looked up from his desk, blinked then stared at them. His eyes moved from one person to the other. "Hey, you're all together!" He shook hands with each and escorted them to a window table. "Is Cascade back in business?"

"We don't care about work anymore." Steve grinned. "We won the lottery."

"You both?" Pat asked Steve and Vera.

"All eight of us." Norma smiled.

"Lucky bunch! Well, I'll be . . ." Pat clapped. "Congratulations. I'll send the waitress over with our best champagne."

Steve gave Vera a weak smile. It'd be just like her to use this celebration as an excuse to drink more. She always said he drank too much, but unlike her, he knew how to handle his liquor. Last week, their sons were suspended for drinking. Granted, moving three times and adjusting to new schools had taken its toll on the boys. He hoped his sons were okay at their weekend soccer camp. Maybe a clean start in Cedarville would help them all get back on track.

After the champagne, Vera had just one glass of wine with dinner. Steve caressed her hand, grateful she hadn't ruined the evening. The waitress cleared their plates and brought the dessert menu, but Norma set it aside. "Guys, I've already made lemon soufflé. And the cards are waiting."

"In that case, let's not waste time." Keith stood and everyone followed.

When they gathered in the Gunnersen's living room, Steve went to the bridge table and ran his hand over the familiar playing cards with Monet's water lily design. "Norma, you haven't played cards since we all left. They still look new."

"I don't take out these cards when we play with others. These are Cascade Bridge cards. Only for us!" Norma asked, "Does everyone want dessert now?"

Alicia and Vera groaned and held their stomachs. Jane said, "I'm too full."

"Then let's play for a while." Norma handed everyone a tally and pointed to the tables. "This is table one. That's two."

Steve sat at table one, happy to have Norma as his partner. Harold and Jane joined them as their opponents. When Steve picked up the hand he'd been dealt, the picture cards stared back at him. Wow! His luck had really turned around. He opened, "Two clubs."

"Pass," Jane, sitting on his left, said. "Norma, what do you want to say?"

Norma turned her eyes away from the other table, fanned her cards and chewed on her thin lips. "What did you say, Steve?"

"Two clubs." Steve glanced at the blue-eyed, sixty-year old woman. She'd never had to be reminded before of her turn or bidding.

"Okay, I'll say three clubs," Norma replied.

Steve responded, "Four no-trumps."

Norma waved her hand, her eyes on the other table. "Pass."

"What?" the three players asked in unison.

Harold stuck his elbows on the table. "Honey, did you hear Steve? You know, he wants to go to slam."

Chapter Twenty Six

"Sorry, Steve. Can I change my bid?" Norma pleaded.

Jane protested, "What's done is done."

"Oh, well," Steve forced a smile. "It's only a game." If it had been Vera, he would have lectured his wife on bidding like that.

"Sorry, my mind was at the other table." Norma scratched her chin.

Steve glanced over there and saw Keith and Bryan shuffling their cards and talking about how Eagle Energy had mismanaged Cascade. Keith said, "There is demand for offshore deck machinery again. American Marine is bringing us orders right and left. And what does Eagle do? They want to sell the Cascade division."

Norma stood. "Remember what Pat said at Chuckanut when he saw us together? He thought Cascade had started up again."

"I wish that were true." Alicia patted Keith's hand. "He keeps saying, 'If I leave my job, what will I do?' We have to find something to keep the men occupied."

Norma went to the other table. "Wouldn't it be great to have Cascade back?"

Steve shook his head. "Norma, you're a dreamer."

"Did we ever dream we'd win a lottery?" Norma raised her brows.

CHAPTER TWENTY SEVEN

NORMA

Norma couldn't concentrate on the game anymore. Pat's words about the old Cascade back in business echoed in her ears.

When she heard Keith talk about Eagle trying to sell Cascade division, Norma wished she could do something about it. She didn't know what or how, but Grandpa and Daddy would be so proud if she and her friends could restart Cascade business.

Norma dropped her cards on the table, walked over to Steve, and patted his shoulder. "Sorry for the horrible bidding." She clapped to get everybody's attention. "Okay, folks, forget the cards, let's go to the dining table and talk. I'll bring the lemon soufflé and coffee."

"I'll help you." Vera stood. "It's hard to keep my mind on the game."

"Tell me about it." Norma chuckled.

When she and Vera returned to the dining table with dessert and coffee, she heard Keith telling Bryan, "Eagle mismanaged, and now they've put our offshore division up for sale."

Jane set out napkins and forks. "Here we are celebrating our lottery win, but some people are still preoccupied with the old business."

Chapter Twenty Seven

Norma piped in, "Well, it hurts that the company that meant so much to us is failing under Eagle. If only we could do something...."

"If the Cascade project books and drawings are up for sale, what will it take to buy them?" Alicia asked.

Norma set the coffeepot on the table. Her friends had talked about investing in an antique store or golf course, but nothing they suggested made sense. "This is the first good suggestion I've heard for investing our winnings." She hugged Alicia and twirled her around. She let Alicia stand by the chair. Giddy at the prospect, Norma held on to the edge of the table. "Hey, guys, did you hear that? What a great idea. Why didn't we think of this before?"

"You mean buying Cascade?" Keith shook his head. "Even our combined winnings aren't enough for that."

"Darn. If we were allowed to keep our full winnings, we could have bought the business." Vera wound her ponytail around her finger.

Harold took a mouthful of soufflé and set his fork down. "Listen, whatever business we start, we won't have to pay it all up front. You know, if we present a specific business plan and prove we have enough cash for a healthy deposit, we could easily get a loan."

"I'm quitting my job and settling in Cedarville. We'll need the winnings to survive, so can't invest everything." Steve frowned. "Frankly, I think the way the market is going, we'd make more money in NASDAQ."

"Well, some things are more important than money." Norma said, "Just think how satisfying it would be if we owned our old business and could work together again."

Alicia rested her hand on the table. "Even if we invest a million per couple, surely we can live comfortably on the rest for several years until the business starts making money."

Bryan looked at Jane. "Our share is divided. Would you want to invest in this?"

Jane smiled. "If the rest of you want to, I'm in. Lottery or no lottery, I'm going to continue teaching. I love my job and the kids at school, and I need the health insurance."

"You love your job?" A knot formed on Bryan's forehead. "Why did you complain so much about teaching when you were in Seattle?"

Jane pursed her lips. "There's a difference between substitute teaching in Seattle and working with the same children year round and watching their progress. Remember it wasn't just my job that drove me away from Seattle."

Norma looked from Jane to Bryan. Were they going to argue about their divorce now? She stood. "I'll get more coffee?" She went to the kitchen and called, "Jane, could you help me?"

When Jane came in Norma asked her, "Are you sure you don't mind putting your share in this joint venture? I so much wish for us to work at Cascade, but you have your teaching job and children's college to think of."

Jane hugged Norma. "Hey, just because Bryan and I are divorced, doesn't mean I don't want this business deal. Bryan and I will add our million if the rest of the couples agree to start the business. I'd love for you all to work together and get your company back."

When they returned to the dining room, Keith was saying, "There are lots of factors. Besides, I need a job, a routine in my life."

Alicia placed her hand on Keith's. "Sweetheart, if you all start an engineering office, you'll have a regular job and a routine. And wouldn't the company have health insurance?"

Harold nodded. "Sure. You know, any business would have medical coverage. It wouldn't hurt to find out how much Eagle wants for the Cascade assets."

"There's no harm in finding out," Steve said.

"I agree," Vera added.

"Me, too." Alicia smiled.

"Yes, Yes, Yes!" Norma cried.

"We need to do more research." Bryan massaged the bridge of his nose. "I want to pull Cascade out of Eagle's clutches, but a lot of work goes into starting a business—a business plan to get the loan, negotiating the sale, setting up an office."

"Could someone volunteer to do that?" Vera turned to Keith sitting next to her.

"I'll have to go back to my real job in three days." Keith paused. "Sorry, owning a company isn't as rosy as you think."

"Sweetheart, I thought you loved Cascade. Why are you being so negative?" Alicia frowned.

"I'm only being practical," Keith replied. "And while I'm at my new job, which I also love, I can't get involved in making plans for a competing business."

Bryan agreed, "I know, it would be a conflict of interest for you."

Norma sank into her chair. Just when she thought everyone was convinced about reviving Cascade, Keith and Bryan, the ones with the know-how, were faltering.

"How about you?" Harold cuffed Bryan's shoulder. "You have an MBA. You do it."

Bryan glanced at the women around the table. "Boeing is not in the same line of products, and it's not a competing business. I'm willing to look at the feasibility of buying the Cascade project books and drawings. But I don't think we'll be able to buy it. And if we do get it, there is a lot more work to start a company."

"I'll help," Harold offered. "Next week, we can get together and work on a rough business plan. You can write about the product and its marketability, and we'll estimate the costs involved."

"Okay, we can try it," Bryan said. "Actually, I'll enjoy the challenge."

Norma relaxed. Her heart raced, thinking about the prospect. Winning the lottery was going to bring the group together and bring back the old times. She rose from her chair and hugged Bryan. "Thanks, you're the best."

CHAPTER TWENTY EIGHT

BRYAN

From his dining room window, Bryan could see the glow of the setting sun on the yellow and orange leaves, ready to sever their connection with the maple tree and drift to the ground. In the corner, a stately spruce stood unaffected by the change in season. Unlike the evergreen, the ups and downs in his relationships and career had made Bryan feel more like a maple.

Winning the lottery was one of those "up" moments, but it also brought new frustrations. He had to make a decision about whether to stay at his job. At the same time, he needed to work on a business plan for buying the Cascade project books and drawings. Then there were his personal problems, which neither the money nor owning a company would solve. The celebration party at the Gunnersens two weeks ago reminded Bryan of the comfort he felt with Jane and his old friends. He had missed that after Jane left. Sure, he had Carol, then Olivia, but nothing had clicked. He was alone again.

When the Cedarville plant closed and the engineering operations moved to Houston, he'd been fortunate to get a job at Boeing. Years ago when he had started his career there he had loved his work, but now it was a drag. Good or bad, happy or unhappy, he had decided to keep working here to get vested in their retirement plan and medical benefits. And now this windfall!

Although his friends were enthusiastic about the prospect of working together again, most of the exploratory work fell on Bryan. He reread the pages he had written about the demand for offshore drilling equipment and how their new company could fill that demand. The business plan listed the expertise and years of experience of the four partners in management, engineering, manufacturing and accounting. He had stated that they could tap into a pool of skilled draftsmen, engineers, and secretaries, who had worked at Cascade before.

Bryan took off his glasses and rubbed his tired eyes. He couldn't proceed until he collected more data about the American Petroleum Industry forecast. Tomorrow, before going to work, he would call his former customers in Houston at 9 a.m. their time to get more details.

He turned off his computer and went to bed. Things were taking shape now. Before he dozed off, he mentally began drafting his resignation letter to Boeing.

* * *

Bryan had polished the business plan and sent copies to his future partners. Within a few days, he heard from Harold, Norma, Steve, and even Jane, who applauded his attempt. But Keith hadn't called yet. What was wrong with that man?

Three days later, Keith called. "I haven't even talked about this to my boss because I need to tell Paul first. He's in Baku, Azerbaijan. He's a good friend. Let's not broadcast this before I tell him."

"What do you mean broadcast?" Bryan slapped his hand on the table. "I sat on my ass for hours and hours, putting this thing

Chapter Twenty Eight

together, and you don't give a damn."

"Bryan, I know you've worked hard. It's just that Paul and my boss, Bill, should hear about the new company from me instead of reading about the deal in the *Oil Industry Journal*."

"We're not at that stage yet. Harold and I will have to get the loan approved and establish a credit line before we approach Eagle. It sounds like you don't want to return to Cedarville."

"Sure I do. Especially Alicia wants to come back. But the thought of telling American Marine about becoming their competitor is giving me cold feet. They've been good to me."

"They're good to you, and we aren't? Just remember, I'm doing this for all of us." Bryan's temples throbbed. "Are you telling me you'd rather be an employee than a co-owner?"

"I wish all this had happened when I was with Eagle. I would have left them in a flash." Keith paused. "Look, buddy, I appreciate all you've done. As promised, Alicia and I will pitch in our winnings with the group. But how am I going to tell American Marine and Paul about it?"

"Well, that's not my problem." Bryan slammed down the phone.

Darn Keith! At least the others were behind him. Harold had made an appointment with the loan officer on Friday. Keith or no Keith, it was time to get the ball rolling.

* * *

Despite the high ceiling in the bank lobby, Bryan felt claustrophobic. He ran a finger under his collar. Was the business plan he had prepared enough to secure a loan? He heard Harold say something and turned.

Harold introduced him, "Mike, this is Bryan Stafford. And Mike Knox."

The slim, tall, silver-haired bank manager in a light-gray suit shook Bryan's hand and led them into his office. He pointed to the chairs across from him. "Please take a seat."

Bryan sat next to Harold and handed the manager the manila envelope. "We've worked up some numbers. With the cost of a barrel of crude going up, oil companies want to drill deeper and farther out to sea to find new oil. They need different kinds of deck machinery. Our former customers say they've received inquiries from as far away as China and Russia."

Knox nodded. "What's your estimated credit line for this business?"

"We have a general estimate of twenty million. That includes buying the project books and drawings, operating costs, equipment and salaries of drafters and office help." Bryan rested his arm on the desk. "We're starting the engineering office and will have our designs manufactured at other plants. The details are all in the business plan."

"We need the loan so we can pay manufacturers up front," Harold added. "You know, the customers won't pay us until the sea trials."

"I'll go over these papers." Knox tapped the envelope. "We need to scrutinize the plan and get an okay from our head office. Many businesses start up and then fold."

Bryan's shoulders slumped. All the work he had put in might amount to nothing. Although reluctant at first, he was eager now to take on the challenge of owning Cascade. He wanted to show Eagle how to succeed in this business.

Harold raised a brow. "Mike, I'm confident that after your head office reviews the plan, they'll go for it. You know, we have experience, and our product is in demand."

"True. But it's cyclical. You remember the oil glut of the eighties?" Mike asked.

Chapter Twenty Eight

"You think we won't get the loan?" Bryan blurted out, forgetting his business-speak.

Mike picked up the envelope. "We'll let the head office decide that. If the loan is approved, your interest rate will be a quarter percent over the prime rate."

When they left the bank, Bryan took a deep breath of the fresh air. He worried that the loan might not be approved. Then he worried that if they got the loan, they would start their business with a huge debt that could be hard to pay back. "It doesn't look hopeful."

"Oh, don't worry." Harold patted Bryan's shoulder. "You know, why don't I call Norma, and we'll go out to dinner at the Peking Restaurant?"

"Sounds great." Bryan would love to see Norma. Maybe her enthusiasm would rub-off on him. It would be relaxing after a hectic day. Besides, it would save him a drive back in rush hour traffic. And maybe, just maybe, he'd run into Jane at the restaurant.

CHAPTER TWENTY NINE

KEITH

Keith sighed and watched the airport runway as the planes took off and landed. Winning the lottery should have brought uncomplicated happiness. But, like the pendulum in his grandfather Ishikawa's old clock, his mood vacillated from one side to the other. His hopes soared whenever he and Alicia talked about the possibilities—buying a house in Cedarville where his mother could move in, and investing in his in-law's bulb farm. The idea of owning and reviving their old business and working with his friends made him giddy. But Keith's stomach churned at the thought of having to tell American Marine engineers and his friend Paul in marketing that he would have to compete against them.

He picked up the *Houston Chronicle* someone had left, tried to read it, then threw it on a chair and stood. Why hadn't the winnings come earlier? He could have left Eagle Energy without guilt. But he loved his new job and his work was recognized here. On the other hand, he couldn't let his friends in Cedarville down. Besides, Alicia was so excited about moving back.

When they had talked about buying back the Cascade

Chapter Twenty Nine

project books and drawings, he was so sure they were just daydreaming. He was surprised when Bryan called and told him they had managed to get the bank loan and that Eagle Energy had tentatively accepted their offer. Now Bryan and Harold were on their way to Houston to finalize and sign the deal.

That also meant Keith would have to make his decision about staying with his job in Houston or joining his friends in Cedarville. He had already agreed to invest some of his money with the group, but perhaps he could continue to work at American Marine. And yet, how could he not work with the old gang? Back and forth with each step, Keith's thoughts swayed with no conclusion in sight.

The Continental flight from Seattle arrived at the gate, and his friends were among the first passengers off the plane. Seeing their cheerful faces, Keith couldn't help but smile. During the ride home, Harold gave him a detailed account of approval of the loan, and negotiations with Axel and the other Eagle Energy CEO.

Alicia welcomed Harold and Bryan with hugs and showed them their rooms.

Later, when they sat down to dinner, Harold said, "Lasagna? You know, I was expecting champagne and steaks."

"Do you think we'd change our lifestyle suddenly?" Alicia passed the bread to him.

"Come on, I was only joking." Harold patted Alicia's hand.

Keith filled the wineglasses with Merlot, and teased, "And here's our no-name-regular-folks brand house wine."

Bryan swirled his glass and took a sip. "Mmm. Nice. Now, tomorrow, after we sign the papers, let's take Harold to that South American restaurant for steak. What was the name?"

"Charusco," Keith said. Any hint of his hesitation would spoil the twinkle in Alicia's eyes, Harold's enthusiasm, and Bryan's plans for tomorrow's meeting.

The choice now seemed simple. Keith wanted to go to Cedarville and work with his friends. He had waited to tell his employers about it, because he needed to tell his friend Paul first. Now that Paul was back from his business trip, Keith couldn't put it off any longer.

After a restless night, at work the next day, Keith tried to think of how he would inform his friend Paul and his engineering boss, Bill, about his decision. Paul came and sat down across from his desk. Keith shook his hand. "Welcome back. Looks like your trip was successful."

"I got several proposal jobs for you." Paul leaned on the desk.

Keith looked at his friend. It was now or never. "There's something I need to discuss. As I told you earlier, I, well our group in Cedarville, won the lottery."

"You lucky guys. You all going on a cruise? Or do you have other plans?"

"Well, we talked about how to invest our winnings, and they wanted to restart the Cascade engineering office in Cedarville."

"They must be dreaming." Paul frowned. "Eagle has let that product slip in the last seven years. Reviving a dying business takes a lot more than money. It'll never happen."

"I thought it was pure fantasy." Keith paused to form his next sentence. "But Bryan and Harold were able to negotiate the sale with Eagle. They're here to sign the contract."

"Bryan is in Houston and hasn't called me?"

"They came in last night. Bryan wanted to call you, but I told him I had to talk to you first about our plans," Keith managed to say.

"What plans?" Paul's eyes probed Keith.

"About buying Cascade project books and drawings and starting an office in Cedarville."

"You'd be competing with American Marine?" Paul's face

Chapter Twenty Nine

turned red. "Why didn't you tell me earlier?"

"The idea was so far-fetched. I was sure Bryan and Harold would never succeed in it. And you were in Baku." Keith crumpled the handkerchief in his hand.

"Cheap excuse. Didn't we talk on the phone every day?"

Keith leaned forward. "I wanted to talk face to face. I've been agonizing over it. I love my work here, but. . ."

"You better tell Bill." Paul's chair screeched as he stood. "You're starting a company with similar products, so Bill might ask you to leave right away." He turned on his heel and stormed out, letting the door slam behind him.

Keith massaged his temples. Now that he had infuriated his friend, he had to take the next step. He took a deep breath to summon his courage, then went to the director of engineering. Bill looked up from his mahogany desk, smiled, and gestured him to sit. Keith recited the story of winning the lottery and his friends buying Cascade project books and drawings.

Bill frowned. "This is quite a surprise. Company policy is that anyone going to competitors must resign immediately."

"I thought I'd talk to you first." Keith gripped the unyielding armrest of the chair. When he didn't get any response from Bill except an icy glare, he said, "I'll write my resignation letter. Would you like me to explain my projects here to someone in engineering?"

Bill tapped his pen. "I'll bring Hank to your office."

Keith wiped his sweaty hands with his handkerchief. The boss who used to joke with him and inquire about his health and family had morphed into an angry man. He said, "Bill, I've learned a great deal from you about managing people and projects. Please rest assured that if the new Cascade bids on proposals that I've worked on here, I'll stay out of it."

Bill pushed his chair back from his desk. "Submit your

resignation and pack up your stuff."

Keith dragged his feet to his office and stared at the calendar. Life had become so complicated in a month. He started writing the resignation letter. Before he had finished, Bill came in with Hank. "Can you explain your projects to him while you pack?"

Keith nodded. After Bill left, Hank sat down. "I'm surprised you're leaving."

"It all happened suddenly." Keith sighed.

He made a pile of files to leave behind and started packing his photographs and books. Keith opened a file and pulled out his notes for the new winch order, to explain to Hank. The way Hank looked at the file made Keith realize the man had been planted there to check what he was packing. How ridiculous! He had the designs in his head. His stomach burned. They had confidence in him until yesterday. Now they didn't trust him. "Here are the calculations for the winches. I'll be in town for several weeks. Call me if you get stuck."

At the end of the day, he said goodbye to his colleagues. The heaviness in his chest that had lingered for two weeks, sat there like a rock as he drove home.

Alicia met him at the door and kissed him. "Sweetheart, it must have been a rough day for you." Alicia squeezed his hand. "Bryan and Harold are waiting in the living room."

"Come on, fellow owner of Cascade Engineering," Harold called.

"So, your meeting with Eagle was successful!" Keith said.

"Of course." Harold popped open a bottle of Dom Perignon and poured the champagne into four glasses. "Let's celebrate in style."

Bryan handed a glass to Alicia and another to Keith. "To a new beginning." Bryan took a sip of his drink. "How did Paul take it?"

Chapter Twenty Nine

"He's very upset. He's also mad that you're in town and haven't called him."

Bryan said, "Maybe I can call and invite Paul and Susan to Charusco."

Alicia handed the phone to Bryan. "Number eight on the speed dial."

Keith wanted to stop Bryan, but gulped his words along with his drink. Perhaps Bryan could explain to Paul why they had decided to buy Cascade Engineering. He might even persuade Paul to join them. A reviving business could use someone like him in sales.

Bryan set the phone on the table. "He didn't want to talk to me."

After several minutes, the phone rang. Keith picked it up. "I figured Bryan had called from your place," Paul yelled. "You stab me in the back and then invite me to dinner. Did you think I would socialize with you or Bryan after what you did?"

"Paul, I value your friendship. I wish you could understand my position."

"Well, I don't." The phone clicked at the other end.

Paul's words stung him. Bryan gave him a questioning look. A lump formed in Keith's throat. "I've hurt him. Badly."

Alicia put her hand on his. "Sweetheart, if you're going to be this miserable, maybe you shouldn't leave American Marine."

Keith shook his head. He couldn't imagine regaining the trust of his friend, Paul, and his boss, Bill, after what had happened. Still, Mr. Blass, the owner, had said that if there was any change in his plans, he could return to this job.

Harold frowned. "Keith, Paul is laying a guilt trip on you. You know if the situation had been reversed and he'd left the company, would you have blamed him?"

"You're right." Keith nodded. Bryan and Harold had

accomplished a great feat today. Instead of being grateful, he was making this fuss. "Sorry, guys."

"Let's go eat now." Bryan patted Keith's shoulder "If you decide not to work with us, I won't be as hard on you as Paul has been."

"Buddy, thanks for understanding."

Keith knew what he wanted to do. He wanted to go back to Cedarville and work with his old friends. But was that what he ought to do? Anyway, now that he had alienated everyone at American Marine, it would be difficult if not impossible to go back there.

CHAPTER THIRTY

STEVE

As Steve drove his sons to their new school, the October sun spread an orange glow across the highway, promising a bright day in spite of the chill in the air. Vera sat next to him, smiling. Steve hummed along with the tune playing on the radio.

"Dad, you like this Grunge music?" Ryan asked.

"Is that what this is?" Steve made a face. Was he really listening to the ear-grinding station that his sons had preset? What the heck! He wanted Xavier and Ryan to be as happy here as he and Vera were in their old surroundings. Steve vowed to be more involved in his sons' school, to make sure they chose good friends and stayed away from alcohol and pot.

In the past, it had always been one step forward and two back. But ever since winning the lottery, everything had moved in the right direction. He didn't need a job anymore, so he and Vera had decided to return to Cedarville immediately after their celebration gathering at Harold and Norma's. At first he hadn't cared whether Bryan and Harold could buy back the Cascade project books and drawings. Now that they were starting their own company, excitement buzzed through him.

Steve chuckled. Money might not buy happiness, but happiness was surely following the lottery money. For the first time, the housing market had worked in his favor. Their Portland house sold the first week it was on the market, and they bought a nice home in Cedarville not too far from the Gunnersens. They would settle there as soon as the movers delivered the furniture this afternoon. It would be nice to live in their home instead of Skagit Inn, where they had been staying for the last five days.

Steve dropped Ryan and Xavier off to school and took Vera to their new house before going to meet Bryan and Harold. He kissed his wife. "Bye, darling. Can you handle the movers by yourself?"

"I've had enough practice. Besides, Norma is coming. Good luck finding office space."

Steve waved, started the car, and tapped on the steering wheel in rhythm to the music. During the moves to Springfield, New Orleans, then to Portland, Vera had sulked. But now she cheerfully took charge of moving and decorating their new home.

Harold and Bryan were waiting in the living room when Steve arrived at the Gunnersens. "Okay, the manufacturing vice president is here. Let's go." Bryan gulped his coffee and set his cup on the table. "Norma, you women are also investors in this business. Perhaps you should come along on our office hunting adventure."

"Well, I thought I should go help Vera," Norma said. "The movers unload so fast, you need one person to take the inventory and another to see if everything is going where it belongs."

Harold jingled his car keys then kissed Norma. "Let's check out our options today, then when we narrow it down, we'll take you for final approval."

At the real-estate office, the agent printed out a list of commercial rentals. They looked at the pictures and descriptions

Chapter Thirty

in the listing and decided to look at four office rentals. As the real-estate agent drove them from one place to the other over the bridge crossing the Skagit River, Steve gazed at the frolicking water, feeling a sense of power. This time, he was going to have a say about where his office would be and how he would furnish it.

One rental didn't have enough storage space, the other lacked parking area, and the third didn't have a lobby. Finally, at the fourth building, they nodded to each other.

Bryan said, "This might work."

Harold turned to the agent. "Stacy, we still need to show this to our bosses. You know, our wives, before we finalize the deal."

On the way back home, Harold said, "Too bad Keith couldn't get here earlier. I wish he knew what he's missing. I mean, we're starting our business from scratch. Renting a place, buying furniture. It's like giving birth."

"Sure, like you'd know that experience," Steve teased.

Bryan chuckled. "Well, at least Keith will be here before the other birthing experience, when we shop for computers and printers."

Steve was glad that finally Keith had decided to come to Cedarville. He was still in Houston with Alicia, packing and trying to sell their house. Since he was already there, Bryan had asked him to supervise and make sure Eagle Energy shipped all the project books and drawings they were supposed to send.

Steve leaned back in the car seat. Working with his old pals was going to be fun.

CHAPTER THIRTY ONE

NORMA

Norma looked at the new carpets and watched the Eagle Energy truck unload box after box filled with Cascade drawings and project books. The prospect of dirt being dragged onto the carpet bothered her for a second, but she ignored it. She was getting a treasure. What a contrast it was from the gloomy day seven years ago, when she and Harold had watched a similar truck take away these boxes. The sun beamed today with an infectious exuberance. Steve, Vera, Keith, Alicia, and Bryan stood with her and Harold in the lobby, as if to greet a long-lost friend.

With all the comings and goings through the lobby, Norma couldn't organize her desk or record a message for the answering machine. She needed some distraction and thought of food. "Hey, guys, are you getting hungry yet? Why don't I order pizzas?"

"Sounds good." Bryan nodded.

Norma picked up the phone and ordered two large pizzas. Just after the Eagle moving van left, a young man delivered the pizza. They gathered in the small kitchen, talking, laughing and eating. Eating together had been a part of their friendship, and now they were doing it in the office they owned.

Chapter Thirty One

Anticipating extra work during the setup, Norma had hired two former Cascade secretaries. When Donna and Michele arrived, Norma went with them downstairs.

Donna picked up a box from the stack. "This one has the files with the parts list. Do you remember how that Eagle autocrat kept interfering and made me cry when we packed?"

"What a nightmare." Norma sighed. "It's over now. This is our new Cascade office."

"Look! That's my handwriting. I packed this one." Michele ran her hand over the cardboard box. "That's old marking. They never opened it!"

Norma sat on a chair next to the box. If it hadn't been opened so far, maybe the engineers wouldn't need it. She called, "Keith, Bryan, could you come down and tell us if we need to empty this box?"

The whole gang, including Vera and Alicia, came to the basement. Norma laughed. "Now, now. I just asked for the engineers. Tell us which box can be left stored like this."

"We're going to open all the boxes and have them available for reference. We won't do what Eagle did." Keith opened the box and picked a project book.

"I think we'll file the parts list in the cabinet by serial number and organize the project books and drawings by their project numbers on these shelves." Norma turned to Bryan. "Okay?"

Bryan shrugged. "Sure, you're the Administrator-in-Chief."

"Ha, ha." Norma chortled. After the company sale was finalized, they had discussed titles for each other—Bryan the president, Harold the comptroller, Steve vice president of manufacturing, and Keith, vice president of engineering.

"And, Norma, you're going to be the Administrative Manager," Bryan had said.

All Norma wanted was to work with her friends in the

business that they had worked before. She didn't care about the title. Smiling at Vera and Alicia, she blinked back tears of joy. The women were partners in the business but not a part of the workforce, as Norma was. Still, all of them, including Jane, who wasn't there, were so enthusiastic.

Norma took a file from the box and caressed it.

CHAPTER THIRTY TWO

BRYAN

For the last two months, since opening the Cascade Engineering office, Bryan had spent his time on marketing and sales. He informed former customers that Cascade had reemerged, visited previous business contacts in Houston and Louisiana, and called potential clients in Europe and Asia. The new Cascade even opened a sales office in Houston and hired a salesman, Albert Morris. So far, nothing had happened. They were able to establish the parts business for older equipment, but they needed to get orders for new deck machinery designs.

Finally, an Italian company, Gimaldi Shipbuilding, asked Bryan to meet the chief engineer in Turin to discuss the proposal Cascade had submitted. Bryan took Albert, the new salesman, with him so he would get some experience handling sales meetings.

After their meeting at Gimaldi Shipbuilding, they went to the Michelangelo Restaurant and settled on their chairs. Albert leaned back in his chair and yawned. "Gosh, I'm bushed."

The yawn made Bryan sleepy. "I'm fighting jet lag too. Did you take note of what the Gimaldi engineers were asking? Right now, Keith and I are doing sales jobs, but when we get busy with designing and you're on your own, be sure to ask the customers pertinent questions, be ready to answer their concerns, and let our engineers know before the meeting."

The salesman nodded. Bryan scratched his chin and pretended to study the menu. He wished he could have hired an experienced salesman, like old Cascade's Sam Bachman or Cascade's former European salesman, Pierre Douquette.

Bryan took a sip of his wine and glanced toward the entrance. He saw his old friend Paul, American Marine's director of sales, with Bill, their director of engineering. Bryan nearly choked on his wine. Paul hadn't talked to him since the outburst two months ago in Houston, when Keith had told him about the new venture.

"Al, don't look at the entrance. Our competitors, American Marine people are here." Bryan put his hand on his forehead and pretended to study the menu.

The waiter came to their table. "Sir, may I take your order?"

Bryan was glad his face was hidden behind the waiter when Paul and Bill passed by their table. Without uttering a word, Bryan pointed to the salt-crusted bass and mushroom risotto dish on the menu. He hoped Albert would take the cue and not talk loudly in English. The young man also put his finger on an item in the menu.

Rubbing his temples, Bryan sat quietly, until he heard Bill call him, "Bryan!"

Feeling trapped, Bryan waved to Bill. Paul was looking in a different direction. "Al, let's go say hello to them." Bryan stood.

To his relief, Paul shook his hand. Bryan introduced the salesman, "This is Albert Morris."

"So, how's the new business?" Bill asked.

"We're making progress. Some parts orders for refurbishing have come in. We're also working on proposals for new traction

Chapter Thirty Two

winches." Bryan didn't know what else to say.

A knot formed on Paul's brows. "Even if you get an order, where will you get it manufactured?"

"We're already using Eagle facilities for parts production." Bryan tried hard not to raise his voice. "Steve has lined up manufacturing companies to work on contract for us."

Bill smiled. "Good to see you."

"Good to see you both too." Bryan turned toward his table. He suspected Bill and Paul were in Turin for the same potential job that had brought him there.

When dinner arrived, Bryan and Albert ate in silence. Bryan wished Albert could be more like Paul, who came up with new marketing ideas and spoke four languages. With American Marine vying for the same job, perhaps this trip was going to be a waste of time and money.

* * *

Two weeks after returning to Cedarville, Bryan called Gimaldi engineers to find out if they had made a decision. "We are concerned about the logistics," the Italian said.

"As I explained before, we have contacts with several manufacturing facilities. We have experienced engineers. Our designs have a proven record . . . ."

"But we've decided to award the job to another company."

"Hope you'll consider our proposals in future. Thanks." Bryan slammed the phone in its cradle and stormed to Keith's office. "Paul must have been bad-mouthing us."

"We didn't get the Gimaldi order?" Keith looked up from his computer.

"Our meeting with Gimaldi had gone well. I told you what Paul said to me in Turin. He must have told Gimaldi people that we don't have proper manufacturing facilities to deliver our products."

"We have other proposals, and something is going to work out." Keith paused. "I wanted to warn you about International Drilling Company. I got a call from someone with questions about the proposal. I told him I didn't work on it and asked him to call you."

Bryan rested his elbow on the desk. "A man from International Drilling had called earlier and insisted he talk to you. I told him you were not available." Keith had worked on the proposal at American Marine, and had promised them he wouldn't work on the same for Cascade. Were they trying to test him?

"Hmm." Keith raised his brows.

"It looks like American Marine put them up to it. Paul is in a destructive mode."

"I still feel guilty about leaving American Marine." Keith sighed.

Bryan drummed his fingers on Keith's desk. "How can you continue to defend Paul?"

"Bryan, I'm not defending him. I'd rather concentrate on other jobs instead if being angry at Paul. I'm hopeful about the North Sea Drilling Proposal. I'll forward my calculations to you."

"If we snag this, it would be large repeat order." Bryan stood to leave.

* * *

For weeks, Bryan answered question after question about the traction winch, from the chief engineer, Ken Olsen of North Sea Drilling. Olsen had said he would call today with his decision. Hoping for a positive response, Bryan had bought a bottle of Mumm's champagne to celebrate with his business partners.

Chapter Thirty Two

As he tried to work, Bryan glanced at the phone, willing it to ring. Finally, when it rang, Bryan grabbed it. "Hello."

"Bryan, this is Ken Olsen. We would like to award you the order for traction winches, but we need a different performance."

"Send us your specifications, and we'll adjust our design." Bryan leaned back on his chair. The changes the customer wanted would increase the engineering hours and cost. Still, they needed the order. First designs were always costly. Hopefully the company would start making a profit on future jobs. "Ken, if we change our gearbox size to meet your performance requirement, are you ready to give us the order?"

"We can do that."

Yes! Bryan pumped his fist in the air and forced his voice to remain calm. "Can you fax a letter of intent?"

Ken said, "I'll send it right away."

"Thanks, Ken."

Bryan dashed to the car, picked the champagne bottle wrapped in a towel, and sneaked it to the kitchen. Fortunately, the cold December day kept the champagne chilled. He took a stack of plastic glasses from the shelf, and went to the lobby.

Norma looked up from her computer. Bryan whispered, "We're celebrating. Can you gather everyone here? Just pretend you need help for the computer or whatever."

Norma called, "Hey, guys, I need help. Something is wrong with the fax machine."

"Not the fax machine!" Bryan hissed. She was going to blow the surprise, but it was too late. He heard Keith and Steve coming down the hall. "Get Harold," Bryan told Norma.

Keith asked, "What's wrong with the fax machine?"

Bryan still bent at the machine, said, "Paper jam."

When Harold joined them, the three men and Norma hovered around Bryan while he guarded the fax machine. The machine resonated and a sheet of paper appeared. Bryan looked to make sure it was the letter of intent. He handed it to Norma. "Read it out loud, please."

Norma took the paper. "A letter of intent from North Sea Drilling!" Her eyes grew large and a smile spread across her face.

"Hot damn!" Steve jumped up and hugged Norma.

Keith put up his hand to high-five with Bryan. "We did it!"

Bryan smiled. He shouldn't have doubted Keith when he defended Paul. Bryan popped open the champagne and poured it.

Harold raised his glass. "To our new business and first large order."

CHAPTER THIRTY THREE

NORMA

After helping set up a desk for her new secretary, Norma returned to her chair, thinking how their business had grown. In the last nine months, the workforce had increased from the five lottery winners to thirty-one, many of them former Cascade employees. Although most of those hired were engineers and draftsmen, or the unisex term, drafters, Harold had hired an accountant, and Norma had hired Donna, who had worked at the old Cascade as secretary. It was good to have someone who knew the procedure and could take over some of Norma's responsibilities.

Norma glanced at her watch. Alicia would be coming soon to look at pictures and newspaper clippings. Last Saturday during their bridge game, her friends remembered the Fourth of July picnics at the old Cascade plant. They decided to have a picnic and invite the old-timers. Vera volunteered to reserve the park, Jane offered to shop for food and drinks, and Alicia said, she'd send a reunion announcement to the newspaper, so ex-employees could join them.

Norma rose from her chair. "Donna, When Alicia comes, send her to the basement."

In the basement, Norma first looked at the scrapbook she had started after they opened the office in October. She reread the article from the business section of the *Cedarville Gazette* dated November 2, 1994: "Company Transcends Time, Space." It continued, "A time/space-moving event was pulled off by a core of former Cascade engineers and development workers." The story listed the company's progress from machine shop foundry and logging products, to grenades during World War II and mooring equipment for floating oil-exploration rigs in stormy waters five-thousand-feet-deep. The article concluded, "Use the time machine and call it Cascade Products, and use the space positioner to move it from Houston to Cedarville, and welcome the return of this business."

Each time Norma read the article, she got a lump in her throat.

She heard Alicia, "Hi, Norma. I see you have already started."

"I thought I'd do a bit of screening for you." Norma opened a page and pointed to a black and white picture of the ten original employees. "This is my grandpa. And this is Mr. Clemens, the owner."

Alicia bent down to see the picture. "Wow! That was more than ninety years ago."

"And here are the pictures of the machines from the time when my dad worked there. I used to laugh whenever I heard 'Gas Donkey' and 'MAC Little Tugger' used for logging."

Alicia took the file in her hand. "I think we should have three photographs, one with your grandfather and the original employees, one from the seventies with offshore drilling equipment, and one of the four men and you, buying the business back. I can write a sentence or two for each of the three time periods. Then I'll give the reunion time and place and our phone numbers. Let me take a picture right now of you and the guys."

They went upstairs. After taking their photograph, Alicia

said, "I'm planning to write a short history and add photos from the past. It might be considered an advertisement, which would cost us."

Harold waved his hand. "Don't worry about that. We want the thing to be eye-catching, so the ex-Cascade employees will notice it and come to our picnic."

"Well, that's great then." Alicia picked up the scrapbook. "Bye."

Norma hugged her. "Thanks."

CHAPTER THIRTY FOUR

KEITH

The broiling heat of the July sun baked Keith's back as he hauled a huge cardboard box from Jane's car and set it on the picnic table with a thud. "Hope I didn't break anything." He wiped his sweaty forehead.

Jane cleared her throat. "You do know that paper products don't break."

Keith laughed. "Thanks for reminding me."

He turned toward the parking lot to get the cooler from Jane's car, but stopped when he saw the Stafford children, Brad and Jennifer, carrying it. Keith ran his fingers through his hair and saw a gray hair stuck to his nail. He didn't feel that old, but the kids were becoming mature adults, so he must be getting old. His daughters were progressing into adulthood, both in New York—one working, the other a student at Columbia University. They were home for ten days and should be arriving to the picnic with Alicia. The picnic was turning out to be not only a reunion of the Cascade employees, past and present, but also their families.

With the help of Jane, Brad and Jennifer, Keith dragged four

Chapter Thirty Four

tables into the shade on the lawn and secured blue plastic table covers with masking tape.

"Here's Dad." Brad ran toward the parking lot. Jennifer followed. They hugged him.

When Bryan came, his eyes were fixed on Jane. They were not arguing so much at bridge games now and seemed to be getting along better. To give them privacy, Keith left to get the gift certificates from his car.

He saw his former boss and mentor, Carl Meyer and his wife. The man limped forward with the help of his cane and embraced Keith, his cane dangling on his arm. "So great you brought Cascade back to Cedarville."

"Actually, Bryan and Harold did the planning."

"Don't be modest, Keith. I have a feeling they couldn't have pulled it off without you." Carl patted his back.

"Thank you." Keith saw Bryan, and moved to the side to make room for him.

Carl shook Bryan's hand. "Hi, glad to see you in our neck of the woods again."

From the corner of his eye, Keith noticed Fred Glasser. Although Keith hadn't seen this man in years, memories of his biting remarks resurfaced in his mind. At old Cascade picnics and Christmas parties, Fred often got drunk and had once called Keith "Boy."

Keith shuddered, as if ants were crawling on his back. Alicia moved to Keith's side and he squeezed her hand. No way would Fred spoil this Cascade reunion. Hopefully the man was not drunk and was going to remain sober, because liquor wasn't allowed at Cedarville State Park.

As Keith turned to go the other way, Fred called him, "Keith, thanks for inviting me."

"Glad you could come." Keith forced a smile. The jerk

seemed to have mellowed in his old age.

Keith looked away in the distance to the meandering Skagit River, glowing velvety green in the noon sun. He thought of the Buddhist saying, "You can't step in the same river water again." People change, circumstances change. There was no need to bring up old grudges. He was the host and vice president of his company, and Fred was just a guest.

As more people came and brought their share of potluck lunch, the picnic tables filled with food. In one corner, Norma's daughter, Anne, started her CD player, and the youngsters gathered around her, swaying, tapping, and singing.

Harold, who was slaving at the barbecue, flipped the hamburgers and announced, "Okay folks, grab your plates and fill them up."

After lunch, while some were still struggling to finish their watermelon and cake, Keith gave Norma the gift certificates he had bought from Gateway Inn and Harbor View Restaurant. The friends had decided that Norma would give out the prizes. After all, no one was more enthusiastic about this reunion than she was.

Harold announced, "Folks, you know, it's time for some important business. Everyone gather around."

In a little while the music stopped and eighty odd participants joined them.

Norma opened an envelope. "Okay, who's the oldest Cascade employee here?"

An elderly woman, in a purple polyester dress and a hat, raised her hand and mumbled something. Norma took her wrinkled hand and gave her the gift certificate for Gateway Inn. "Esther is eighty-nine years old. She was a secretary way before I joined the company."

Norma waved another envelope. "Now tell us, who has

Chapter Thirty Four

traveled the farthest distance?"

Amid replies of, "Oak Harbor, La Conner, Seattle, Olympia," one man shouted, "Mobile, Alabama."

A round faced, heavy man in overalls, came forward. "I'm Chad Morgan. I worked here from '69 to '72 in quality control. I'm visiting my son in Cedarville, and my wife saw the reunion announcement in the Gazette."

Norma gave him the gift certificate. "So what're you doing in Mobile?"

"I work for a manufacturing facility in quality control. They produce similar machines to what we used to build at Cascade," the man replied.

Thinking the company might be the kind of manufacturing plant they were looking for, Keith whispered to Steve, "Find out about the exact products their shop makes in Alabama."

Steve nodded. "I was thinking the same thing."

* * *

Summer was over, the fall was almost at its end, and the workload was growing, with deadlines fast approaching. Keith picked up a pile of resumes from his desk and went to Bryan's office. He had not found a single qualified person. He never thought he would complain about the booming economy, but that was the real culprit. With so many job openings at Boeing and Microsoft, who would come to work for a little company in this small town? Besides, most engineering graduates were studying high tech and couldn't translate those skills to traditional manufacturing, or as some called it, "Dumb iron engineering."

Keith set the resumes on Bryan's desk. "I don't think any of them suit our needs."

"No new applicants after the ad in the *Seattle Times*?" Bryan raised his brow.

Keith shook his head. Although the design office now had twenty-eight draftsmen and engineers, anticipating more orders, Keith had suggested they place want ads in the *Seattle Times* and contact universities for graduating mechanical and electrical engineers.

Bryan had objected, "We can't justify hiring more people yet."

Now that they were swamped with orders, Bryan was bugging Keith to hire more engineers ASAP.

"Bryan, I can't wave a magic wand and produce qualified workers in this tight job market. We should have done that earlier, but my hands are tied."

Bryan frowned. "What do you mean your hands are tied? I've never objected to anyone you hired."

"We placed the ads so late that most of good candidates were taken by other industries. Shuttling between Italy, Norway and Houston delayed my projects. If I had a project manager I could depend on, we could have completed the designs," Keith said.

The phone rang, and Bryan answered. "We'll be there." He set the receiver down. "It's Harold. They're waiting for us in his office to discuss the bonuses. Don't worry, we'll definitely work on getting a few more engineers."

Keith had forgotten about the meeting. He followed Bryan and sat down next to Norma and Steve across from Harold.

"Here's the Cascade Financial Report." With his suit and tie, Harold looked like a banker, especially now, with a little extra weight and his balding head. Putting on his glasses, Harold unfolded a pile of papers. "The net profit before final adjustments for some pending office expenses is around $287,000."

"Wow!" Steve sat up straight in his chair, almost to the edge.

Chapter Thirty Four

"Considering that most businesses don't expect profits in the first two or three years, this is great news."

Keith's pulse quickened. "In fourteen months, I knew we exceeded our expectations for orders, but I had no idea we were doing this well."

Bryan leaned forward on the desk. "Harold and I have been discussing whether to divide the profit among us or give bonuses to all salaried employees."

"I like the idea of sharing the bonus with everyone," Norma said.

Steve replied, "It will be difficult to distribute. The employees have different pay scales and were hired at different times."

"Well, I can figure that out." Harold tapped his pen. "The contract people won't be included, but the twenty salaried employees could get a percentage of their pay as bonus. My question is, are you willing to share?"

Keith watched everyone for signs of nodding or frowning, but couldn't figure out if they wanted to share the bonus or not. "At a time when qualified workers are hard to find, a little bonus would boost their confidence in the company. Without them, we couldn't have accomplished this. But I also feel we should pay up our loan with this profit."

Harold cleared his throat. "The interest rates are low right now, and having the loan gives the business a tax break. So, I think we should distribute the profit, either just among us or share it with other employees."

"I think it would be a good gesture to give a bonus." Keith thought of the backlog. "But remember, we may not get more orders if we can't deliver on time. We need to hire at least two engineers."

"You're right, Keith. I'll talk to a few customers in Houston and see if they suggest some candidates." Bryan turned to Norma. "You place ads in the newspapers after the holidays."

"I'll do that." Norma nodded.

"How are the plans for the Christmas party?" Steve asked.

"I've reserved the banquet hall at Rainbow Inn for December 19. With the contract workers, regular employees and their spouses, we'll be seventy people."

"Good. We leave that planning to you, our administrator-in-chief." Bryan laughed.

"Hail to our administrator." Steve clapped. "Hey, we're all stressed about work, but let's celebrate the profit and enjoy our Christmas party."

"I agree." Keith smiled.

CHAPTER THIRTY FIVE

STEVE

Steve pushed his chair back from the computer and picked up the ringing phone. He heard Vera's voice. "Darling, Ryan wants to come to Brazil with me after his graduation. To visit his *avos*. My parents will be so happy to see him. What do you think?"

"He has to shape up first." Steve took a deep breath. "That's what we decided after he was caught drinking in the school parking lot."

"Well, that was almost a month ago. He's been good, doing his homework and everything. What's wrong with a visit to his grandparents?"

"What's wrong with you, Vera? Gosh, are you rewarding him for bad behavior?"

"Do you think I'd promise him anything before checking with you? Have you even noticed the change in him? We told him he can't go with his friends to Europe. I thought it would be a good compromise if he visits Brazil with me." Vera sighed. "Graduation is four months away. This might give him an incentive to stay sober. I can't discuss anything without you jumping on me."

From the sudden click on the phone, Steve knew Vera had cut

the connection. Steve set the receiver down and looked out the window at the cloudy gray evening. It was so different from the February he had spent in Brazil. Almost twenty-two years ago, he had heard the melodious voice on the phone that had prompted his search for Vera. Their marriage and their lives, just like the trees and clouds outside, had some dark and some bright spots. They had struggled through the rough times, but unlike Bryan and Jane, they had stayed together.

Just as he was reaching for the phone to call Vera, Bryan walked into the office and asked, "What's happening with the castings?"

"They'll get to New Orleans." Steve scratched his head. He had found a plant in New Orleans that could assemble their large traction winches. Still, it was a drag to keep track of castings from one supplier, machining from the other, and gear-cutting from the third. "Why can't a darn single plant do every aspect of production, like old Cascade?"

Bryan sat on a chair. "Yesterday I talked to Chad Morgan. Remember, he was at the picnic and won a prize? He says their shipyard in Mobile does almost all aspects of production."

"When I did a web search for machine shops and foundries, Alabama shipyard didn't come up. If it's a small plant, I doubt they can handle everything."

"Many businesses are not advertising on the Internet. It wouldn't hurt to contact him." Bryan shrugged and left.

Steve got Chad's calling card from his Rolodex, but it was late evening in Alabama and almost quitting time here. Besides, he needed to go home and placate Vera.

While driving home, Steve thought of the day two years ago, when Norma had called with the news of winning the lottery. Foolishly, he had thought that the winnings could solve all his problems. For sure, he and Vera were happier to be back in Cedarville among their friends and away from his interfering family, but the boys still had their problems. Xavier was now going to Cedarville Community College, and Ryan would soon get his high school diploma. But would they ever be financially responsible on their own?

Steve gripped the steering wheel. At least there were no financial worries now. Not only was he earning a lot, he had invested his lottery share in tech stocks, which had doubled his portfolio, making up for the losses in the stock-market crash of ten years ago, and then some. He smirked, remembering his father's critical words after Black October. Now that he had his own business and was making money in investments, his father hadn't given him any credit for it. Steve shook his head. Did he sound like his father when he put his sons down? He'd go home and make things right.

* * *

Three days after his talk with Chad Morgan, Steve arrived at the Alabama Shipyard. The huge complex reminded him of the old Cascade shop. Although the flat land by the Gulf of Mexico was different from the Cedarville area, the manufacturing facility at the shipyard was similar to old Cascade's plant.

Chad Morgan introduced him to Eugene Simpson, owner and president, and Duane Landry, the chief engineer. After coffee in the president's office, they proceeded to the tin-roofed shop. The plant had a foundry, pattern making, casting, welding and painting facility—everything they needed, except a gear-cutting machine, which Simpson said they had ordered.

"Looks good." Steve turned to Simpson. "When I searched for deck machinery plants on the Internet, I couldn't find your company on lists of manufacturers."

"That's because we were in the service industry, just refurbishing parts. Now, we're expanding our business to manufacture and assemble larger offshore drilling equipment." Simpson pointed toward his office. "When we go back, I can show you photographs."

After discussing Cascade's manufacturing needs, Steve requested copies of photographs and description of their machine tools, foundry capacity and quality control procedures for Bryan and Keith. He put the papers that Duane gave him in his briefcase, and shook hands with the short stocky owner and the tall engineer. Their firm handshakes convinced him that he had found the right fit for Cascade designs. It would be nice not to have to run all over the country to micromanage the production.

CHAPTER THIRTY SIX

BRYAN

Bryan printed the latest contract from Alabama Shipyard to review at home. Ever since Steve had contacted them and given them the traction winch orders, the plant had been manufacturing most of the parts for Cascade. He put the contract in his briefcase and waved to Norma. "Don't want to be late for Jenn's performance."

"Tell her we'll be there tomorrow to see the play," Norma called back.

Bryan started the car and tapped his fingers on the steering wheel. No matter how rebellious his daughter got, today he wanted to be in the audience, cheering for her as she made her debut as Juliet in the Bellingham Shakespearean Theatre. While driving to Bellingham, Bryan compared Jennifer's progress to Cascade's achievements. In 1995, the year after their group started their business, Jennifer graduated from high school. Just as their business had faltered initially, then succeeded, Jennifer, too, seemed to be doing better.

She had dropped out of college for a year, but enrolled again last year. Still, when she declared drama as her major, Bryan's jaws had tensed. He had caused another rift with his daughter, when he asked if a degree in drama could feed and clothe her. On the other hand, his son Brad was a down-to-earth man, working and living in an apartment on his own. Although Bryan had set up trust funds for both his children, he wanted them to learn the value of money.

But Jane gave in to Jennifer's every demand. She told him that she was paying for Jennifer's trip to Thailand this summer. Bryan shook his head. Since Jane was spending her money, he had to keep quiet.

Bryan parked his car and strode in the theatre lobby. Inhaling the aroma of percolating coffee, he passed a few laughing teenagers and some adults ambling in the hall, then saw Jane in a corner with a young man in T-shirt and jeans. Bryan scratched his chin. Was the man her date? Compared to the young guy, Bryan felt old and overdressed. He slid his finger under his collar to loosen his tie.

Jane's azure blouse enhanced the sparkle in her eyes, and her auburn hair shone in its French twist. Bryan's mind traveled back to their first encounter at Boeing, almost thirty years ago. He knew what had drawn him to her, but he could barely remember what had pushed them apart. In the last few years, he and Jane met often with their friends to play bridge or for dinner. They didn't argue as much as they used to. Perhaps living separate lives and being together socially worked better for them than the day-to-day grind of married life.

This evening, they were alone together in a crowd, parents sharing their pride in their daughter. Jane looked more beautiful than ever, but there was this hunk hovering around her. While he was debating whether to greet his ex-wife or stay away, his eyes met Jane's. She waved for him to join them.

"Hi, Jennifer just went inside to get ready. Bryan, this is Bobby Karr." She turned gracefully in her ankle-length black skirt and

Chapter Thirty Six

high heels. "And this is my ex-husband, Bryan."

"Hello." The man shook Bryan's hand. "You have a talented daughter!"

"Well, thank you." Bryan wondered how and what did the man know about Jennifer.

"I better go backstage. Nice meeting you, Bryan." Bobby left.

Not being able to contain his curiosity any longer, Bryan asked, "Who's this guy?"

"He takes care of lighting and electrical stuff for the theatre," Jane replied casually.

That didn't answer Bryan's question about Jane's interest in the man.

Later, sitting next to Jane during the show, a current ran up Bryan's spine whenever he glanced at her. He resisted the temptation to reach for her hand. When the show ended and they stood for the applause, the tears he saw in Jane's eyes caused a lump in his throat. As they made their way backstage through the cheering crowd, he put his arm around her shoulder.

Bryan spotted Jennifer in the corridor. Jane dashed over. "Oh, honey, you were superb."

As the women embraced, Bryan caught Jennifer's eye and smiled at her. She let go of her mother and ran to him. "Dad, did you like it?"

"It was wonderful. You played your part very well." Bryan patted Jennifer's shoulder.

"Hey, Jenn, you were awesome!" A voice came from the corridor.

Bryan saw a curly-haired girl in a short skirt and sleeveless blouse standing beside them. Jennifer turned to her. "Thanks, Tracy. This is my dad."

After the introductions, Jennifer said, "Dad, you promised a dinner after the performance, but my friends are going to the

Ferry Terminal. Mind if I take a rain check?"

Bryan nodded. What could he say to a twenty-one-year old? With Jennifer it was the same story—partying. And for all he knew, Jane might have plans with that electrical guy.

Jane gave Jennifer's cheek a peck. "Honey, remember what I told you."

"Y-e-e-s, I'll be careful. I'm not the only one. There are other girls from my dorm."

Bryan opened his mouth and gulped some air, as if to eat the words he would like to say.

"Dad, could you give Mom a ride back?"

"Sure, if she needs one." Bryan looked at Jane.

He expected her to say that she could get a ride with that Bobby fellow. Instead Jane explained, "Jenn and I came together, so I didn't bring my car."

"No problem. Are you ready to leave?" Bryan asked.

He had wanted a family dinner, and his daughter took that chance away. There was emptiness inside his stomach and it wasn't all because of hunger. Outside, the cool May evening made Bryan shiver. He started the car and asked, "Do you trust Jenn's friends?"

"Tracy is a very responsible girl. I've met her mother, and I know Jenn's new friends are not into pot or drugs. Haven't you noticed a difference in your daughter?"

Bryan hadn't paid much attention. "I have to take your word for it and hope for the best."

"I've learned that Jenn does well when I don't try to push discipline down her throat."

Bryan frowned. Was Jane implying that he didn't know how to handle his daughter? He changed the subject. "I'm hungry. Would you like to eat something?"

"I was hoping you'd ask." Jane smiled.

Chapter Thirty Six

The emptiness he had felt a minute ago evaporated. He drove to the Pacific Heights Restaurant. Dinner for just the two of them!

At the restaurant they share not only a carafe of wine before dinner and a blueberry cheesecake afterwards, but also the trials and triumphs of their jobs. He had forgotten that when Jane wanted to, she could be a good listener. He took her hand in both of his.

Bryan didn't want the night to end. When he took Jane home, she opened the door and waited for him. He kissed her. She invited him in.

* * *

As the morning light filtered through the drapes, Bryan opened his eyes and smiled. He counted the Friday nights he had spent with Jane in her house since the evening of Jennifer's performance. This was the tenth weekend of their togetherness. He used to be the last one to leave the office, since there was plenty of work and no one waiting for him at home. But now, on Fridays, he would bolt out of the office to be with Jane in Bellingham. Once when he was leaving in a hurry, Norma asked him if he had a new girlfriend. He just laughed.

Bryan gazed at his ex-wife's face, surrounded by her auburn hair on the pillow. The old melody, "Reunited," echoed in his mind. Their relationship was more complicated than those singers could have imagined. As passionate as they were in bed, he was unwilling to reveal their reunion to his family and friends. He and Jane had gone through a divorce. If they got back together, he would be admitting the divorce was a mistake. And what if it didn't work the second time around? He wasn't willing to accept an error in judgment twice.

He could see her breasts through the lingerie, rising and

falling with each breath. Bryan brushed his lips against her arm, then her neck, and drew her close. "We don't have to limit this to Friday nights."

As he leaned forward to kiss her, a knot formed in his chest and constricted his throat. He rested his head on the pillow and massaged the invisible fist that had gripped his heart. Pain radiated to his arm and back. Unable to breathe, he sat up, then slumped on the bed.

When he opened his eyes, Jane was wiping perspiration off his forehead with a towel. "You passed out. I've called the ambulance."

By the time they reached the hospital, his breathing had returned to normal and the pain was gone. After several rounds of blood tests and an angiography, Bryan told Jane, "If I didn't have a heart attack before, I'll surely have one now."

The cardiologist came into the room, carrying several papers. He showed a graph to Bryan. "Mr. Stafford, you have blockages in three arteries. We should schedule bypass surgery as soon as possible."

While Jane went in and out, talking to the nurses, Bryan waited in his hospital bed. He wished he could eat something, but the doctor had told him he must not. Poor Jane must be hungry too. When she came in, he told her, "Why don't you get something from the cafeteria?"

"I'm not hungry." Jane sat on a chair by the bed.

"At least get some coffee and toast." Bryan pushed against the uncomfortable mattress. "We should call the kids, Mom and Dad, and the bridge group."

Today was their once-a-month bridge game. In June and July, after their Friday night sleepovers, Jane had suggested they drive together on Saturdays for the card game, but Bryan had made up excuses about work and told her he would meet her there.

Chapter Thirty Six

"I've already called your parents and Brad. I didn't want to worry Jenn in Thailand." Jane paused. "I'll call Norma and let her know we won't be there for bridge. Don't worry, I'll say you came in the morning to discuss the children's trust fund and got sick."

"I don't mind if you tell them about us." Keeping their relationship secret didn't seem so important anymore.

"Really?" Jane looked at him. "That's a switch. We always meet in Bellingham and you don't like to go to Cedarville together . . ."

Bryan interrupted, "That was because I felt we needed to iron out our differences first."

"And, Mr. Therapist, did Friday night trysts help resolve our problems?" Jane squeezed his arm and smiled. "I was only joking."

A nurse came in with a syringe to take blood samples. Bryan closed his eyes. He had nothing to do but wait for the surgery tomorrow.

The next day, a chlorine-like odor awoke Bryan. He tried to sit up but couldn't. He was trapped in the bed with an IV, catheter and the oxygen mask. A nurse patted his arm. "Mr. Stafford, you are in the Cardiac Care Unit. Your wife was here all night. She just stepped out to talk to your friends. I'll get her."

Wife? Bryan scanned the dimly-lit, windowless hospital room. What day was it? Was it evening or morning? He closed his eyes. A gentle hand touched his shoulder. "Jane?"

"Yes." Jane caressed his hand. "The surgery went well."

"Mrs. Stafford," someone called.

No wonder the nurse had thought Jane was his wife. She had kept her married name after the divorce. He didn't mind the misunderstanding now.

* * *

A week later, when Bryan was released from the hospital, Jane brought him home, fixed lunch for him and tucked him into his bed. "Rest now, I'll come back tomorrow. I'm available for three weeks before school starts."

He took her hand in his. "Thanks for everything. Will you move in with me?" The words Bryan had resisted for so long tumbled out of his mouth. "I love you."

Jane's eyes grew moist. "Let's not rush this. I'll come often until you're better."

Over the next two weeks, with Jane taking him for checkups, daily walks, and cooking nutritious meals, Bryan was recuperating well. Jennifer was back from Thailand and Brad was visiting for a few days. Their presence made Bryan remember the old days, especially when they played games together.

After lunch, Bryan sat at the dining table with his ex-wife and children to play Pictionary. Brad drew a picture—something that looked like world map, and he made vertical lines on it with numbers. Jennifer guessed, "Time zones!"

"You kids are just too smart. Enough of the game now." Jane collected the papers and clues and put them in the box. "Jenn, could you please bring us some iced tea?"

Jennifer returned with glasses and tea pitcher. "In Thailand, they serve milk-iced tea. Would anyone like to try that?"

"Yuck." Brad wrinkled his nose. "Who would drink that stuff? No wonder Mom doesn't trust you to take care of Dad by yourself."

Jennifer crossed her arms. "Dad, college doesn't start until September 21, so I can stay with you while you recover." She glared at Brad. "But he thinks he should take time off work and stay here when Mom's school starts. He thinks I'm not responsible enough."

Touched by his daughter's desire to help him, Bryan patted Jennifer's shoulder. "Okay, you all, Jenn is quite capable of helping

Chapter Thirty Six

me while you both go work. I'm feeling much better. By next week, I can probably go to the office for a few hours."

A warm feeling came over Bryan. He took a deep breath. His heart attack had brought his family together, and he would try to keep them that way.

* * *

As summer heat faded into a rainy, chilly autumn, Bryan, now fully recovered, was happy with his family life. Ever since Jane had moved back in with him, things at home were great. Now he concentrated on the new development at work.

For the last two years, the Alabama Shipyard plant in Mobile had been manufacturing for their company. Recently, the owner of the Mobile plant had offered a consolidation with Cascade. Bryan expected this merger to be as beneficial for all concerned.

Harold told Bryan that he favored combining the forces of engineering and manufacturing. Now they needed to convince the rest of the group, so Bryan decided to invite all eight partners to his home to discuss Alabama Shipyard's offer. He cleared the table and brought his briefcase in preparation for the meeting.

CHAPTER THIRTY SEVEN

NORMA

Norma traced the grain of the dark wood of Bryan and Jane's dining table. How many decisions and discussions had this table witnessed? More than four years ago, they had gathered around this table in Seattle, cheering and laughing, before going to collect their lottery winnings. That day had set them free—especially Bryan, Steve and Keith, who could leave their jobs and return to Cedarville. For Norma, the fact that her friends used their winnings to bring Cascade back from Houston was more fulfilling than the money they got. Each new order, each success at work made her heart swell with joy.

And here they were, all sitting at the Stafford's oval table, pondering the merger of Cascade with Alabama Shipyard.

Norma focused her mind to what Bryan was saying, "The more I think about Eugene Simpson's offer to combine our design office with their production facility, the better It looks. We have been giving them contracts for the last two years." He looked at Steve, who oversaw production, "You are satisfied with their job performance."

Steve nodded. "They do a good job, but sometimes they cut

Chapter Thirty Seven

corners. Like, I had asked them to paint the inside of the drums to prevent rusting but they had neglected to do that first."

Bryan raised his brows. "I thought you settled that problem early on."

"Yes, they paint it now, because someone from our Quality Control is always there to observe." Steve paused. "And they realize they won't get our business otherwise."

Keith scratched his chin. "If we agree to the merger, they'll get our orders no matter what their performance. That's why American Marine never joined any manufacturer. But they renewed their contracts each time. That way, there was accountability in production."

Bryan frowned. "Let's not talk about American Marine."

Norma clasped her hands. Bryan seemed irritated whenever Keith mentioned American Marine. But, she too had her doubts about the merger.

Harold cleared his throat. "Guys, several businesses have merged. You know, Lockheed-Martin Marietta, and recently Boeing-Macdonald Douglas. They are doing well. We can too."

Alicia put her hand on Keith's and looked at Bryan and Harold sitting across from her. "The mergers you're talking about are between competitors, not manufacturers and engineers."

"I know you are concerned about this," Bryan said, "But we all know that old Cascade was efficient because it had the plant and offices together."

Norma spoke up, "At old Cascade, engineers and shop staff were in the same compound and started out as one unit. With Alabama Shipyard, it won't be walking distance for the engineers to go check or for them to come ask you anything."

Vera stuck her elbows on the table, "What if they decide they want to have the engineering office near their plant and move Cascade to Mobile?"

Alicia nodded. "Yeah, it happened with Eagle, when they moved to Houston. Are we going to pack up and move again?"

Norma was glad the women voiced her fears.

Harold raised both his hands. "Okay, ladies, if you're concerned about having to move, you know, we can make a stipulation in the contract against relocation."

Norma saw the three women smile. She said, "If you promise that, we might consider this merger."

"That's the main condition, for sure." Bryan turned to Harold. "Now tell us about the advantages from the financial side."

"I'll get some coffee." Jane rose from her chair. "You keep going. Give us the good, bad and ugly so we can make an informed decision."

Jane hadn't expressed her views, so Norma followed her to the kitchen to get her opinion. While the coffee percolated, Jane said she thought the merger idea was okay. She set the mugs, creamer and sugar on a tray.

On the way back to the living room, Norma heard Harold. "One advantage of the merger is that they'll take over our loan."

"What happens to our investment of four million?" Alicia asked.

"Yes. What about that?" Norma returned to her chair and elbowed her husband.

Harold tapped the pencil on his pad. "It's a merger, you know, not a buyout. They won't pay us immediately, but they will handle our loan and will return our investment in installments."

Jane passed the coffee mugs around the table. "All this sounds complicated. We should consult a lawyer."

"Of course, we'll do that," Bryan said. "Another advantage is that the oil industry is cyclical. By joining forces, we can do engineering work on their cranes and refurbishing jobs when the deck machinery business is slow."

Chapter Thirty Seven

"That's true." Keith paused. "Although we could diversify on our own too."

Another disagreement between Keith and Bryan! Norma wondered what was going on between the two old friends. To her surprise, Bryan calmly said, "When I was in the hospital, I started thinking it was too much pressure on all of you, especially you, Keith, to handle the orders by yourself. But if Alabama takes over some of the administrative responsibilities, we can concentrate on engineering and design."

"One more thing," Harold jumped in, "Have you thought about what will happen to the company when we retire? You know, our children aren't interested. At Alabama Shipyard, the owner's son and the chief engineer's son are being groomed. If we merge, the company has a better chance of survival."

For Norma, that was the winning argument. The company must go on, as the old Cascade had for almost a century before the takeovers. She reminded herself that this was not a takeover. The company would still belong to them. "If the merger goes through, what would the company be called?"

"Probably Cascade/Alabama Shipyard," Steve replied.

"Or Alabama/Cascade." Bryan glanced around the table. "They might want their name first, since they'll have a greater share because of their plant and manufacturing facilities."

"What? It's so out of place. What is it called?" Norma tried to remember the word. "Anachronism?"

"That's for misplaced time," Jane corrected her. "This is . . . oh it'll come to me."

"The teacher flunked the test!" Bryan put his arm around Jane's shoulder.

They all laughed. As the evening progressed, Norma was relieved that they didn't argue too much. Even those who had aired their hesitations agreed that if a corporate lawyer approved the terms, they would go ahead with the business deal. Norma wondered if others hoped that the lawyer would advise against it. All she wanted was success for Cascade and the amiable relations among her friends that had sustained their bond for years.

CHAPTER THIRTY EIGHT

KEITH

Keith turned away from his computer, rubbed his eyes, and stared out his office window at gray November clouds. Last year, their corporate lawyer, had told them that the merger contract between Cascade and Alabama Shipyard was a good deal.

Now, Keith wasn't sure. Not only had the name of the company changed to Alabama/Cascade Products, but their job titles had changed too. Eugene Simpson, the owner of Alabama Shipyard, became the president of the new company, because his manufacturing plant had a larger investment. Bryan became vice president and Keith's title changed from vice president to director of engineering. Keith had been assured that the Alabama Shipyard's small engineering division would come under his control, but Duane Landry, the manufacturing vice president in Mobile, kept interfering with his designs and tried to control other engineers in the Cedarville office.

Feeling a burning in his stomach, Keith reached for his Tagamet and a glass of water. Darn Alabama Shipyard had given him this ulcer. He'd have to confront Duane, even if it increased his heartburn and stomach pain.

The recent winch design Keith had sent to Mobile included a preassembled unit of motor and gearbox ordered from Olympia Gears. Duane insisted he could get a motor from another source and make the gearbox at the plant. Keith had asked for specs, and the number of hours this job would take compared to the cost of the preassembled unit. The jerk hadn't replied.

"Keith!" Fred, the project engineer called.

He swallowed his medicine. "Come on in, Fred."

"The spare part design Duane wants is going to take too many engineering hours." Fred sat across from him.

Not only was Duane interfering with Keith's designs, the man had sent his other proposal job directly to Fred without first discussing it with Keith.

"We've worked on a similar design before. Why can't we use the old one with a few modifications?" Fred asked.

"I agree." Keith nodded. "I'll talk to Duane."

"Thanks." Fred pushed his chair and left.

Before Keith could reach for the phone to call Mobile, the phone rang. "Hi Keith, how is it going?" Bryan who was at Alabama Shipyard, asked him.

"I was about to call Duane regarding the motor and gearbox design that I sent."

"I'm in his office." Bryan cleared his throat. "We're on the speakerphone."

"Hi, Keith," Duane said, "I explained to Bryan that we can do this job for much less if we get the motor from Mobile and make the gearbox ourselves."

"How much is the motor alone?" Keith shifted in his chair.

"I'm getting bids now. But it'll definitely be cheaper than the pre-assembled unit."

Keith tried to control his rising voice. "How much cheaper? And how much time would be spent on the gearbox? We're

Chapter Thirty Eight

getting a good deal from Olympia Gear because we have ordered the assembly. I've already designed the dimensions for their unit."

"I'll make sure the dimensions are the same," Duane responded.

"Send me a sketch and your numbers." Keith tapped his pencil against the desk. "Also, Fred discussed with me the spare part proposal you asked him to do. He has some good cost-cutting suggestions. We should talk about…"

Duane cut in, "Don't worry about that. I'll call Fred."

Hearing the click at the other end, Keith dropped the phone into its cradle. Immediately, the phone rang again. Still angry, he picked up the phone and heard Bryan's booming voice. "What the hell is the matter with you? Why did you tell Fred to ignore Duane's instructions? And you're being stubborn about the motor and gearbox."

Keith couldn't believe the overbearing tone. God knows what Duane the Double Face had told Bryan. "If they want to make changes in my design, they should have a valid reason. Either a better design or cost saving."

"You're not being a team player," Bryan barked.

Keith's grip tightened on the phone. Not a team player? Heck, ask anyone at work, especially the twenty-three engineers and draftsmen working for him, and they would disagree. "You trust Duane's judgment more than mine?"

"Don't get all worked up. We'll talk about it when I return."

"Fine." Keith slammed the receiver down and massaged his burning stomach.

What a mess. Ever since the merger of the two companies, Bryan had acted like a heavy-handed boss. He said Keith was the technical expert, yet his opinion was disregarded.

Keith's mind went back to the Oil Technology Conference in Houston. Bryan had just given a customer golf ball with the

ALABAMA/CASCADE logo. The man had a question about the new winch, but instead of consulting Keith who had designed it, Bryan asked Duane to explain it. That had been only six months after the merger, so Keith thought Bryan was trying to include Duane in their group. But now Duane's interference was getting to be too much.

Within an hour, the phone rang. Seeing Alabama Shipyard's caller ID, Keith ignored it. The rings persisted, so he grabbed the receiver. He heard Bryan, "Guess what?"

Prepared for more admonitions, Keith sighed. "What now?"

"You'll be happy to know that I negotiated to get some of our investment back from Alabama," Bryan said in a cheerful voice, "Eugene agreed to pay out two-hundred-thousand for each of us by December. That's one-fifth of our investment."

"Hmmm." Their contract had specified that in addition to their salaries, the four couples would get yearly installments as payment for their investment.

"Keith, you are the first one I'm calling. Can't you show some enthusiasm?"

"Thanks. Did you forget your last phone call, Bryan?"

"Well, I have a lot on my plate. We'll talk later. I need to call Harold and Steve. Bye."

Keith pounded his fist on the desk. What was the matter with Bryan? Scolding him one moment, then calling cheerfully the next.

Keith leaned back in his chair. At this rate, he'd have four more years of aggravation before recovering his million. Maybe he should use part of the money on a nice vacation around Christmas. If he planned it right, he wouldn't have to deal with Duane Landry and Eugene Simpson at the Cascade Christmas party on December 17. He couldn't stand one more minute of their phony pep talk.

Chapter Thirty Eight

He called Alicia. "Hi, Sweetheart, would you like to go to Fidalgo Bay Inn for dinner?"

"Sure. Any special reason?" Alicia asked.

"Alabama Shipyard is transferring funds to pay the first installment on our investment. We should celebrate."

"That's good news. About time we get some of our money back. I'll be ready at six."

On the way to the restaurant, Keith told Alicia that he would like to get away before the company Christmas party. Later, at the restaurant, they got a table by the window facing the Fidalgo Bay. He saw the dock-lights churning in the raging waters, like his agitated mind.

After ordering their dinners, Keith raised his wineglass. "To our trip! So where would you want to go? Holland? You always wanted to go to your parents' birthplace."

Alicia took a sip of her wine. "Holland would be cold. Besides, the girls will be home. We don't want to leave your mom or my parents during Christmas. And don't forget, your Aunt Suki is coming to spend the holidays with your Mom."

Keith scratched his chin. "How about if we all go—Kayla and Kerry, Mom, Aunt Suki, and your parents."

"That's an idea." Alicia nodded. "Did you know that Steve and Vera are going to Brazil to spend Christmas with her parents? They're leaving the day after the office party to go to Quito and the Galapagos Islands, before going to Brazil."

"Hmmm, Galapagos!" Keith smiled. He wouldn't mind sharing part of their vacation with Steve. It might give him a chance to vent his work frustrations. "I'll talk to Steve to see if we can coordinate our trips. But I'd like to go the week before the office party. We can go somewhere else in South America, then join Steve's family for Quito and Galapagos trip. What's near Ecuador—The Amazon, Colombia, Peru?" Keith tried to recall his geography.

"Kerry had always wanted to see Peru, especially Machu Picchu. And I would love that too." Alicia placed her hand on the table. "Remember *Chariots of the Gods*?"

Keith squeezed her hand. In the early 1970's, they had read the book and seen photographs of the Nazca Lines. They had been convinced that the lines must have been created by aliens. "Peru is it then. Why don't you call the travel agent tomorrow?"

Alicia gently stroked her earring. "Let's talk to everyone first to see if they want to go."

Keith swallowed the hard crust of the bread he had been chewing. His father's wish, to travel together to Hawaii and Japan flooded Keith's mind. That never happened. There'd been a shortage of vacation-time and money. But now they had the money and he deserved some vacation. It would be an interesting experience taking both the older and younger generations, but he wouldn't care. Whatever happened, it would be worth it to escape the office party.

* * *

Keith stood in lines of travelers snaking through customs and immigration in Lima, and put his arm around Alicia. The tourists ahead of him turned back and surveyed them. They must be wondering about the unusual mix—he, an African-Japanese-American, alongside his Japanese mother and her cousin, and his in-laws speaking English with a Dutch accent. Or maybe they were admiring his beautiful daughters with their blend of races and cultures.

When they left the customs area, Keith and his daughters loaded everyone's luggage in two carts, then went outside. Looking past throngs of signs—Inca Tours, Andean Adventures, and such, Keith spotted a man holding the sign—"Peruvian Experience Travels" and approached him. A small, brown-skinned, slightly balding man came forward. His blue eyes stood out against his brown complexion, suggesting he was a mix of native and European races. Keith strode toward him. "I'm Keith Wilson. We have a group of eight."

"I'm Julio Estaban. Your tour guide." Shaking Keith's hand, he smiled and nodded to the others, now surrounding Keith. "I take you to the van. Yes? The driver will take you to your hotel. You rest. Tomorrow, after breakfast, we have orientation meeting at nine. Yes?"

Amused at the man's affirmative questions, Keith smiled. "Yes."

His father-in-law, Zosef Devries asked the guide, "Hey, does the driver know English?"

"Grandpa, he knows the road." Kerry said, "If you need anything, I'll translate for you."

Keith patted his daughter.

The next day, while his elderly relatives chose to relax at the hotel, Keith, Alicia, and their daughters went on the plane to see the Nazca Lines. Keith closed his eyes. Why had he bothered to take this part of the tour? It cost a bundle, they had to get up early and catch a flight to Nazca then take another small plane over the area to see the drawings scratched into the earth. He yawned and turned to his daughter sitting next to him, "I should have stayed at the hotel."

"Oh, Dad," Kayla poked his ribs.

Alicia who was sitting with Kerry in the aisle across from them, said, "Sweetheart, once you see the figures, you'll be glad you came. I can't wait to take photographs."

Keith hoped Alicia would get good pictures that some magazine would publish. Although she had photographed her father's bulb farm for their catalog, she hadn't been successful in selling her prints to national publications. Sometimes, he couldn't understand why she still submitted her photographs and faced rejections. But then he could ask himself the same question. Why did he continue to work? Just as designing winches and fairleads had become his routine, photography was Alicia's passion. At least her rejections hadn't given her ulcers.

Soon the pilot announced, "The 2000-year old geometric figures of birds and animals we will see are spread more than thirty-seven miles."

As they neared the Pampa Colorada, or the Red Desert, the fog and mist cleared. On the ground beneath them, spread across the terrain, were the drawings of a massive condor, a monkey with a curled tail, and geometric shapes. The plane tipped to one side, then the other, to let the passengers view the designs. Keith's stomach lurched. He had been on small planes before; even ridden baskets on cranes to get to the oilrigs, but this was hard on his stomach. He popped a candied ginger in his mouth that Aunt Suki had given him. Why would the Nazca people construct these figures and roads leading to nowhere? In the *Chariots of the Gods*, Erich Von Daniken had theorized that the drawings were signs, and the lines were landing strips for astronauts. Some people thought they were ancient ritual centers. It still didn't make sense that ancient Peruvians spent so much time on something they couldn't even see or appreciate from the ground. He thought of his work. Would scientists of the distant future see oilrigs in the ocean and wonder about their utility or purpose?

Two days later, on the train to see the ruins of Machu Picchu, Keith took in the view of the gorgeous mountains and green valley dotted with red-roofed homes below. Keith turned and caught a glimpse of his mother's salt and pepper hair. Mom, sagging in her seat, clasping her wrinkled hands, looked old. Why hadn't he

Chapter Thirty Eight

noticed that his mother was getting old and his daughters were becoming independent? He remembered his Buddhism class— Like the water of the stream, nothing remained the same. Neither Cedarville, nor the Cascade office and his friends.

At Ollantaytambo when they got off the train, melodious flute music welcomed them. Keith paid a few solas to the musicians. The women gravitated toward the craftsmen and people in bright red, yellow and green clothes, selling alpaca sweaters, mufflers, and painted Christmas ornaments. Keith could imagine their tour group showing off their bargains later on the bus ride.

After lunch, they took the city bus to Machu Picchu. The bus climbed up the hairpin curves and switchbacks, making Keith's stomach roil. However, as soon as they arrived at the ruins, he felt better and followed the guide to see the enormous walls, palaces, temples and sundial of the "Lost City of the Incas." He took a deep breath. How much persistence and strength had it taken to chisel gigantic stones that fit so precisely into each other? How many generations had worked on it?

Alicia, walking beside him, asked, "People say visiting Machu Picchu is a spiritual experience. Sweetheart, what do you think?"

"Those experiences are only in books like *The Celestine Prophecy.*" Keith caressed Alicia's arm. "I don't even know what spiritual feels like."

"Keith Wilson, you're so darn logical."

"I'm in awe of the architecture. The flute music at the station really moved me. Is that spiritual enough?" He leaned over and kissed her.

He heard their guide, "We're going to see the sacrificial stone where women—especially virgins—were sacrificed. Their heart and other organs were removed…"

Keith put his arm on Alicia's shoulder and whispered, "So much for the spiritual!"

On the ride back to the town, Keith watched through the bus window as a young boy ran down the steep hill. It looked as though he was dropping off at the edge of the hillside. As the bus negotiated a switchback, he raced it again. It happened at every hairpin curve until the bus arrived at a level road. The driver stopped the bus and let the young boy in. The passengers clapped and gave him a few solas. The lad was grinning; the tourists were smiling. This was the human spirit—spiritual or not—that touched Keith.

CHAPTER THIRTY NINE

STEVE

Steve covered his head with his hands to ward off the broiling sun. Their guide had told them to bring hats to the Middle of the World monument in Quito, Ecuador, but Steve had forgotten. Other tourists in their group, including Keith and his extended family, were used to carrying their hats and water bottles after spending a week in Peru, but Steve had arrived last night with his family. Unlike him, his sons and wife donned sunglasses, sunscreens, and hats, and cheerfully followed the young Ecuadorian guide, Maria Cardenas.

"The equator line actually runs through this area." Maria stopped by the steps of the monument. "This site is surrounded by shops, folk art and restaurants. You want to do shopping or use the facilities. Right? We meet here in half an hour. Right?"

Steve told Keith, "Let's go to the café while the wives shop."

Keith laughed. "Not just the wives, the kids and the elderly are off shopping too."

They found a corner table in the café and ordered Pepsi. Steve asked, "Did you enjoy Peru?"

"We had a good time." Keith took off his hat and fanned

himself. "I'm glad we could take this part of the trip with you. How was the office party?"

"Okay. Eugene Simpson bragged and took credit for all the business we received in the last few years. Bryan and Harold sat there smiling, telling them about how hard they've been working. No mention of you or me."

"Am I glad I didn't have to sit through that." Keith gulped his drink. "What's happening with the gearbox?"

"I'd sent Ron to Mobile to follow up on the progress. He said they ordered a motor that didn't fit the foundation. Duane's son, Curtis, has started his engineering office in the same compound and is now redesigning the foundation for the gearbox."

Keith frowned. "They should have stuck with the assembled unit I'd ordered. Duane insisted on making the frame and said the assembled unit was too expensive. Now they've spent extra labor hours and money. Well, I warned them. Now it's their headache."

"Forget work." Steve shifted uncomfortably in his chair. He didn't want to ruin Keith's vacation by telling him that Duane claimed that the job was delayed because Keith had designed the frame using the wrong gearbox.

They walked toward the steps to meet the rest of the group. Alicia's father, Zosef Devries, called to Steve, "Hey, you need a hat, son." He took a handkerchief from his pocket, knotted its corners, giving it a round shape. "Put this Dutch hat on your head."

"Thanks, Mr. Devries." Steve fitted the handkerchief on his head.

At their next stop, Mitad del Mundo—"Middle of the World," Maria, the tour guide explained, "At latitude 0-0-0 degrees, the equator line is far from the center of gravity, so you have less resistance. Right? Let me show you." She looked around. "I need a volunteer."

Twenty-two year old Xavier pushed forward. Steve and

Chapter Thirty Nine

Vera exchanged glances. He had noticed how their son seemed enamored of the young woman. Xavier grinned as the guide touched and pushed his hand while he tried to resist. Probably he would have continued to tug on her hand, but she stopped and moved to show them two sinks. Xavier followed closely. The guide explained, "The water flows clockwise and counterclockwise on the north and south of the equator line. Right?"

Keith muttered, "In America too, north and south go in different directions."

Steve winked to acknowledge Keith's comment.

* * *

Back in Cedarville, the house felt empty. Leaving his son behind in Rio de Janeiro was difficult for Steve. But after their Ecuador trip, all Xavier did, was talk about becoming a tour guide. At first Steve and Vera had laughed about their son's fascination with the Ecuadorian guide. But when Xavier said he would like to find out about the Tourismo courses in Rio, Vera's parents introduced him to a nephew who was studying to be a tour guide. Xavier immediately enrolled in Portuguese language and tourism classes, starting in January.

Steve almost told his son that being a tour guide wasn't a career, but he bit his tongue. Xavier had shown an interest in studying history and language. He had a goal, and Steve couldn't discourage him. Besides, as Vera said, being away from Cedarville and his drinking buddies would be good for their son.

When Steve returned from work, he looked for Vera and not finding her in their bedroom or kitchen, he went to Xavier's room. She was sitting on the bed, her eyes red and puffy. Steve took her in his arms.

She said, "Xavier wanted me to send him his books and jacket.

I was looking for those."

"You want me to help you?"

Vera shook her head. "No. I'll do it later. When Ryan comes he can help me. Even Ryan is lost without his brother."

Steve sighed. "I miss him too. But remember what you told me in Brazil? Our son is serious about this course and we have to let him go."

"I know that. And I know my parents will take good care of him. In fact they are glad for the company. But I won't see him for a year." Her voice cracked.

Steve held his wife's hand as they walked out of the room. He had to leave tomorrow for Mobile. He didn't want to go, but he had no choice. As much as he wanted his children to grow and live independently, he was glad his younger son, Ryan, was living at home and going to the community college.

* * *

In Mobile, as Steve left the plant manager's office, he heard someone call him. He turned and saw Curtis, son of chief engineer, Duane Landry. Curtis had started his own business, Landry Engineering, in the Alabama/Cascade compound.

Shaking his hand, Steve asked, "Curt, how does it feel to be your own boss?"

"Come over and see my office sometime." Curtis clutched a drawing in his hand. "I'm delivering this to the shop."

"That's where I'm headed," Steve told him.

"I forgot something." Curtis immediately turned back toward his office.

"I'll come see your office tomorrow," Steve called after him.

Continuing toward the shop, Steve wondered at Curt's odd behavior. Alabama Shipyard was also manufacturing for his

Chapter Thirty Nine

Landry Engineering, but Cascade was designing new winches, and Curtis was working on spare part designs. So there was no competition or conflict of interest.

At the test site, the supervisor told him, "Sorry, Steve, the testing is going to be delayed by a couple of hours."

Hurry up and wait again. Steve sighed. "Okay, I'll be back at eleven."

Since he had a few hours, Steve decided to visit Curtis.

At the Landry Engineering office, he poked his head in the open door and called, "Curt." When he didn't hear anyone, he walked in and saw Curt at his desk. "Hey, you asked me to visit, so here I am."

Curtis had a startled look on his face. He turned off his computer. "But you said you'll come tomorrow."

Steve scratched his forehead. People usually didn't turn off their computers when they had visitors. He said, "Testing is delayed, so I thought, I'd check your office."

"What do you need to check?" Curtis frowned.

"Well, see your office. You invited me earlier. Didn't you?"

"Oh, right. Come on in. Let's go to the kitchen and have coffee." Curtis led him to the opposite side of the drafting and designing area.

"I thought you were going to show me your work place. Are you into cooking or what?"

Curtis laughed. "We're reorganizing the computers and drafting boards, so I'll show that some other day."

He poured coffee into two cups and handed one to Steve. After a short tour of the kitchen and lobby, they returned to Curt's office. When Steve sat down, he dropped his napkin. He bent to pick it up and noticed a disk under the desk with a "C" marked on it. Could it be Cascade?

Immediately Curtis bent, grabbed the disk and shoved it in a drawer. Steve sipped his coffee. What was the man trying to hide? Was Curtis like his father, Duane-the-double-face? The disk must be a duplicate of the computer aided design that Cascade had sent to the Alabama plant. It was for those who manufactured winches and components designed by Cascade, not for another engineering firm. He suspected Curtis and Duane were copying Cascade's calculations and drawings but he needed some proof to confront them. He would talk to Bryan and Keith about it.

CHAPTER FORTY

NORMA

Norma shuffled the cards for another round of bridge. Bryan slapped the table with his palm. "Keith, if you had returned my lead, they would have been down."

"Oh sure. Anything goes wrong, it's is my fault." Keith glared at Bryan.

Long ago, the monthly bridge game had created a bond among the four couples, but recently, playing caused more arguments than laughter. Norma pressed her fingers against her temples to ward off a headache. "Even if Keith had played a club, I would have trumped it."

Jane patted her husband's arm. "Forget the last hand. It's time to play this one."

Bryan frowned and picked up his cards. Keith chewed on his lip. Bryan spoke often about how he had played bridge with Keith since their college days. But lately, the buddies of thirty-seven years seemed at each other's throats—at play as well as work.

Norma felt that something similar was happening between her and the McGills. When Steve had first brought his Brazilian bride to Cedarville, Norma and her mother had helped Vera adjust to the move and had taught her to play bridge. Vera had always been like a younger sister, but recently she had become very political, and a liberal at that.

Vera's strident voice brought Norma's attention to the other table. "Gore won by popular vote. He should have been the president. The Electoral College is antiquated. It should be abolished."

Alicia said, "Even with the Electoral College, Gore would have won if they had allowed the recount in Florida."

"Come on now," Harold raised his voice. "This is not some third-world country. You know, just because Ozone Man didn't win, you want to change our system?"

Steve laughed. "Remember the hanging and pregnant chads? There's a rumor that President Bush is going to appoint Kathleen Harris the ambassador to Chad."

Norma heard their laughter, then the sound of a screeching chair. She turned and saw Harold's red face. His blood pressure would go through the roof. He threw his cards on the table.

Leaving her table, Norma went to her husband and massaged his shoulders. "Guys, let's finish this round and have dessert. The pain-killers are making Harold very tired."

Steve cuffed his arm. "Come on Harold, we're joking."

"Sorry, Harold." Alicia patted his hand. "Our friendship is above politics."

"I'll play this round but no more." Harold picked up his cards.

Norma reluctantly returned to her table. Her friends didn't become Democrats overnight. While two of the couples quoted NPR radio and supported the Brady Bill, she, Harold, Bryan and Jane listened to Rush Limbaugh and were NRA members. These differing opinions had never bothered her before. She always thought she had more in common with Alicia and Vera than with some Republicans, but her friends were becoming more critical.

Chapter Forty

And Harold snapped easily these days. Maybe he was nervous about his upcoming hip replacement surgery.

* * *

Norma tied a Valentine balloon and a "Get Well Soon" balloon to the leg of the coffee table. Harold needed cheering up after his surgery. She had cooked salmon and scalloped potatoes—his favorites. She took the plate to the living room where her husband was resting. She kissed him. "Happy Valentine's Day."

"Oh, honey, you know, I can't even take you out to dinner." Harold's voice cracked.

Norma put her arm around his neck. "We have our own party here. Here's a quiz for you. How many years ago did you first take me out on Valentine's Day?"

Harold shifted on the couch, pain etched on his face.

Norma caressed her ring. "I'll give you a hint. It was the same year we got married."

A broad smile crossed Harold's face. "Forty-five years ago, you know!"

"You proposed to me that day." Norma squeezed his hand. "We survived the changing of the century together."

Harold nibbled at the food Norma had prepared. At the office, Steve had said he and Vera would come over with Harold's favorite carrot cake. Bryan and Keith wanted to visit too. Norma had warned them, "No politics or office talk."

Just as they finished their dinner, the doorbell rang. The three couples strode in, arms filled with carrot cake, books, and balloons for Harold. Norma's eyes traversed the faces around her. Bringing Cascade back, though exhilarating, had taken a toll on everyone. Bryan had had a heart attack three years back, and had a stent put in last year. Keith was struggling with ulcers. Steve had recently been diagnosed with a prostate problem and was scheduled for biopsy. Norma rubbed her forehead. Her headaches were becoming more frequent. In spite of the doctor's assurances to the contrary, Norma had nightmares about having a brain tumor.

Most of their ailments came after the merger with Alabama Shipyard. Or were the men already developing their illnesses, and the symptoms surfaced within the last few years? As she rubbed her palms together, she stared at the back of her hands. They looked so wrinkled.

* * *

Although Harold had recovered well after the surgery, today, Norma couldn't concentrate at work as images of smoke billowing from the World Trade Center and the Pentagon that she and Harold had watched on television in the morning, flashed into her mind. The silence in the office added to her anguish. No phones rang, no faxes came.

Finally, a ringing phone broke into the silence. Norma picked up the phone and heard Keith, "Norma, I'm going to be late today. Alicia and I are waiting to hear from Kerry or Kayla."

Norma's hands trembled. "How far do they live from WTC?"

"Their apartment is near Columbia University, which is pretty far. But they're not answering their cell phones."

Norma tried hard to find reasons for the absence of communication. "Probably they forgot to charge them. Keith, do you want me to come over?"

"I'll call you if we need your help."

Norma busied herself with arranging her files. Some people from the office were in other cities or countries and couldn't come home because all the flights were grounded. They would eventually get home. But Kerry and Kayla? Norma shivered.

Chapter Forty

After more than an hour, when the phone rang, Norma grabbed it and heard Alicia.

"Alicia." Norma didn't know what to say.

"Wanted to let you know Kayla called. My girls are safe." Alicia's voice broke.

Norma sat up straight as if a heavy rock had been lifted from her back. "Oh, Alicia that's great." She blinked back her tears of relief.

* * *

Even a month after the attacks of September 11, whenever Norma checked her e-mails, there were several patriotic messages. It amazed her how people from different backgrounds and differing ideologies came together to grieve and recover. Bryan and Keith were getting along better too. She started rethinking her priorities. Job was fine, money was fine, but she was thankful her children, friends and their families were okay. And she was glad seven months after his surgery, Harold had fully recovered.

At work, Norma took a fax to Bryan's office.

Just as she got there, Harold came in huffing. "That Simpson fellow says he can't repay us this year."

Bryan shook his head. "He's been arguing about money for some time."

Harold threw the printed e-mail on the desk. "Read it. According to Eugene Simpson, a financier has expressed an interest in taking over Alabama/Cascade. You know, Eugene thinks he needs to let the financier take over, so they can pay the loans."

"But you can't let another company buy Cascade." Norma began to wring her hands, wanting to cry.

What next? First Alabama Shipyard merged with Cascade

and absorbed its loans. Now the Alabama president claimed he couldn't pay the loan or return their investment. If a new firm bought Alabama/Cascade, the company would be removed one step farther from her. Would her friends have to leave Cedarville again?

CHAPTER FORTY ONE

BRYAN

Bryan tried to keep up with the reams of faxes and ringing phones from customers and associates. Besides completing designs for the orders they already had, they were busy with new proposals. Oil companies were exploring farther and deeper, more than a mile beneath the surface in the Gulf of Mexico. This deep-sea drilling required thicker, stronger wire ropes for winches and sophisticated electronic equipment, cameras, and remote computer controls to fit into their designs. A company in Minneapolis—Minnesota Precision Electronics—provided similar equipment to aerospace industries. Keith had gone there to discuss how they could modify their equipment for Cascade deck machinery.

Bryan picked up the fax detailing the electronic schematics that Keith had sent. It seemed a good fit for the Cascade winch, so he told Keith to give them the order, and to tell the Cascade engineers to specify MPE as vendor for a proposal job.

In the midst of all this Bryan had to take time from work to meet with Alabama Company's owner, Eugene Simpson, and the new owner/financier, Greg Mixen, who were arriving this afternoon. A month earlier, when Eugene Simpson had informed them that Mixen & Boyer had offered to buy Alabama/Cascade, Harold had investigated. He found out that the financiers bought industries with good prospects and turned troubled companies around. The firm's ventures in steel and other products appeared to be prospering. So in the interest of the financial health of their business, the Cascade group had agreed to this business transaction. If the finances were sound, there was a better chance for him and his friends to recover their investments.

The phone rang. It was Simpson, telling him that he and Mixen had arrived at Sea-Tac airport and were on their way to Cedarville.

When the Alabama president and the new financier arrived, Bryan took them around the office and showed them the projects Cascade was working on. Then they returned to the conference room for a meeting with Harold.

Mixen settled in a chair, one hand clutching his navy blue tie, the other massaging his square jaw. He asked, "Why do you have three separate operations? It's not cost-effective."

Biting back a sarcastic response, Bryan explained, "Well the shop was already in Mobile. Most of our customers are in Houston, so sales and marketing offices have to be there. Cascade stays here because there's an experienced pool of engineers and drafters who are unwilling to leave Cedarville."

Harold leaned forward on the table. "Greg, you know, sixteen years ago, Eagle Energy closed the plant here and transferred the Cascade project books and drawings to Houston. The business faltered because experienced engineers didn't move. Changing location didn't work then. It's won't work now. Eugene must have told you that our group bought the Cascade project books and drawings from Eagle, and, you know, the business is thriving because of our hard work."

Chapter Forty One

"Having everything at one place has certain advantages. Unlike the plant in Alabama, the engineering could easily be moved." Mixen raised his brows. "I'm not suggesting that yet."

"Yet?" Bryan muttered, his hand shielding his mouth.

Harold turned to Eugene, "Have you told Greg about the Alabama guarantee of no-relocation and of payment of our investment?"

Simpson ran his hand over his balding head. "Greg knows that. We had higher debt to pay when we took over Cascade's loan, and we didn't have enough profit last year."

Bryan stared at a brown spot on the wall. What was Simpson up to?

Mixen said, "Before we bought Alabama/Cascade, my attorney looked at your merger contract. There is a clause about payment of your investment, but it's dependent on profits."

Bryan's chest tightened. Were Mixen and Simpson suggesting that with the new ownership, the clauses were null and void? Could they change the rules of the game?

* * *

After a quiet Christmas with his family in Spokane, Bryan returned home with Jane and the children. Although his job was getting more stressful with the new financiers, Bryan was grateful he and Jane were together, Brad was progressing at work, and Jennifer had finally completed her bachelors and had a job. He hoped next year would bring better luck at work, and the Company's new financiers would cooperate with them.

Just as Bryan grabbed his briefcase and headed for the door, the phone rang. Jane picked it up. "Hi, Alicia." She put her hand over the mouthpiece. "Keith's in the hospital."

"What?" Bryan dropped his briefcase and reached for the

phone.

"Bryan wants to talk to you." After a pause Jane said, "Call me if you need anything." She set the receiver down. "Alicia is in a hurry, she couldn't talk. She said last night Keith bent over in pain and collapsed, so he was taken to the emergency room. His ulcer is bleeding."

"You get dressed. We'll go to the hospital." When Jane went to change, Bryan paced the kitchen floor.

At the hospital, Bryan saw Keith in a wheelchair, his wife and mother by his side. Bryan hugged Alicia and Miyoki, then lightly punched Keith's arm. "I know you wanted to avoid Duane. But you didn't have to go to this length."

Keith's black eyes sparkled, looking bigger on his ashen face.

When the nurse wheeled Keith away, Bryan felt a guilty knot in his stomach. He'd been ignoring his friend and had not noticed his deteriorating health or the stress he was under.

Jane whispered, "I'll stay with Alicia and her mother-in-law. You go on to work."

Bryan waved to the three women. "I'll be back at noon. If you need me before that, call."

Back at the office, Bryan saw Duane standing over a drawing from Minnesota Precision Electronics. Why was he scrutinizing Bryan's papers? Bryan recalled Steve's suspicion about the Cascade Computer Aided Designs in the office of Duane's son, Curtis. Bryan didn't take it seriously, because Alabama Shipyard had access to their drawings since they were manufacturing for Cascade. They didn't need to steal designs. But was Duane passing the information to his son or others?

Duane looked up. "I want to check if anyone in Mobile makes this equipment for less."

Bryan frowned, recalling the gearbox that Duane had insisted on manufacturing, which turned out to be more expensive. "MPE is known for their electronics. We can't take any chance with this unit."

"Well, I thought we should try to save cost. I guess Keith likes the MPE unit better."

Heat rushed to Bryan's face. So many times he had listened to Duane and snapped at Keith. He wouldn't do that to his buddy again. "Based on the customer requirement, I decided we'd buy the remote unit from MPE. In future, if you want to check my papers, give me a call." Bryan leaned against the door as Duane walked past him. "By the way, Keith is in no position to answer your questions, He's in the hospital. I just came from there."

"What happened? Can I visit him?"

Bryan shook his head. His friend's ulcer might explode at the sight of Duane. "He has internal bleeding and has to go through several tests. He can't have visitors." Bryan put the MPE drawings in the file cabinet and locked it.

CHAPTER FORTY TWO

STEVE

Anxious about his biopsy results, Steve couldn't concentrate on his work. He took his lunch bag to the car, drove aimlessly, then stopped at the park. He got out to walk but returned to the car, sat there and nibbled on his sandwich. He had been having frequent prostate infections, and according to his doctor the blood tests indicated a higher than normal PSA. Last week he had a biopsy, actually, several biopsies—the doctor nicked him in several places. That pain was gone but what about the diagnosis? The big "C?" He didn't want to think about it.

He returned to the office and went to get a glass of water. Norma asked, "Feeling okay?"

"Yeah." Steve gulped his water.

"Be positive. Most of the time tests are done to rule out certain things," Norma said.

"I know." Steve trudged to his office.

His partners had their health problems—Harold's hip replacement, Bryan's heart attack, and Keith's bleeding ulcer. They were fine now, but if the diagnosis for him came with the dreaded "C," he would never be the same. He was the youngest

Chapter Forty Two

in their group. Why him? He shivered. The doctor might call today. He decided to go home early. From the parking lot he saw yellowed maple leaves on the tree. Their life cycle will soon end. Would his life end too?

When he reached home, Vera was in the garage. "Darling you came home early." She kissed him. "Are you feeling okay?"

"Did the doctor call?"

"Not yet." Vera took his hand and walked to the kitchen. "Would you like some tea?"

"I don't think so."

"I was about to go to the health club, but if you like, we can take a leisurely walk instead. It's a nice day. The doctor said light walking is good for you."

"I'm tired." Steve flopped on the sofa. He didn't feel like plunging into exercise or other activities until he got his results. In case there was a malignancy, exercise would be futile. Why waste precious time?

Vera sat beside him. "Most probably the biopsy will be negative. If not, there are good treatments. You know that Bob had cancer ten years ago and is fine, working, playing golf. And remember that man at your work?"

"I remember. I don't need pep talk now!" Steve sighed and stood. "You go for your workout. I'm going to rest."

Vera hugged him and left. As Steve headed for the bedroom, the phone rang. He picked up the receiver. "Is this Mr. McGill?" the nurse asked. When Steve answered in affirmative, she continued, "Your biopsy results are back. Good news! There is no malignancy."

Steve exhaled with relief. "Thank you, thank you. So when do I come for my checkup?"

The nurse said, "There is no need for visit until your next annual exam."

"Thanks again."

Steve set the phone down. Feeling a burst of energy, he pumped his fist in the air. "Woohoo!" He picked up the phone, wondering whether to call his parents first or Ryan. His parents had been worried about him. They were not the old critical selves now. He called them and waited for Vera to return before calling Ryan in Seattle and Xavier in Brazil.

Steve tapped his fingers on the armrest of the sofa. Finally, everything was working well. Both his boys were settling down. Xavier had earned his "tourismo" license, and Ryan would soon get his associate degree. Best of all, he didn't have a deadly disease.

* * *

For several months, Steve hadn't been to Mobile, letting the plant manager handle the quality control. Now that he was well, he went to Alabama Shipyard to observe the test for brakes and gears before the final certification for American Bureau of Shipping—ABS—and the Norwegian Det Norske Veritas—DNV, the maritime standard-setters. The customers were now demanding certifications from both bureaus of shipping to ensure that the equipment would work anywhere in the world.

Mel, the shop manager approached him. "Steve, we'll be ready in a few minutes. It will go fast. We're doing fifteen-minute tests for each phase."

"What?" Steve's voice rose before he could check it. "This must meet maritime standards. You can't burn-in brakes in fifteen minutes. How will we know that the brakes will hold the test load? The gearbox oil and bearing won't rise to full temperature in that time. ABS people are going to be here this afternoon and if anything goes wrong, the tests will have to be done over." Without waiting for a reply, he turned and hurried toward the office.

Chapter Forty Two

What was happening to Alabama Shipyard? They did good work for Cascade before the two companies merged. Now they were taking shortcuts and ignoring the shipping bureau's recommendations. Eugene Simpson and Duane Landry would probably argue that it saved on labor costs and that shorter testing didn't really compromise anything.

He heard someone call, "Steve, where you going, huffing and puffing?"

Steve stopped and greeted Chad Morgan. "Nowhere. That's the problem. Am I glad to see you."

"Come sit on the bench here. Now, tell me what's up."

"I, I need to explode!" Steve sat beside the friendly Alabama machinist who had originally suggested this manufacturing plant.

"Okay, explode away." Chad laughed.

Steve told him about the shortcuts the shop was taking. Chad nodded. "Yes, it seems they're bent on cutting expenses one way or the other."

"It's penny-wise and pound-foolish—cutting and chopping where it's important." Steve felt the heat of his blood on his face.

"I'm also tired of them. Sometimes I feel sorry I suggested this plant for Cascade. Something changed after the companies merged." Chad lowered his voice. "I've heard that Duane and Eugene told the financial bigwig that if they move the engineering office to Mobile, it'll save them a bundle."

Steve shook his head. "They can talk, but no one from the Cedarville office would move. Where would they find experienced design engineers like Bryan and Keith?"

"They're saying they don't need the Cedarville engineers." Chad raised his brows. "Haven't you guessed? Duane's son has been poring over the Cascade calculations. Between Eugene and Duane, there are sons, brothers, cousins with their businesses who are willing to take over the Cascade engineering jobs."

Steve glared at Curt's office across the compound. Alabama now had all the calculations and Computer Aided Designs. They could make minor changes for repeat orders, but what about the new, more complicated ones? Emptiness filled his stomach, thinking of all the work he and his partners had invested to make Cascade a success. What would happen to their company?

CHAPTER FORTY THREE

NORMA

Norma pushed her chair away from her desk and stretched her arms. She had spent more than an hour trying to get flights for engineers. Booking airline tickets ought to be left to the travel agents, but six months ago Mr. Simpson sent out a memo that secretaries would now handle the reservations, because the travel agencies were charging fifteen dollars per ticket.

Norma sighed. Things were getting tough. The Mobile office had ordered her to lay off one of the three secretaries. That meant that beside administrative duties, Norma had to take on some clerical work that Lisa handled. Norma was glad to learn that the single mother of two had found another job.

"Is it time for lunch yet?" Harold's voice boomed down the hall.

"Any time is lunchtime," Bryan replied as he strode to the kitchen.

Norma laughed and joined them. She got the sandwiches she had packed. Bryan warmed his diet dinner in the microwave, and they sat at the small table.

Bryan poured some sauce over his brown rice and broccoli

dish. "Mixen and Simpson are using the same tactics Eagle used in '86. They've asked for a list of engineers who are willing to move to Mobile."

Norma quickly swallowed the bite she had taken from her sandwich. "But, but, it's in our contract that they can't move us."

"Honey, they don't want us, you know. Just the engineers." Harold wiped his forehead.

"But this is our company." She gulped some water. "Do you think they'll lay us off?"

"No, they can't do that." Bryan frowned. "But Duane and Simpson will make it hell to continue working here. I bet they're expecting us to resign. I wish Keith and Steve were in town. We need to discuss it with them and talk to our lawyer."

Harold stood and got a can of Pepsi. "You know, Eugene and Duane have convinced the new owner they don't need us and they can provide the designs much cheaper in Mobile."

"I thought Mixen was smart enough to figure out who was more competent." Bryan set aside his fork. "Well, when we're out of the picture, the financiers will realize the truth. We have eight months until our building lease expires. I doubt Mixen will agree to renew it."

Norma's temples throbbed. How could this happen to the company they had brought back from Houston and revived? "Will we get our investments back?"

Bryan rose from his chair. "We'll make sure we get the money they owe us. I'm going to make an appointment with our lawyer."

* * *

On an unusually hot Monday in early September, Norma listlessly filed papers. The summer was approaching its end, and so was the Cascade office.

Chapter Forty Three

Steve came to her desk. "Norma, can you update my resume?"

Norma looked up at his slumped shoulders. "You're not moving. Are you?"

"No. A friend told me about a boat building company in Anacortes. They're looking for a manufacturing manager. Thought I should apply." Steve handed her a couple of pages. "Here's my old resume and the details of my work experience at Alabama/Cascade."

"I'll have it ready for you this afternoon, Steve."

Steve's boyish face looked haggard. Everyone else seemed to have plans after their forced retirement—traveling, visiting their children or grandchildren, spending time with aging parents, and helping them in their business. Why couldn't Steve live on his savings and the lottery winnings—the part they had not invested in the company?

As if reading her mind, Steve said, "It'll be five more years before I'm eligible for Medicare. I'll need to work to keep our health insurance. I guess I shouldn't have played the stocks, especially NASDAQ, which has tanked."

"I heard that, Steve." Harold approached and elbowed Steve. "You know, when you get your money back from Alabama, I'll help you set up your investment."

Norma tried to encourage Steve. "Maybe you, Bryan and Keith can start your own consulting firm."

"Can't do that." Harold shook his head. "You know, there's a clause in our contract that does not allow us to form a competing company for the next two years."

"Frankly, I just want a regular job without any headache." Steve asked, "Harold, do you think we'll get our money back from Alabama?"

Harold nodded. "You bet. Otherwise they'll have a lawsuit on their hands."

Norma wasn't sure. In this post-Enron, post-9/11 era, there were no guaranties. She clasped her hands. "Steve, at least you made it back to Cedarville and we worked together for eight years."

"Yes, we came home." Steve smiled. "And my sons are on the right track now."

* * *

Norma picked up the framed pictures of her children and grandchildren from her desk, wrapped them in paper and put them in a plastic bag. She looked out the window. The autumn morning was as clear and bright as it had been the day they had gone to collect their lottery winnings. She went to the basement and surveyed the boxes of project books and drawings. Her heart burned with sorrow. It was like saying goodbye to dear friends.

She plodded back upstairs to Harold's office. He was collecting files to take home. Returning to the lobby, she saw Steve with Vera in his office, putting his diploma and other items in a box. She wandered to Keith's office, where Alicia had started filling a box with Keith's engineering books.

Bryan came to the lobby and called, "Hey, guys, don't worry about your stuff right now. We have the lease here for ten more days."

Keith and Alicia came to the lobby, Steve and Vera followed them.

The door opened, and Jane walked in. Bryan's face lit up. "Love, you're not in school?"

"I took the day off." Jane kissed Bryan, then came to Norma and embraced her. "Anything I can do?"

Norma needed that hug. "Your being here is a big help."

The eight of them stood in the lobby, but no one talked. The

Chapter Forty Three

silence was more grating than the loud complaints Norma had heard over the last few months.

The silence broke when the Alabama/Cascade moving van arrived and the movers started taking boxes to the truck. When the project books, drawings, computers, printers and fax machines were loaded, Norma went to the parking lot. Harold stood behind her and put his arm across her shoulders. Fifteen years ago, she and Harold had watched the Eagle Energy truck rumble out of the old Cascade plant. She remembered the emptiness in her stomach as she had watched the truck leave. A big part of her was leaving again, but thankfully, this time her friends were right here with her.

Bryan asked, "Can you imagine Alabama/Cascade Engineering and Manufacturing?" He chuckled. "It's as bad as the Chicago-based-Boeing."

Her friends laughed. Norma, too, gave a half-hearted chuckle.

After the truck left, when they returned to the office, she said, "I'll order pizza like I did the day the Eagle van brought our stuff here." Without waiting for a response, she picked up the phone and called for the delivery.

When the pizza arrived, they sat in the conference room to eat. After lunch, Norma took out the broaches with Cascade logo that she had ordered. She gave one each to Alicia, Jane and Vera. They gently fingered their broaches and took turns hugging Norma.

Steve made a face. "Not fair. Just the gals got the gifts."

Norma smiled and took out bridge tallies and decks of cards from her bag. She had made the tallies by cutting eight pieces of felt and gluing a picture of a Cascade winch on top. She gave that along with the cards to the men.

"Thank you, thank you, thanks, Norma." The men's voices came at once. Harold squeezed her hand.

Norma blinked back her tears. One lesson she had learned from bridge was that she had no control over the cards, but she had to make the best use of what was dealt to her. If she didn't have a slam hand she couldn't bid one, but she could play her cards well and cherish the process of the game. She had no control over the company where her grandfather, father, and she had worked, but she had experienced the thrill of owning Cascade with her friends for eight years.

"The business is gone, but we are together." Bryan poured Pepsi in their glasses and raised his glass. "To our friendship!"

Norma took a sip of her drink. In this lottery, they had won each other. They were back together, they were healthy, and their children were doing well. She raised her glass. "May we all have a life of grand slam!"

THE END

THE HISTORY OF SKAGIT STEEL

In 1996, a core group of engineers in a small Northwest town were given a contract to restart a product line for a company that had been once dominant in the marine and offshore equipment. The business was subsequently purchased and moved to the South. Their story, however, started many years before that, demonstrating the dedication of workers and the support of the community for a local business.

In 1901, John Anderson established a neighborhood machine shop, Sedro-Woolley Iron Works. A year later, he approached the town council to make it a publicly traded stock company. Within half-an-hour, local investors bought shares and raised the capital to continue the project. The company took on any job, "... from making iron stakes for the city surveyors to overhauling and repairing locomotives; from making iron pulleys 36 inches across to building 8,000-pound log jacks."

A young machinist, David McIntyre, purchased shares in the business in 1906, and changed its name to Skagit (a Native American word for strength and power) Steel and Iron Works. A few years later, McIntyre purchased Fuller's and Fritsch's shares, and became owner of the company.

During World War I the company filled the contracts for ship builders, making pinions, rudders, propeller hubs and struts. The number of employees grew from 12 to 70 and the production increased to more than 250 percent of the previous year.

When McIntyre's son, Sydney, completed his degree in drafting and engineering at the University of Washington he came to work at Skagit Steel and Iron Works. He designed a gasoline powered hoist, called MAC Little Tugger, to be used along with a Fordson tractor for logging and land clearing. The innovation sold so many tractors that Henry Ford himself traveled to Skagit County "to see where all his tractors were going."

By the end of the 1920s Skagit Steel and Iron Works provided equipment for locomotives, railroads, logging, oil field wells, and castings for the electricity generators at the Seattle City Light Diablo Dam Project.

David McIntyre passed away in 1939, and his son, Sidney, became the company president. During World War II, Skagit Steel produced winches for the Navy, shafts for the B-29 Bombers, and rifle shell casings for the Army, and the company employed close to 500 people. The government used Skagit yarders for logging operations on Guadalcanal and other South Pacific bases. Residents of Skagit Valley who were overseas during the war often reported seeing Skagit equipment.

In 1943, the company started an apprentice program of machine shop and classroom work for high school students. The Federal Manpower Commission praised it as a model in "war industry plants." When the war bonds program began, while most employees pledged 10 percent of their wages, foundry worker Yosef (Joe) Hassan, a Palestinian immigrant, pledged his entire paycheck. He said he could get by with his garden, cows and chickens until the war was over, and didn't mind "giving 100 percent when the boys overseas were giving 110 percent." For such dedication, Skagit Steel earned the Army and Navy "E" award.

Chapter Forty Three

As the war wound down, Sidney McIntyre shifted the emphasis from Navy deck machinery back to logging equipment, which helped the company survive and succeed. The engineers designed new yarders, and manufactured logging engines, drum sets and replacement machines for the ones damaged in the war. It was discovered that in the Philippines, the Japanese had removed the drums and shafts from the machines built by Skagit to make gun barrels. The employees took it as a "back-handed compliment" for their product.

After the war, since business was slow, the company obtained a research and development contract from the Army Transportation Corp. To meet the contract requirements, the McIntyre family ranch was changed into a test facility for lifting and moving heavy equipment. After some modification to a yarder, it was used by the Army to tow tank gunnery targets. The machine was also used as a dredging hoist. In the fifties, Skagit Steel exported logging equipment to Africa, India, and the South Pacific. One man in India told them "the machines were capable of doing the work of ten elephants."

In 1953, Skagit Steel received a three-million-dollar contract to produce 106 mm recoilless rifle shells for the Army. Since it required construction of an ordnance facility, the management searched for other locations. To keep the business local, the community leaders solicited donations and options on property adjacent to the plant. The residents helped. Mayor Stendal declared August 11, 1953, a town holiday to "celebrate the overwhelming response."

Because of the variety of quality products, Bendix Corporation bought the family-owned business in 1969. Dave McIntyre, David McIntyre's grandson, said, "Everybody's got factories for sale, but Bendix wants our people, our skilled tradesmen."

With experienced workers and Bendix management, Skagit

became a blend of "the best of the old and the new, the big and the small." The sales of offshore drilling equipment were strong, but Skagit diversified by taking on the challenge of designing, building and installing the Schachle Wind Turbine near Palm Springs. It began generating power in December 1980.

Houston-based Continental Emsco, a division of LTV Steel, acquired Skagit Steel from Bendix Corporation in 1980. A few years later, LTV filed for Chapter 11. From a workforce of over 850, only 100 remained. Eventually, the Sedro-Woolley plant closed and the project books and drawings were taken to Houston. Engineers were asked to move to Houston, but most didn't go.

When the Continental Emsco division of LTV was sold to another firm in mid-nineties, the new financiers tried to revive the offshore product line and inquired about experienced engineers. Four former Skagit employees took up the challenge of restarting the product, with a prerequisite that the business be located in the Northwest. Former Director of Engineering, Edward Mangold, set up a marketing plan and they started the office in Mount Vernon, Washington. Each member brought specific expertise to the business that allowed Skagit to become viable again.

Within two years, the business grew beyond their expectations, employing more than 50 engineers, draftsmen and salesmen. Since their products were manufactured at various plants, they merged with a plant in Louisiana for efficiency. After a few years the company in Louisiana convinced the new financiers that they could provide the engineering services at a lower cost. The company closed the Mount Vernon office.

In 2012, a decade after the Mount Vernon office had closed the Louisiana plant contacted the former employees who had revived the product line, asking them to start an engineering office in Skagit County again. Most of them were retirement age and declined to work for this company. The Louisiana plant sent an engineer to open an office in Sedro-Woolley and hired several draftsmen and engineers who had worked for either the old company (Skagit Steel, Bendix, Continental Emsco of LTV) or the Skagit office at Mount Vernon, Washington.

Mr. McIntyre's words, "Bendix wanted our people, our skilled tradesmen," still rings true, albeit for a different company and a different generation of workers.

History of Skagit from 1901 to 1976 taken from *SKAGIT/ 75 IN '76—Pulling Together/Bendix/Skagit Corporation,* which was published to celebrate 75th anniversary of the company.

About The Author

Hemlata Vasavada was born in Jodhpur, India, where she earned a master's in philosophy. She immigrated to the United States in 1968 with her husband and their then one-year-old daughter. She has been a Girls Scout volunteer and an ESL tutor. She has conducted workshops through the Literacy Volunteers of America to train volunteers in English as a Second Language teaching techniques. She is a member of Skagit Valley Writers League, where at various times she has held offices of president, vice president and treasurer. Her articles and humor essays have been published in *The Seattle Times, Houston Chronicle, Syracuse Post Standard, Northwest Life & Times, Tea A Magazine, Everett Herald*, anthologies of Skagit Writers, *India Currents* and *Khabar*—magazines for Indian-Americans, and *I Should Have Stayed Home—Food*, anthology from RDR Books.